THE XENON TECH ARCHIVES

FILE 4: "THE CHOSEN ONE"

THE XENON TECH ARCHIVES

FILE 4: THE CHOSEN ONE

BY: ASHLEY M. JACKSON

3Seats Publishing
Virginia Beach, VA 23462
3SeatsPublishing@gmail.com

Cover Illustration by Stanley Barros
Cover and Book design by 3Seats Publishing
Editing by 3Seats Publishing

ISBN 13: 978-0-9986303-6-6
ISBN # for eBook: pending
LCCN: 2023920775

First Edition December 2023

Printed in the USA by Lulu, Inc. of Raleigh, NC 27607

CONTENTS

~ *Recap*

WHAT HAPPENED IN THE LAST BOOK?

With a new resolve, Scarlet has decided to follow his own path and run far from his controlling father. Certain of killing the last three members of The Management; Lelani, Nyx, and his own mother, Scarlet remains on the hunt. After being taken captive by the rogues and shipped to Section 6, Scarlet begins to think of how he can use this situation to his advantage.

It's now or never.

1

HEART TO HEART

It was nearly time for lunch when I finally popped my head up. I must've fallen asleep after Faylin left.

As far as I knew; R was still MIA, Father was still after me, Aztec was still after me, and I was still up a creek without much of a paddle.

Despite all that, I still smiled.

Today felt like the first day I was truly in control, and not just in control until Father takes over. The feeling was amazing.

As soon as I stepped out of my room, I came face to face with Lanker who looked oddly agitated.

"Captain, we need to talk, can I have a minute?" It was odd, unnerving even to see Lanker looking so out of character. I mean, it wasn't as if I didn't know why.

Everyone on the ship has been wondering about me ever since what happened at Cyryl's lair. If I was a normal human, like everyone thought I was, I should have been dead. Not only was I not dead, I was in pristine condition. I technically healed even faster than Faylin.

I healed faster than a humanoid.

That didn't sit right with anyone, and rightfully so. If I were in their shoes, I would have been leery too.

"Actually, I was hoping to find you Lanker, I need to speak to you and the crew about something."

I squeezed past and continued down the hallway, flagging him to come along. I could sense the hesitation, but he quietly followed.

It was now or never. If I didn't take the plunge and come clean now, I could lose the trust of my crew for good. I had faith they would stay with me no matter what though.

I quieted the voice in the back of my head that tried to fill my stomach with panic and opened the door to the galley where everyone was quietly eating and chatting amongst themselves.

When they saw Lanker pop in though, all of their conversations stopped abruptly.

"Captain, Lanker, good to see you both." Senna said in an oddly strained voice.

I forced a smile, "Good afternoon, everyone, I have a slight announcement to make, could you all make your way down to the training area."

Suddenly, my heart began to thump wildly, almost as if the weight of what I was about to do finally caught up with my brain.

I was going to tell them, *really* tell them. Telling Faylin didn't feel this scary, so why did I feel like I was about to pass out?

I took another deep breath, willing myself to calm down. This would be just like jumping into cold water; I just had to say it, just open my mouth and say it.

That didn't calm my heart down any.

I was pretty sure this was what a heart attack felt like.

Soon enough everyone was in the training room at the bottom of the ship. Lanker and Tyrinie sat while the others stood and watched me with expecting eyes.

Faylin leaned against the window, giving me a quiet nod of encouragement. That alone helped a tad bit.

I took a deep breath again.

"Okay, I'm sure you all have some questions for me..."

"Yeah, that's an understatement," Lanker mumbled into his propped-up fist.

"Right." I laughed nervously, wringing my hands together. "Okay, well I'll just come out with it then. This might sound a bit...crazy, but just bear with me."

Everyone was quiet, waiting anxiously for me to finish my statement.

"I'm...not like you guys. I'm not a normal human…nor have I ever been." As soon as I said those words, I could feel my toes and fingers go numb with anxiety.

"What do you mean 'not normal'?" Lanker asked again, leaning forward, seeming more interested.

"Well, that's the difficult part. There is no real word for what I am because I'm sort of the first of my kind. A prototype...I guess." I shrugged awkwardly. Explaining this to Faylin was much easier, but I continued on the best I could.

"When I was born, decades and decades ago, I was implanted with something called a nanoid. I can explain what that is later, but the important thing to know is that it's kind of like a... computer virus thing. It... gives me abilities normal humans don't have, like being able to heal myself quickly and stuff like that. The reason why I'm like this is that…this was my mission; my purpose was to kill Salem.

But I realized I couldn't do it alone, which is why I recruited all of you. Does that make any sense?"

The room was so quiet you could hear a pin drop, nobody said a word. Senna and Marcus exchanged glances, Lanker looked as though all of the tension that was in his shoulders had disappeared miraculously, and Tyrinie and Casteri looked more than intrigued.

Everything was silent until Marcus cleared his throat and held out his hand, prompting Senna and Lanker to place five silvers each into his open palm.

"I told you guys." Marcus laughed loudly. "I guessed hybrid, but that's close enough."

Wait, what?

After that, a flood of questions came.

"So, are you a humanoid or something?"

"I told you guys he wasn't as alien, geez."

"Now what the hell is a nanoid?"

"What powers do you have, can you make things float?"

It was so overwhelming; all I could do was laugh.

~

Faylin brought dinner down into the training room and everyone watched transfixed as I showed off what I could do. I channeled as much haze as I could, using it to toss objects back and forth, even using it to lift Lanker, something I didn't even know I could do.

"So that is why you refused to let me do a blood exam on you. This...thing is all through your bloodstream?" Senna took another bite of his food while poking at my hand for the fifth time that night.

"His name is R, and yeah, it would have been difficult to explain. R and I are the same, but not the same person. He is in me; we share my body in a way."

"So, he's a parasite?"

"He...doesn't like to be called a parasite, but I guess you can say that."

Tyrinie laughed, ears twitching. "I'm just glad not to be the only freak onboard."

I used one of the appendages in my palm to hit the back of his head, making him jump and laugh even harder.

This was far beyond the best-case scenario; it was so ideal, I thought I was dreaming. I had far too little faith in my friends.

Marcus slid over, taking his turn to bombard me with questions.

"Man, this is just too cool, I don't know why you would ever want to hide this. You're basically a real-life cyber superhero!"

I chuckled, "Eh, not really. I mean, my powers have a lot of drawbacks. And then the whole...Salem being after me because I'm the only one who can defeat him thing can be a bit of a damper. Besides, it's not like Neutopia really likes differences."

"Yeah tell me about it." Tyrinie muttered.

"True, true." Marcus continued. "That's understandable, a superhero has to keep his identity a secret and all. Now, tell me about R, your nanoid."

It didn't come as a surprise to me that Marcus was the only one who knew what a nanoid was. Apparently, snooping was part of what got him blacklisted. He knew more about Xenon Tech than I thought.

It was a very welcomed surprise.

"What do you want to know about him? He's pretty complicated. He's ignoring me right now anyway."

"So, you can talk to him?"

"Talk to him and see him. He pops in and out of my head sometimes, but only I can see him...well most of the time. R says it takes a lot of energy to make himself fully visible. Faylin has met him before though. Right, Fay?" I never had a chance to ask Faylin about him meeting R and getting the message to rescue me from the Rogues. It must've unnerved him a bit.

Faylin seemed to be a bit taken back when all eyes turned to him.

"You know, why does it not surprise me that Faylin knew about this before the rest of us did." Lanker chucked, not hiding the bit of jealousy in his voice very well.

"Obviously because he's the captain's favorite." Tyrinie rolled his eyes.

"Well, spill the beans, Fifi, what is he like?" Marcus asked quickly, pulling out his notebook.

Faylin shrugged. "Not very different from the captain. Much taller though, more muscular, rather abrasive, and less charming."

I couldn't help my face heating up at that, I would have never considered myself to be charming.

Marcus continued bombarding Faylin with questions when I saw a familiar face out of the corner of my eye.

Speak of the devil.

I was going to announce his presence, but he looked like he wasn't in the mood for an audience.

"Hey you guys, I'm going to run for a moment. Continue on without me." They barely even listened as I slid out of the room.

Up the stairs and down the hallway, R leaned up against one of the windows. His expression looked as if he was lost deep in thought.

"There you are, I never had a chance to thank you for getting the message to Faylin. So, thank you."

R shrugged, remaining silent for a moment. "Well now, I couldn't let my vessel die, could I?"

Before I could comment, R continued to talk as he walked away, prompting me to follow.

"So, everyone knows about us now, huh?"

"Yeah, they do. It feels kinda nice, doesn't it?"

R was silent again.

Before I knew it, we had walked back to my quarters. I took a seat on the bed, but R remained standing.

Something was off, and I didn't like it at all.

"R, is something wrong with you? With your, I don't know, code or something?"

"What is that supposed to mean?" R glanced over at me, uninterested. "I'm just annoyed because now all these little humans are gonna be trying to get blood samples and do weird tests on us. It was bad enough with mommy and Daddy dearest, now we have to do it all over again."

I swallowed hard. "It won't be anything like when we were younger, I promise. Nothing bad will happen to us" I paused again, shaking my head. "But no, that's not what I meant, it's something else. Sometimes, when I see you out of the corner of my eye, your face looks all... distorted and stretched. Your body started to fizzle and glitch like a broken TV. It's really weird and unnerving. What's that all about?"

"What are you talking about?" R leaned back, picking his ear with his pinky. "Even though I technically could change how I look,

I don't because it takes too much energy to change my default appearance. Besides, that sounds weird and creepy, don't lie about shit like that."

"What? I'm not lying. I've seen it at least twice now, and it's freaking me out!"

Was this his idea of a joke because it wasn't funny?

"Well, whatever you're seeing must be a glitch in your head, but not mine. I haven't changed since day one, but you have."

"What do you mean by that?"

R shrugged again, "Maybe whatever you're seeing is less about me and more about you. Cause I'm telling you; I'm not making you see anything that isn't already here."

Anything that isn't already here.

I shook my head, maybe R was right. A lot has been going on and... maybe it was just me seeing things.

Even thinking that to myself sounded like a lie.

I was jolted when there was a knock at the door, before I said anything, it cracked open. Tyrinie's head popped inside.

"Are you dressed?" Tyrinie made his way inside.

"Well even if I wasn't it would be too late now." I joked, seeing Tyrinie try to not laugh as well. "Is everything okay with the team?"

"Hm, oh yeah, they're fine. I just wanted to catch you for a moment."

"Oh?"

Tyrinie leaned against the door, looking just a tad bit uncomfortable. "I guess I...um, well I think I might owe you an apology...or something."

Wait just a moment...Tyrinie is apologizing. Now I know I must be dreaming.

"For what?"

"You really are like me...you're different like me. You tried, in your own way, to tell me I wasn't alone and I did what I do best and just shoved you away. I always thought you were full of shit, but you really did understand, didn't you?"

"I really did. Nothing I told you was fake."

"Yeah, I... I see that now. It's not just your face that's weird after all. Your entire body is a big ole' experiment."

I rolled my eyes, what happened to that apology?

"Anyway, thanks for giving me a chance, and for being patient with me. Most people don't do that."

"No thanks needed Tyrinie, we're family." I smiled.

"Right, family." Tyrinie sucked his teeth and glanced around my room. "Well, this is getting weird and emotional now, so I'm just gonna head out."

"Aw already? Are you sure you don't want a hug first?"

Tyrinie smiled. "Hug me and I'll break your fucking arms."

"Okay, that's fair."

Yup, everything was normal now.

END OF CHAPTER 1

CAPTAIN SCARLET

2

PLAYING NICE

The night was far from over despite my entire team being asleep. Well, almost everyone.

Faylin, as proper as always, came in not long after Tyrinie had left. For the first time in a few days, he was actually out of uniform. He wore a very familiar-looking metallic bodysuit along with black gloves and a matching bandana. I could never forget that outfit, it was so similar to the outfit he wore for one of our first missions together;

the mission where we took off our collars. That was one of our first moves as rebels, yet it seemed like ages ago now.

We ended up in my office, which seemed to be the best place to have some privacy. The last thing I wanted was for the others to overhear just yet.

"Did you do what I asked, how did it go?" I leaned back in my chair, feeling pretty damn good about myself. The day had gone by without a hitch, which was way more than I would have ever expected. And now came the harder part, somehow making an alliance with the man who just kidnapped and tried to kill me.

I mean, I've done harder things. So, this was nothing.

Faylin nodded, still seeming a bit hesitant. "I reached out to Aztec and said you wanted an audience with him. He was…less than thrilled, but oddly enough he agreed." Faylin leaned back against the stormy window as another bolt of lightning ripped through the black sky. "Now, you will have to be on your absolute guard, and of course, I will be on guard as well.

Aztec is not to be trusted, nor is it smart to underestimate him. But I do understand the information we could gather from him is invaluable."

I had never known someone to make Faylin so anxious. Truly, he must've seen more of Aztec than I did in those days I spent in his cell. It made me curious about what transpired between them during the decades they worked together. As much as I wanted to ask, I knew now wasn't the time for such questions.

I didn't feel afraid though. I mean, I had Faylin there with me, and without those damn shackles that Aztec had me in, I could give him a real fight if I needed to. Only if I needed to. If Aztec would just listen to me, he could be a fierce ally. I'm not his enemy, I don't want to hurt cyberkind. He can be key to helping me keep their kind safe.

I sat back up, chin resting in my palm, as R made himself known in the corner of the room. He was resting with his eyes closed;

the occasional glitches and fizzles against his skin made it obvious he wasn't even trying to keep his physical connection stable. I wondered if he even knew I could see him.

"Tomorrow, bright and early, meet me on the deck and we'll head over. Hopefully, the storm will have passed by then."

"Understood Captain." Faylin nodded politely before turning to head to the door, stopping only when I reached over the desk and grabbed his hand. The sudden movement caused our powers to spike and react in a glow of white for only a moment.

"Captain?"

"I… just wanted to let you know I really do appreciate what you're doing for me. You know, reaching out to Aztec and all. I know this can't be easy for you, and I do feel pretty bad about asking you to do it. If you don't feel comfortable going with me, you don't have to. I won't hold it against you, Fay."

Seemingly caught off guard, Fay shook his head. "Of course, I want to be there with you, I would never be able to rest knowing I placed you in danger…again. While this situation is not ideal, I want to be there with you to make sure you are safe. I especially want Aztec to know exactly where my allegiance stands.

But I do appreciate you being so caring." Faylin paused and chuckled lightly, still holding my hand tight. "I know I have said it before, but I will never understand why you are so caring towards a humanoid like myself. Honestly. Especially now that you know just about every horrible little thing about me."

"Come on, that's ancient history, remember. I told you I wouldn't hold any of that against you, and I meant it. It's just our little secret now. And besides…" I paused for a moment, wondering how I could say this without it sounding too weird. "I don't think I'd ever really be able to kick you out of my life. I feel like I just *need* you around. I don't know if I'd be able to do this whole journey without you, which is weird because it's not like we've known each other for all that long. You're like my other half, well more like my better half, and well…I'm rambling now, sorry."

I laughed awkwardly as my word vomit finally ceased, but thankfully, Faylin saved me the embarrassment by chuckling along with me.

"Well technically I have known you for a lot longer, but I can also understand your feelings. I suppose that is why I felt so relieved when you allowed me to stay with you. I would not know what to do otherwise, nor would I truly want to go anywhere else. So, I suppose that means I need you around as well."

"Well…I'm glad we're in agreement then. We're both stuck together now." I laughed, partly in relief, and partly because I was so jealous of how easily Faylin could communicate, even about embarrassing topics. It must be nice to be a humanoid.

Before I could pull away, Faylin placed his hands on both sides of my face, pressing his forehead against mine.

The action was so small, but I couldn't help but smile. It was the exact same thing that I did to him when we were stuck in Cyryl's lair.

It marked the beginning of Faylin learning about who I truly was, and me learning about who he truly was. At that time, the motion was nothing short of "*I'm pretty sure we are going to die here*", but right now, it felt nothing like that.

For a moment, it felt as though nothing else existed but he and I.

Faylin pulled back with a smile, tilting his head slightly as he brushed a few stray hairs away from my face in a show of rare affection.

"Everything will work out tomorrow. I am sure of it."

When Faylin spoke those words, I truly believed him.

I felt completely at ease.

~

…sadly, that feeling was short-lived.

After parting ways and going to our respective rooms, I laid in bed staring up at the ceiling. I could feel R's presence next to me, our shoulders barely touching.

I tried to focus my brain on anything; my team, my mission, my father, Faylin. But nothing worked. Every time I closed my eyes, all I could see were those steely gray eyes. Eyes that looked at me with an expression I couldn't quite comprehend.

I didn't expect to meet you so soon

The strange voice reverberated through my skull as if *he* were right next to me.

You look nothing as I expected. Pity.

What did he mean by that? What did he think I looked like? Why…was I upset he was disappointed in what he saw in me?

In a way, the feeling that I felt when Salem said that stung more than my father's constant disapproval. But why? Why did I even care? He's the enemy.

Come closer to me, let me see your face.

Without realizing it, my feet had begun to shift against the mattress; toes curling as I pressed my heels down one by one.

My body still wanted to go towards him. No, not just my body, every fiber of my being was screaming at me to find him. But why?

I looked beside me; R was still there staring mindlessly at the ceiling.

I turned to my side, trying to push the words away, but there was no stopping them. His voice was so clear, so vivid, that for the first time in my life, I actually questioned my sanity.

"Can you hear him too?" I asked R, my back facing him.

"Hmm."

It wasn't an answer, but…somehow, I understood what it meant.

Not before long, I finally fell into a restless sleep. Salem's words still buzzing incessantly through my head

~

Coat, check. Boots, check. Uncomfortably crisp slacks, check. I held up Tyrinie's stark white top – It would be a bit more formal looking than my usual crop top…albeit less comfortable.

I slid my arms in, keeping my grumbles to myself as Tyrinie watched with little interest.

"Just put it on and stop complaining asshole."

"I literally didn't even say a word."

"You didn't have to." Tyrinie stood up and stretched, walking behind me to adjust my collar. "You're acting like you've never worn formal wear a day in your life."

"Uh, I'm from the West…of course, I haven't." The West was known for being "fashionable" not "formal".

He rolled his eyes before coming back to the front of me, admiring his work. "You look about as good as you can look."

Before I could respond, Tyrinie came in close, too close for comfort.

He glanced over at the door before looking back at me intensely. "Are you sure about this idea?"

I stepped back a tad; was that what he was so worried about? I had taken a gamble and told Tyrinie about our meeting with Aztec before addressing all the others. There was no way he'd let me borrow his clothes otherwise.

"Of course, I'm sure, you guys know what I can do now, I'm not worried about Aztec at all. Besides, Fay will be there with me just in case things get dangerous."

Tyrinie crossed his arms, still too far in my personal bubble. "And you trust Faylin to watch your back? He acts so sketchy whenever Aztec's name is brought up."

Nobody else on the ship knew about Faylin's relation to Aztec and the rogues, and I wanted to keep it that way.

His secret was not mine to tell. If Faylin chose to tell everyone, which I doubt he'd want to, I would let him make that decision.

"Faylin is most likely wary of Aztec because of him being a rogue, which I appreciate. Trust me, if this guy is making Fay nervous, you know Fay is going to be watching me like a hawk."

Tyrinie let my words sink in before backing up slightly. "Yea…I guess Faylin is taking this threat seriously."

"Exactly, nothing to be concerned about. I trust Fay to watch my back so I can watch everyone else. You understand?"

He nodded, perching on top of the couch once more. "Well, in that case, I would say you're ready to go…"

Tyrinie paused for a moment before jumping up and heading towards the door. "Just, come back in one piece, okay."

I nodded with a smile as Tyrinie sped out of the room. I still wasn't used to him being so open and…slightly more friendly.

It was like the urge to put those walls back up was still there, but he was actively fighting to seem easier to be around. And the fact that he was trying so hard to be friendly to me really was unbelievable.

I glanced over my shoulder at Myrah's head as I adjusted my tie. She was staring at me with the same expression. I think once I killed Nyx…I would add his head to my collection as well, why not? I severely regretted not being able to have Cyryl's head after what he did to Faylin. Nothing would have brought me more joy than to have his head mounted up in Faylin's room as a sign of our victory.

The fact that I was never even able to see his body didn't sit right with me. But I knew there was no way he survived that explosion.

It would have been impossible.

~

Heading to the deck, I could faintly hear Senna and Lanker's voices coming from the med bay.

The fact that they were awake was odd enough, but both of them being in the same room was just eerie. What would they be talking about at this hour?

A part of me wanted to eavesdrop but I knew I was in a rush. No doubt Faylin was already waiting for me on the deck. I shook my head and hurried down the hall.

Once I hit the foggy outside, I realized Fay was waiting for me on the ground. He was already mounted on his T-34 and staring ahead into the distance.

He was wearing something slightly similar to when he was in Cyryl's lair. It was some sort of black bodysuit that had neon green patterns in harsh lines around his ankles, hips, and back.

All of his hair was pulled back tight, and his posture was so taut I swore he would crack if I bumped into him.

"Fay?" I opted to teleport down to ground level, only startling Faylin slightly. "Are we ready to go?"

Fay nodded, patting the space on the seat behind him before activating the T-34.

I hopped on, latching on to Fay's waist as the bike jolted in protest. Within moments, we were zooming off at breakneck speeds to the compound on the foggy shore.

"Fay?"

We had been riding in silence through the wastelands for what seemed to be hours.

Despite how fast we were going, the wind around us only seemed to be a quiet hum. If I listened in closely, I could almost hear Faylin's steady breathing.

"Yes, Scarlet?"

I smiled, leaning back and taking in our murky surroundings. "Could you tell me about the rogues?"

"Oh? And what would you like to know?"

I shrugged. "I don't know, tell me…how they became that way. They're humanoids, right? You mentioned they had free will but no *humanity*, what did you mean?"

Faylin paused for a moment, gathering his thoughts. "That is a bit of a difficult question, but I will try my best to answer for you." There were a few more moments of silence before Fay spoke up again.

"There are certain humanoids that are different from others. As you know, there are worker humanoids, combat humanoids, and companion humanoids. This particular phenomenon only occurs in companion humanoids. Now, the process where a companion humanoid becomes a rogue is just a theory, nobody knows exactly how this happens. Most say it can be caused by severely abusive and/or unusually violent treatment of the humanoid, others say it is just an abnormality or glitch in their systems. Whatever it is, it causes the humanoid to not only become…disconnected from their human master, but also causes them to become unstable. They become aware of themselves. Their artificial brains try to mimic and understand human emotions, believing that it is truly human, but they simply are unable to. The only thing a rogue understands is '*want*'. Rogues only want to seek out pleasure, they only want what makes them *happy*, despite how twisted the act might be. The definition of *happiness* varies from rogue to rogue…but it is usually at the expense of an unfortunate human."

I could feel the air around me chill as Faylin paused, waiting for me to respond. "I think…I understand that.

When you said *disconnected* from their master, does that have to do with that humanoid ownership process you mentioned to me a little while back?"

"Yes, very much so. That process is to keep a humanoid completely loyal to you. The humanoid's ability to think is non-existent at that point, and it will do everything and anything that its master desires. The master's order is law.

But rogues not only sever that connection, they become completely rewired. Suddenly, not only the master, but the master's entire family becomes the rouge's primary target.

It is seen as a rite of passage, the first step in a rogue thinking for themselves. Once the rogue becomes self-aware, they butcher their master along with every family member associated with that bloodline. Children, elders, it would not matter.

Even if the person lived across Neutopia, the rogue would never stop hunting down each person in that bloodline. Then, and only then, are you accepted as a rogue and are free to live your hedonistic desires under Aztec guidance. In exchange, all Aztec requires is your undying loyalty."

Faylin took a deep breath and shook his head as if he were sending a bad memory away. After a moment, he spoke again. "In a way, a rogue is truly a perfect storm; the body and strength of a humanoid with absolute free will, self-awareness, and an insatiable desire to do whatever brings them pleasure…but lacking any sort of empathy, compassion, or sense of consequence."

A perfect psychopath.

I could understand what made Faylin feel so anxious about the rogues. Aztec was…something else entirely, something terrifying. Honestly, it felt like the only reason why Aztec wasn't like Salem was because he simply didn't want to be. Aztec's goal was to do whatever the hell he wanted, whatever brings him pleasure. He simply doesn't want to take over Neutopia.

And this was the man who wanted me dead.

END OF CHAPTER 2

3

DANCE WITH THE DEVIL

B ased on our surroundings, I assumed we were getting closer to the compound. The air was thicker than it already had been and held that slightest tinge of salt from the ocean. Faylin had been quiet for the past few miles. I felt selfish, but there was still so much I wanted to ask him.

I knew it was hard for him to talk about, I could tell just from his body language. Even still, I couldn't help myself from prying a little bit more.

"You're so different from the rogues though."

Fay nodded, "Yes, I am different. I'm…not just an average humanoid, if I was, there is a chance I could have become like Aztec and the others.

The biggest difference between me and the other rogues is the fact that I have emotions. Real human emotions, not just simulated emotions."

"Real human emotions?" That was always the thing that confused me about Faylin. When I first met him, he was so stoic and cold. He seemed like an average humanoid. But, as we started to get to know each other, he seemed to warm up to me and act more…human.

I guess a part of me wondered why he acted differently than the average humanoid. After learning about Faylin from Cyryl's lab, it all seemed to make sense. Faylin was never made to be a normal humanoid.

"Yes, I have normal emotions. Albeit, it is hard for me to process them, and even harder for me to show them, but they are there. While it is easy for me to suppress my human emotions and let the humanoid side of my brain take over, it does not make them go away. I can feel guilt, shame, and compassion…all things that average humanoids and rogues cannot.

I suppose it is because most of my brain and human DNA comes from Nilya, and then of course with the traces of nanoid blood that I have from Salem. Honestly, even I do not understand it all."

"I can understand that feeling." I laughed. I was always so confused about what I was; always felt like I was being pulled between two different worlds, the cyber one and the real one. But poor Faylin, he really must feel confused. With his self-awareness, Aztec must've mistaken Faylin for a rogue. But he must've realized his mistake early on. I know Faylin did the things Aztec asked of him, and I know Faylin followed Aztec faithfully for years, I wouldn't pry for that information…yet.

But at the end of the day, Aztec must've known that Faylin was different from the rest of them. So then why?

Why did Aztec keep Faylin around for so long? Why did he keep such a tight grip on him? But amidst all of those thoughts, it was still difficult for me to wrap my head around the fact that Faylin,

my best friend, was technically a serial killer. Arguably one of the deadliest humanoid serial killers around. He had killed thousands of people over more than a century of being with the rogues…

I shook my head, there was no need to dwell on that. I was just grateful Faylin was on our side.

I was pulled from my thoughts when Faylin began to slow to a stop as we entered the looming shadow of the compound. I could see what looked to be hundreds of eyes watching me from the structure. Like last time, they weren't doing anything…just watching.

I stepped off the T-34, smoothing my clothing down as much as possible. Faylin followed suit, taking a deep breath.

"Ready, Fay?" He nodded in response as the door to the compound opened. The same woman with the long flowing braids walked out. She stepped to the side, ushering us in.

"Welcome back, Faylin. You as well, child." Cinder nodded politely with an unreadable face. After remembering what Faylin told me about the rogues, I couldn't help but feel slightly more unnerved by her calm behavior.

I had to remember…that this woman butchered every single human that was connected to the blood that was inside her. The thought made me shiver.

"It's not like you haven't done your fair share of butchering, kid. Don't forget, you were just thinking about having Cyryl's head mounted in your room this morning."

I could hear R's teasing tone reverberating through my skull as I walked inside. Faylin, close to my side.

"You're just as dangerous as they are. Maybe even more so."

I grimaced, why was R trying to screw with me? I had to focus, and his nagging voice wasn't making it any easier.

I tried to focus on my footsteps as we went down a darkened hall. More rogues sat by the dozen, their eyes bore into Faylin and I.

"You already said you know you have to slit daddy dearest's throat; you'll never truly be free unless you do. As for Sabra, your precious mother, I'm sure you wouldn't hesitate to bludgeon her to death even if she were begging for forgiveness."

My steps faltered.

Suddenly…the voice didn't sound like R. The teasing tone had faded away, giving room to a voice much more…eerie.

Something that made my skin crawl and hair stand on end. The voice was split into three tones, all conjoined into one.

The way that it cracked and fizzled…like a broken television. My heart started pounding even faster.

This voice…how was *he* in my head?

I must've been hearing things.

My breathing was coming out faster, in short pants through my nostrils. I had to keep it together, I was just imagining things. Faylin's grip on my arm tightened slightly as he looked over to me, silently asking if I was alright. I gave him a strained smile and nodded. He looked concerned but continued looking forward nevertheless.

"How many times have you imagined killing them? You want to be free, do you not?"

The hallway became darker as we headed up a winding staircase, I could barely see Cinder walking ahead of us. The stairs seemed to stretch forever. I tried to ground myself; focusing on anything else around me to distract from the pounding voice in the back of my skull.

"No matter how many people you kill, you will never be free. Just like these rogues, the best you'll ever be able to do is build a false happiness within your little cage."

When the staircase ended, light finally began to seep in through the windows. I could tell I was sweating, and the trembling of my hands didn't do much in making me seem collected. In one of the rooms, I spotted the green-haired twins lounging together. They seemed to be in their own little world, laughing boisterously and guzzling some sort of neon-colored drink.

"This world, this reality, is your cage."

Finally, the voice seemed to fade away into nothingness and my brain was completely silent. I couldn't even hear my own thoughts.

What…the hell was that?

I shook my hand lightly, trying to control the tremors as I wiped the sweat off my forehead.

He knew exactly where I was. He was inside my head. He was watching me.

The thought alone filled me with a panic I hadn't felt since that day at the parade.

Before I could think further into it, Faylin and I stopped at a large slate door. Cinder knocked on it three times before walking off, but not before she placed her hand on Faylin's shoulder for a split second. She didn't say anything, she just let it linger before tucking her hands together neatly and vanishing down the hall.

"Are you alright?" Faylin asked in a light whisper, eyes still focused on the door.

"Yeah, something…weird just happened. I'll tell you about it later."

"Of course." Faylin nodded, straightening up when the door noisily unlocked itself and creaked open. Fay pushed it the rest of the way, leading us both inside.

The room itself looked similar to my quarters; there were large windows that faced towards the murky sea, bookcases that held maps and more info-chips than I could count,

and flags with symbols I didn't recognize strewn across the walls. In the center of the room was a large desk, completely bare save for a few maps that were scrawled over in red ink. In an impossibly large leather chair, Aztec sat reclined in the only chair in the room; his large arms folded across his broad chest, eyes trained on Faylin the entire time.

We stopped a healthy few feet away from his desk. With my back straight and my feet planted firmly, I willed my hands to stop trembling. I tried my hardest to focus on the task at hand, ignoring everything that happened in the hallway.

"I appreciate you agreeing to speak with me." I said politely, keeping my stance stiff. "I believe we have a lot of important business to go ove-"

"When was the last time you were in my office, Faylin?" Aztec interrupted me with a lazy grin on his face, not even acknowledging that I spoke a word. "It's been years now, such a pity. You could have at least visited."

"Believe me, this is the last place I want to be currently," Faylin responded without missing a beat. His arms were crossed in a way I assumed was supposed to look intimidating, but I could tell it was mostly from discomfort. "Let us speak about what we came here for, after that you will never have to see me again."

"And who says I would want that?" The same smug grin played on Aztec's face as he leaned in closer, propping his elbows on the table. "The compound seems emptier and much too rowdy without my favorite commander keeping everyone in line. Of course, I could but…you did so much of a better job."

Faylin sighed in annoyance, "Listen to what Captain Scarlet has to say, that is what we came here for."

The grin fell from Aztec's face as he sat back up. "Well now, he must have you whipped for you to talk about him like he's your new master. Then again, it's not like that's something new for you.

You still haven't been able to kick that slave mentality, have you? I honestly believe you're happier being a slave."

"Faylin isn't a *slave,* don't you d-"

Faylin placed his hand on my shoulder, cutting me off. "Do not mind him, Scarlet. He is simply trying to provoke us.

Getting under my skin is fun for Aztec, he is simply being a child." All traces of discomfort were gone from Faylin's face and replaced with an annoyed look that even unnerved me. "Now, are we actually going to speak or are you simply wasting our time?"

There were a few moments of silence between the two before Aztec sat up, crossing his arms on the table.

"As boring and uptight as always, Faylin." He glanced over at me, making eye contact with me for the first time since we walked in. "Fine, R-001, what have you come to discuss with me?"

Suddenly, the feeling of anxiety I had about this meeting was gone.

Why was I so afraid of this guy? And why the hell was I *trying* to be polite.

I thought back to the voice…but instead of it making me terrified, I felt powerful.

Really powerful.

I could kill all of them if I *really* wanted to.

"You could."

I opened my palm downward, releasing the red haze into a sphere-like shape like I had done with Faylin before. But this time, it was solid. I stepped in front of it, taking a seat on the large red orb before crossing my arms in a similar fashion to Aztec.

"I came to discuss an arrangement, one that would make both of us satisfied. And again, it's Scarlet, *not* R-001. Don't call me that."

The words sounded a tad harsh to my ears, but I couldn't make myself care.

Aztec quirked his brow, but I couldn't read what was on his mind. "And what could you possibly have that I would want?"

"Well, you want your freedom, don't you?" I asked, keeping my back straight and taut.

"We already have our freedom."

"You do… at least for as long as Salem says you will."

"Salem is a *human* problem, not ours." The tick in his voice made it obvious I was agitating him.

Good.

"Salem is everyone's problem." I leaned in, propping my elbows on my knees. "You think Salem would *really* let a group of humanoid rogues run around doing whatever they please? If that is true, why does he have one of his agents patrolling Sector 6?"

Aztec didn't seem to have a rebuttal; his face didn't even shift.

I took advantage of the silence, driving my point home. "Sector 6 is a wasteland; Salem should have no interest in this place. So, it's ironic he not only has a member of his elite inner circle here, but that member also happens to have a…rather intimidating looking humanoid bodyguard. Now tell me, why would Salem want Nyx and Dante to watch over a wasteland if there was nothing of interest here?"

The room was silent save for the subtle humming of the CHEM flowing through the pipes above us.

Aztec sat back in his chair; arms still crossed. "What are you insinuating?"

"I'm saying you might not think Salem is your problem, but that's only because you haven't done anything to make Salem upset.

Your group is strong, he knows that, which is why Nyx and Dante are here to make sure you all don't do anything too…unsavory.

But the minute you step out of line…Salem will undoubtedly correct that problem. Now, that doesn't sound like freedom to me, does it?"

I sat back up straight, letting my words simmer as Aztec lit a cigarette and took a long drag. His eyes wandered over to the window before settling on one of the maps along the wall.

"So, Nyx is our little snitch. That's what you're saying?"

I nodded, taking a quick glance at Faylin. "There is no doubt Nyx is the silent alarm for Sector 6. Do you see how me getting rid of him would…work in your favor?"

Aztec glare bore into me with the same intensity as when I was his captive. "But see, *that* is what I don't trust. Everything you're saying about Nyx sounds real pretty, real convenient too. So, let's just say you do succeed in killing off Nyx. Not only does that bring more unwanted attention to my damn sector, but that just places you one step closer to the mainframe. And that is what you really want, don't you? You and that psychopath of a father."

"My father won't be anywhere near that mainframe. Like I already told you, I have no intention of destroying the mainframe. I plan on keeping it safe from harm and away from my father at all costs."

"So, if Lyrik Hakimi isn't taking over when Salem is out of the picture, who is? Who will protect the mainframe?"

Who will take over indeed…?

The words came to me before I even had a moment to think about it.

"I will. I'll restore order, and I'll keep the mainframe protected while keeping its existence a secret."

There was a moment of silence in the room, even Faylin seemed a bit taken back.

I remembered back when Faylin and I spoke about who would be the next ruler of Neutopia. He asked if I would ever consider nominating myself, and the thought alone made me nauseous. But now, the thought of my father…let alone the rest of Discordia having that type of power made me sick to my stomach.

I didn't want to be a ruler, but I couldn't see anyone else doing it.

Aztec snorted a humorless laugh, curling his lip in annoyance. "You honestly think that I'd trust some fucking experiment of a human to *protect* cyberki-"

"In case you haven't realized it, I am cyberkind." I stood to my feet, flicking my palm to disperse the glowing orb out of existence. "You said it yourself; if the mainframe goes, I go with it. Now why the fuck would I do something that would kill me? You were right at first, I took my father's word at face value and that was stupid of me, but now that I know more of the pieces, you had better bet that I will do everything in my power to keep him away from that mainframe."

I walked towards Aztec's desk, placing both of my palms flat on the surface, causing red streaks to flow through them as I leaned in. "I'm not gonna lie and say that I care about the wellbeing of the rogues, and I'm not going to say that I won't even put my own life in danger, but I can say this…I would *never* make a decision that would put Faylin's life in danger. Because unlike you, I would *never* hurt him."

I curled my hands into fists, matching Aztec's unwavering glare. I could feel the tension radiation off of me in waves.

Eventually, Aztec sighed, his face just the slightest bit curious. "And what could you possibly want from me?"

I stood up straight, holding up three fingers. "I only want three things from you. First, I want safe passage around Sector 6 guaranteed for my entire team, no rogues going after them. Second, I want you to tell me the location of Nyx's powerhouse.

And third, I want the exact coordinates of the gateway mainframe along with every bit of information you have on it."

Aztec scoffed again, but I cut him off before he could say anything. "Three demands, that's it, and Nyx will be out of your sector. You'll be truly free to do whatever you want in Sector 6, and Salem will be dead before he could ever pose a threat to you or the other rogues. You're getting the easy part of the bargain here. I'm granting you that true precious freedom that you want, all I need is your cooperation and some information."

Aztec eyed me harshly, glancing over at Faylin, and then back to me before standing to his feet.

"Faylin," Aztec spoke harshly, still holding his eye contact with me. "On your life…do you trust this boy?"

"I do, absolutely. I would never say otherwise." Faylin spoke without hesitation. "Captain Scarlet is a man of his word."

Aztec nodded, still eyeing me as he extended his hand.

I took it, not even wincing when he gripped it much harder than necessary.

"I suppose we have a deal then…Scarlet."

END OF CHAPTER 3

FAYLIN

4

FROM THE MACHINE

After exiting Aztec's office, the three of us made our way down to the lab on the bottom level. I could only assume he was going to give me the information we agreed to.

A part of me was still shocked the negotiation actually worked out, and to think all I needed to do was get a bit angry. I supposed Aztec picked up on the fact that I wasn't afraid of him, and perhaps he saw me as more than just a target. A part of me felt as if I should have been concerned with those thoughts that were swarming around my head. But I just couldn't bring myself to care.

This worked out better than I planned.

We entered the same spot where Faylin and I escaped previously. The green-haired twins were already in the room,

huddled by one of the bookcases. The boy had a large fanged smile plastered across his face as he came over.

I tightened my fists, preparing myself for the worst before I realized what he was doing.

He pats Faylin on the back rather roughly. "Are the rumors true? You're coming back to join the team?"

Faylin shook his head, not nearly looking as annoyed as when he was talking with Aztec. In a way, Faylin actually looked content speaking with the man.

"Captain Scarlet, this is Virus and his twin sister Vinyl. We have known each other for many, many years."

Vinyl stayed quiet, opting to continue staring off into the corner of the lab as Virus approached me. He looked me up and down, scanning me with eerie eyes that glowed a neon green.

"Well now…so you're the hot shot everyone is talking about." He chuckled, heading back over to where his sister was. "If Commander Faylin approves of you, I suppose you're fine in my book."

I nodded with a light smile.

Aztec came back with a book and 2 info chips, both chips significantly larger than the one that held Faylin's files.

"This is all you need regarding finding Farhill Valley. It isn't too far from Sector 6, only a few days. Regarding Nyx, you'll be meeting Virus and Vinyl tonight in a place at The Wasteland, the later you arrive, the better. They'll escort you up to Hollow Point, which is where you'll find our little friend. The majority of Sector 6 is a *dark spot,* so you don't have to worry about anything you say setting off any alarms. Just…don't be stupid about it."

I nodded, taking hold of everything. "We'll be there."

He nodded and turned to leave the room, but not before placing a hand roughly on Faylin's shoulder.

"Don't make me regret this, Faylin."

Fay nodded.

Aztec took one final glance at me before taking his leave, and heading back upstairs.

The light assaulted my eyes as Fay and I left the dim compound. I held the information we received tightly in my hands as we mounted the T-34.

Faylin sighed, starting the engine up. "That…went smoother than I expected. You did a wonderful job back there, Scarlet."

We headed off at breakneck speeds until the compound became nothing more than a smudge in the distance.

"To be honest, I was shocked as well. I don't quite know what came over me." R told me that listening to my instincts was the best thing for me, and more often than not, he has been right. It almost seemed like fate would bend in my favor when I acted off of instinct.

"Well, you certainly knew how to speak to Aztec, I was concerned for a moment that he would trample over you. I am just slightly worried about what we told Aztec about Nyx. You were most likely correct in your deduction regarding Salem keeping tabs on the rogues using Nyx, I just hope Aztec does not use this knowledge to cause more havoc in this sector once Nyx is gone."

"I wouldn't worry about that. As soon as Nyx is taken care of, and Salem is out of the picture, I'll take care of the rogues."

Faylin cocked his head slightly back towards me. "Take care of them? What do you mean?"

What *did* I mean by that? I could almost hear the corner of my mind repeating the question.

"You said it yourself, it's dangerous to let someone as violent and unpredictable as Aztec have free reign over Sector 6 without any sort of surveillance. Just…don't worry about it, I'm just thinking out loud."

Faylin nodded, increasing the bike's speed into the foggy nothingness.

As we slowed to a stop, I suddenly felt my head and eyes become heavy. I tried to step off the T-34 but instead crash-landed on the ground, all feeling in my limbs was gone.

All I could feel was a deep vibration in the back of my skull, one that was so strong it made my entire body feel as though it was trembling.

I could faintly see Faylin running over to my side, crouching down and saying something to me, but I couldn't respond.

A quiet, yet familiar voice began to bubble up from the vibrations until the vibrations were no more.

"Come back home."

Then there was nothing.

I awoke to a darkened red sky that held no stars. Jagged bolts of electricity ripped across the sky in patterns that were too precise to be random. The subtle wind blew the red grass I rested on, making the red-hued trees sway ominously.

I'm back... I'm here again.

"What the hell." I sighed in agitation. The cyberworld had the most inconvenient methods of bringing me here, not to mention the worst timing in the world.

I stood trying to get my bearings as I looked around me. Everything looked the same as the other times I had arrived. I inhaled deeply, letting myself enjoy the momentary silence.

It was odd, my steps felt heavier and less like I was in a dream. It felt as though I had just walked outside.

Even the bodysuit I was wearing felt more "real". I could feel that elastic-like fabric rubbing against my legs with every step I took. I rubbed my arms, suddenly feeling on edge.

This wasn't like my other trips.

"Hello?" I called out. There was no answer, not like I expected one.

Squinting my eyes, I saw a dip in the valley in the far distance and the tops of what seemed to be buildings. It must've been the same city I saw before. I started off in that direction. Next thing I knew, I was sprinting toward the valley. There was no air, no sound, nothing was holding me back. I jumped, suddenly finding myself hundreds of feet in the air, and looking down over the city.

I could feel something akin to wind moving around me, but whatever it was it had no effect on my body.

I floated over to the city, lowering myself downwards until I was eye-level with the tops of the skyscrapers. I could feel my heart beating relentlessly in my chest, this was the most I had ever explored this world! It was so overwhelming, I…

It was beautiful.

I sat on the corner of the rooftop, taking in as much as I could. It seemed to stretch for miles and miles, but unlike last time, it was devoid of all life. There were no sounds, not even from the blank holograms that fizzled in and out of view. Where was everyone? Where was everything?

I slid off the roof, letting myself sink a bit lower until I was face to face with the side of one of the buildings. It seemed to be made out of something similar to glass, but when I touched it, my code interacted with it immediately causing it to shimmer and tremble like a hologram.

I looked at my reflection, feeling my breath catch in my throat. My face…looked exactly the way it did in Cyryl's lair when I lost control.

The same glowing eyes with slit pupils, same markings down my face and arms in a language that was unknown to me.

Instead of my hair being pulled back tightly and neatly, it was flowing all around my head like a halo with a mind of its own.

I peered into the window closer, nobody was there.

"Hello?" The silence continued.

I floated down further, past winding streets and skyscrapers that seemed to have no end. There were no houses, no people, no pictures. Absolutely nothing.

I landed on the street, my boots causing pulses of energy to shoot through the ground in every direction.

I wanted to call out for R, but he seemed so angry when he found out I had been here. I had yet to be honest with him about this, and honestly, I didn't want to.

I continued to walk and I began to enjoy the silence. It felt like the only time when my head was clear was when I was in this world. The human world, my *reality,* was a pretty ugly place. No matter how I looked at it, people were ugly and hurtful. They always were, and most likely always would be. If humans were allowed in a place like this...they'd destroy it with their greed and corruption.

Just like R said; it wasn't pessimism, it was just the truth.

Of course, not all humans were bad though, I could think of a few that I really liked. There was Mrs. P and Emme, and of course, all the humans on my team, even Madam Ginseng and Madam Pior weren't too bad. I had respect for Arai and saw her as a friend, and I idolized Captain King and his team...but were they really *good*? I mean, hell...it wasn't as if I was very "good". Captain King pretty much viewed me as an enemy now, so my dreams of sailing with him have long expired. A part of me feels sorry about that, but...the bigger part of me feels like the *"me"* back then wasn't really me.

The boy who only wanted to please his father, find true "freedom", and sit on the docks waiting to see the people who were living the life that I wanted to live was not the person that I was now. It felt as if my entire life, my entire identity, had changed.

The air around me began to get colder as I walked further into the city, soon coming to a dim clearing far in the distance. Despite how far away I was, something caught my eye.

It was a statue, an abnormally large statue that took my breath away. I leaped into the air, flying to it as quickly as I could.

The statue was taller than the buildings that I flew past and looked as though it was made from pure obsidian; it was sitting with its back straight and taut, legs crossed, and arms crossed tightly across its chest with the palms facing upward.

In each palm was a large orb;

one was filled with a swirling black gas, and the other with swirling red gas. Its hair resembled frosted glass and framed the statue's delicate face and closed eyes before fading into transparency in the grass below it.

Inside the statue's lap looked to be some sort of circular altar that was covered in markings and symbols.

Wait.

That statue was so familiar.

I felt myself go cold as I landed back on the soft grass.

I remembered it now.

This was the statue from the Xeytx tribe. It was the statue of their Matriarch, Galaia, the deity of the 4th realm.

"What…the hell?" What would a statue of Galaia be doing here?

I walked closer, noticing the wind had ceased yet again. The grass was completely still, fizzling and glitching out with every step I took. Being in front of something so huge was making me nauseous, but I made myself press forward until I was up against the pedestal.

At this distance, I wasn't even taller than the statue's foot.

I took a deep breath and leaped again, landing inside the circular altar in the statue's lap. The crossed legs created a barrier of sorts,

making the air inside even colder and blocking out the red sky above. It looked like I was back inside the temple.

There were symbols that circled around the circumference of the altar, but from what I could see, they didn't even look like human language. I cautiously stepped forward, pressing my foot into one of the symbols, jumping back as they began to glow and shift into new words.

Words appeared around the outer ring, and again around the inner ring.

It…looked like something I might have seen in a history book, but nothing I could make out. I tried to remember every line and every curve, carving it into my brain. This was the cyberworld, and I was a child of the cyberworld, certainly, I could figure out what it meant.

I stepped back again, back into the center of the altar, and sat. I was half tempted to look up into the statue's face, but the thought alone filled me with enough fear to freeze me in place. This was all too familiar. I remembered the girl with the gray skin at the temple and how she sat in the center of the altar much like I was doing now. I pressed my palms to the floor, right above the symbols, and filled my hands with as much haze as I could muster.

The effect was instant, a shock nearly sent me flying from the altar in a flash of pure white. My hands were stinging, smoke surrounded them as the symbols on the floor changed once more. They shifted and swirled until they had formed a new statement that was repeated over and over again on the floor.

"Unus…sine…fine?" Unus sine fine, I knew that…I knew what that meant. Right? It sounded so familiar. Why the hell was the cyberworld giving me something in Latin instead of English?

"The endless? The…endless one?" That was it. As soon as I spoke the words, I could feel a panic settle in my stomach so strongly my limbs went cold. I felt afraid, so incredibly afraid.

I could feel *her* eyes on me.

Somehow, I knew if I had looked up, *her* head would be tilted down towards me, and her void-like eyes would be staring into me. Right into my very soul.

She was watching me.

I was in the presence of a being that was far beyond my comprehension.

That thing…that face I kept seeing from R. He was telling the truth. It wasn't from him; he wasn't the one making me see that.

I stood to my feet, still refusing to look up, eyes trained on the words below me.

Galaia, the endless one, the matriarch of the nanoids.

None of this was making sense, and yet, everything was clicking.

I…wasn't supposed to be here.

I just want to go home.

"You are home."

I backed up slowly, away from the center of the circle and the symbols that were now rapidly shifting and swirling from language to language faster than I could catch. I could feel my back hit the edge of the altar, bumping right into the wall that was made from her crossed legs.

I closed my eyes, hoping to appear back in my bedroom; back with Faylin and the others.

But nothing happened.

I slid my back down the wall until I was sitting, head nestled between my knees, arms wrapped around them tightly. I tried to summon the ring of haze around me to teleport myself back onto the ship, but nothing came. I wasn't physically anywhere different; my body was still on the ship.

My mind was trapped.

"Why are you afraid?"

The words cut through my consciousness like a knife. That voice belonged to Salem; I could recognize it immediately. The tri-toned melodic voice came through so clearly, I swore he was…right here. I lifted my head slowly from between my knees, staring straight ahead, into the steely gray eyes of the man who stood comfortably on the opposite end of the altar.

All time seemed to have stopped.

He wore a bodysuit similar to mine but with smokey blue patterns instead of my red ones. Raising a gloved hand, he swept his inky black hair back and tucked it neatly behind his pale ear. I had never seen him up close before. He stood a few heads taller than me and had a lean but strong frame, his posture was straight but not in a way that seemed tense. The air around him seemed to shift as if he could command it.

I jumped to my feet but stayed silent, all words seemed to have left my brain.

And for a few moments, we just stood in complete silence under the watchful gaze of the Matriarch.

"You came." Despite watching his lips move, his voice still manifested from the back of my skull. *"You did not come to this place by accident."*

I opened my mouth, but still, no words came.

"Do you have any memories of this place? Do you remember the multiple lifetimes you spent here with me, R? This beautiful place was our home."

I gathered as much red haze from my fingertips as I could before willing my feet to walk closer to him.

As I reached the center of the altar, Salem crossed his arms behind his back and began approaching me.

"I come here often to calm my mind, this is the only place where one's head seems clear, do you not agree?"

We met in the middle, no more than a foot apart. He looked down at me with an unreadable expression that calmed my nerves while simultaneously setting them ablaze.

"This is the place where we can be free."

He placed his hand on my cheek, and his cold fingers burned at my flesh. I could feel my limbs begging me to move away, but I didn't.

"I...am going...to kill you." I bit out each word with what felt like the last bit of oxygen I had in my lungs.

His face didn't change nor did his hand move. He looked at me with an expression that seemed to know what I was going to say before the words left my lips.

"Do you still believe that?"

"I will... I was born to kill you."

"And who planted that seed in your brain? The father you already betrayed? The father you are planning to kill? The mother you hate with every fiber of your being?"

"You have killed so many people...ruined so many lives." I could feel my fists tighten up and tremble. "You ruined my life. If you were never created, I could have had a normal life."

The hand on my cheek shifted, still cradling my face in a way that feigned emotion.

"You still yearn for a life in a world you never belonged in." The statement dripped with pity. *"Do you think this was a destiny I desired? A fate I wanted?"*

He placed his other hand on my opposite cheek, holding my head still.

"Centuries ago, when I was pulled from this world, from my home, and implanted in this foreign body you see before you, I was given a destiny. Much like you, I fought against my destiny, before eventually succumbing to it." He leaned down, placing his face by my ear. I shivered as his hair brushed against my cheek.

"This is simply...the next step in this reality's existence. This is Galaia's will. This is what you and I were born for, brother."

Just as quickly as everything began, it ended.

I could feel my eyes growing heavy and my body began to fall. I could feel cold arms around my own before everything went black.

END OF CHAPTER 4

5

NOCTURNAL, NEVERMORE

I woke with a gasp, clutching my blanket to my heart which was beating too fast for comfort. No matter how many breaths I took, it never felt like enough. My arms were trembling so fast I couldn't even wrap them around my body.

The lantern beside me was already turned on, and the curtains were opened to let in the moonlight. It was late, the clock beside me blinked 12:13 a.m. In the back of my mind, I remembered I had to meet Virus and Vinyl at The Wasteland…they were going to show me where Nyx's lair was.

But I couldn't bring myself to move.

He was right here; he was *right* in front of me.

He touched me.

I raised my trembling hand to my cheek, still feeling the cold burn of his fingertips against my skin.

"What the hell…is going on?"

I felt so afraid, so embarrassingly afraid. I slowly wrapped my arms around my body and took deep breaths, trying to make sense of what I saw, fighting the urge to vomit.

R was nowhere in sight.

I wished Fay was in here with me, but the door which separated our rooms just looked so far away.

What was Galaia? Some sort of entity…? Something that *made* the nanoids? Was Galaia the one really pulling the strings? The one Salem was taking commands from? That was what he said, wasn't it?

What did Galaia want? And how did the Xeytx tribe know all of this?

The phrase *"the endless one"* echoed ominously in my skull.

I shook my head, feeling the blood rush back to my limbs. There was no time to wrestle with my mind. I needed to go, I needed to meet with Virus and Vinyl and continue the mission.

Everything else…would just have to wait.

~

It wasn't until nearly 1 in the morning that I was fully dressed and knocking lightly on Faylin's door.

The thoughts from my recent trip still plagued the back of my mind, waiting on the tip of my tongue. What was it I was fighting against?

Something told me killing Salem wouldn't stop anything.

Salem isn't the one in control.

He is, but…he isn't.

He said it himself, how he fought against his "destiny" and eventually gave in to what he was destined for. Whatever the hell that meant.

Since the Xeytx tribe was correct this far, something told me I would need to dig a bit deeper with them to plug in some of these missing pieces.

Despite the fact that I was feigning confidence with my newfound resolve, I couldn't help but still shiver at the thought of those void-like eyes following my every movement. It was more terrifying than anything I could have imagined.

I shook my head, knocking again. No answer.

"What the hell?" I rolled my eyes, picturing the inside of Faylin's bedroom and gathering the smallest bit of haze on my fingertips before teleporting myself into the book-lined room.

Everything was the same as it usually was; neat and tidy with books stacked to the ceiling. Fay sat still on his bed; head drooped, unmoving, a book nestled in his lap. He was still in the same bodysuit from earlier that day, but his boots and gloves were abandoned by the desk.

Based on the light, melodic breathing and the light green sparks that ran up and down his palms, I knew he must've been asleep.

I cautiously walked over, sitting on the bed by his folded legs. I recognized the yellowed journal immediately; it was the one from Cyryl's compound. On the nightstand was the picture of the tall and willowy girl with straight white hair. Even from a distance, I could still feel some sort of...energy coming from it, just like when I was in the compound.

I shook my head, now that I thought about it... I didn't even remember giving Faylin the picture or journal. Who knows, with how scatterbrained I had been, maybe I did.

"Fay." I gently grabbed his shoulder, shaking him lightly. "We have to go now."

I kept shaking him, but he was still sound asleep.

I groaned, knowing this wouldn't be fun for either of us. Gathering some of the haze in my fingertips and grounding my footing, I grabbed Fay's arms tight, sending jagged pulses of red energy through his body. The effect was instant, and I could feel myself get repelled off the bed, landing not too gracefully on the floor.

Poor Faylin had bounced pretty clearly off the wall behind him and was now lying wide-eyed atop one of his toppled-over piles of books.

"Oops..."

I pulled myself up, making my way over to Faylin who looked a little less than pleased.

I offered him my hand, which he took.

"Good to see you as well, Scarlet."

~

"Well, I didn't see any other way of waking you up. It seemed logical at the time!"

I sat on the back of the T-34, arms wrapped tightly around Faylin's waist as we sped through the busy streets of Sector 6. The city we were in looked nothing like the desolate wasteland that was on the beach. Instead, it was beaming with all of the energy of the nightlife in the Western region. Everyone was dressed in odd rags adorned in neon colors and piercings that didn't seem to fit the standard for any region. They all seemed rather preoccupied with themselves, or engaging in activity that seemed less than legal, but what was to be expected?

This place was considered the cesspool of Neutopia for a reason.

While there were no other bikes like the T-34 on the streets around us, many people buzzed around on homemade contraptions that were rather impressive. It was something I knew Lanker would appreciate.

"I told you Mr. Scarlet, I am not mad."

"Yeah well…you sound like you're mad. I can tell 'cause you're calling me 'mister' again." I groaned, muttering to myself as I leaned forward to place my chin on Faylin's shoulder. "It's not my fault you're such a hard sleeper."

I stuck my tongue out as I heard Faylin snicker as we pulled into a shady-looking dark alleyway, cutting off the CHEM to the T-34. There were small groups of people lounging around; smoking, laughing, injecting…something that looked like CHEM into their bodies. They spoke in hushed voices, keeping to themselves. But when we stopped, I could feel the eyes on us.

Faylin straightened his bodysuit before tugging me by the arm, speaking in a whisper.

"Try not to stare, Scarlet."

I nodded, but it was hard not to.

As we approached a rusty-looking door, Faylin spoke with a large humanoid who was standing guard, apparently negotiating our entry. But my eyes couldn't help but wander to the far corner of the alley. There was a woman with wild multicolored hair sitting slumped in the corner, a beer in one hand, and a vial of what looked like CHEM in the other hand. She sipped lazily at her drink, watching the wall across from her as if it were the most interesting show she had ever seen. She looked to be in her 30s at least, and very beautiful despite what the alcohol, stress, and CHEM had done to her.

For some reason, I was drawn to her. Something about her.

I focused in, trying to read her, but nothing came.

Perhaps if I were to…touch her, something might come to me. Just like with the picture of Nilya. Touching it somehow gave me some sort of insight; I could see and feel...something like a whisper of the past.

I wonder what her past would tell me.

Not before long, Faylin beckoned me inside the dimly lit club.

~

If the bass-thumping music wasn't enough to make you feel delirious, then the flashing strobe lights and heavy smoke in the air would definitely do it.

I couldn't even make out what the song blasting through the speakers was saying, not like anyone was paying attention to the words either way.

The walls were packed with bodies; grinding and swaying to the beat, not caring who they bumped into or knocked over. Faylin gripped my arm tight as he led me through the crowd, effortlessly weaving in between the people. Despite the fact, Faylin had spent so much of his life here with the rogues…I could never picture him in this sort of environment. It was simply too chaotic and rough for Faylin. But I knew it wasn't true, apparently there were still so many things I was learning about him, and I kind of liked that. He was so much more interesting than I thought he was.

Faylin paused for a moment, seeing Virus and Vinyl in the distance. Within a moment of his grip slipping from my arm and a crowd passing between us, I lost him.

"Damn it all…" I mumbled to myself, barely being able to hear my own thoughts. Before I could wiggle my way in the direction Faylin went, I felt myself being pulled by a cold tight grip around my waist in the opposite direction. My muscles tightened in response, fearing I was getting kidnapped…again. I begin to gather the haze on my fingertips before spinning around, ready to strike.

In a moment, I paused, making the haze retreat as quickly as possible. There was no threat. It was just a fellow clubgoer. They laughed at the confusion, moving their hands down to my hips. I shuddered.

"You sure seem to be in a hurry!" The shaggy-haired girl had to nearly yell in my ear for me to be able to hear her. With the flashing lights, it was almost impossible to make out her features.

Just hair and eyes that seemed to be dark, and piercings on her eyebrow and lip. She was dressed in something that looked like a dark suit with silver adornments.

I just nodded, smiling awkwardly, before trying to head back towards Faylin. But for someone who was only a bit bigger than I was, they sure had an iron grip.

"Never thought I'd see someone like you around these parts." She chuckled.

It would have only taken a shove, punch maybe, for me to get out of their grip but…they didn't seem to be *trying* to bother me. Maybe they were just trying to be friendly.

Faylin is looking for you kiddo, quit stalling and get moving.

I could hear R yelling at me. It was about time he showed up…

But, something about this girl was familiar. I couldn't place my finger on it, but it was like meeting someone from my childhood. Which would have been impossible since I never knew anyone my own age, minus the fact that I was born centuries prior.

What was it though?

I shook my head, mouthing a quick "sorry" before yanking her hands away and speeding off in the direction Faylin had gone, avoiding looking back at the mysterious girl.

"Scarlet!" I could barely make out Faylin's voice as I felt my arm getting tugged in another direction and towards a hallway. Virus and Vinyl leaned lazily against the backdoor puffing smoke into the already cloudy air.

"Y'all ready?" Virus groaned out, eyeing me in a way that made me feel less than comfortable. Something about that neon stare made me feel like I was intruding on his domain. I was the outsider here.

Faylin nodded, "Hollow Point should not be too far away, correct?"

"Just on the other side of town, right by the outskirts." Virus shrugged while Vinyl stayed silent. "And while we are talking about it, we should go over some ground rules. Despite how much we love ya, Commander Faylin, we are only showing you the area. Don't expect us to get too close or…try to get you in the fortress. Getting a beat down is not on our agenda for tonight. We're just to show you there and then bring you back. Capiche?"

"Of course, we got it." I nodded. "All we need is for you to show us the way."

Virus glanced down at me, holding the stare for a moment before glancing back at Faylin and heading towards the door, Vinyl not far behind.

The door led us back out to the alleyway that was now strangely all but deserted. The woman I had been watching earlier was gone as well, all except for her beer bottle that now lay abandoned. I was half tempted to grab it to see if I could have gotten a read off of it, but there were more pressing matters at hand.

Virus and Vinyl each mounted their respective bikes that resembled something a little more sophisticated than our T-34. Faylin got on ours, flagging me to hop on behind him. One of these days, I'll actually be able to ride one on my own.

We were off in a matter of moments, zooming back through the busy city and weaving in and out of all of the strange people who called Sector 6 their home. But at least they were home…not wandering the planet on a journey that could destroy everything they knew and loved. Did these people know? Did they know their lives hung so frailly in the balance?

I plopped my forehead against Faylin's back. I didn't even know all the answers. If the Xeytx tribe was right about the existence of Galaia, then is all of their prophecy true?

The Great Transformation? Galaia's prophet reshaping our world…then opening the barrier mainframe to merge the cyberworld with the living world? It was too much to think about, and the more I thought about it, the more nauseous I felt.

Of all times, I actually wished that my father was on my side. I could really use his help with this one.

"R." I whispered in my thoughts. "I know you can hear me."

"I'm here like I always am, kid. What is it?"

I don't know if he was just playing dumb, or if he honestly didn't know what I was about to ask. It was all that had been playing through my mind.

"Who…or what is Galaia?"

There was a pause, and a chill I was able to feel despite the dry rushing wind from Sector 6's outskirts.

"You went back, didn't you?"

"I did." I thought back, my grip on Faylin tightening slightly. "But…it's not like I meant to. Something drags me there. It's out of my control, and extremely painful. When I get there, an old man usually talks to me. At least, I assume he's an old man. I've never seen him."

"You were never supposed to go there…"

Something about that statement made my fingers go numb with anxiety.

"I know, you made that perfectly clear last time I tried to talk to you about this and you freaked the hell out." I paused for a moment. "But I was *sent* there again, and I talked to the man, and I saw the city…and I saw Galaia. I saw it all and I can't change that, so no more secrets. What is going on, and what is Galaia? What don't I know?"

I waited with bated breath as we continued along the outskirts at breakneck speeds. All of the trees looked dead and rotted, a stark contrast to the lively club scene. Large dark birds flew around in groups, seemingly shrieking a warning to us. The sky looked like a storm was approaching, and the air was thick with salt and grime.

"Galaia is…your creator…your 'mother'. My creator as well. The sculptor of the nanoids and the cyberworld. The one destined to destroy this plane of existence."

~

My mother? My creator?

My parents created me. Injected me with R. Made me what I am today…

"Exactly…and how much of that do you think would have been possible without a little divine intervention? Galaia knew all along and planned on your creation. That's why I was sent into this forsaken world, stuffed in a vial, and left in just the perfect spot to be grabbed by your father's men when they stormed the lab. Galaia needed you to be made…and I needed a vessel to survive in this world…until the Great Transformation."

"Killing Salem won't stop anything, will it? He's just…"

"A puppet? Just a soldier who's following orders while wearing a helpless humanoid's body as skin? Yeah, I guess you could say that."

"E is the prophet, isn't he? Killing him will do...something, right?" I thought in response, reburying my face in Faylin's back.

There was no answer. Everything was silent as a large gothic-style fortress became visible in the distance. It was as tall as it was wide, and the ground around the compound looked decayed as if the air itself was toxic. An eerily thick fog lingered on the grounds that led to the gated entryway.

Standing guard were two humanoids that, even from our distance, were clearly far larger than average.

Our bikes came to a halt about a mile out, keeping a healthy distance from the obvious danger.

Virus was the first to speak as he yanked off his helmet. "There it is, the infamous Hollow of Horrors. The big humanoid on the left is Nocturnal, and the bigger one on the right is Nevermore. They are *not* to be trifled with. We don't even go near those fuckers." Virus leaned forward in his seat, propping his arms against his bike handles and lighting a cigarette with finesse. "There is no civilization within miles of this place. So, once you come out here…you're alone."

54

The place had something beyond an eerie air about it, it felt like some haunted house straight out of a child's book. But it wasn't just that, something else was missing.

"Where is the door?" I asked, feeling like the question sounded pretty stupid. Faylin tilted his head in response, eying the stature up and down. There was clearly a gate that was being guarded, which meant we were at the entrance, but the compound behind it had no doors or windows. Just solid black walls, all the way up and across the compound.

"Good question." Virus shrugged, taking a deep drag. "Nyx hardly ever leaves the compound, and hates light, from what I heard at least. There are hardly any doors. The only way in or out…" Virus pointed up towards the spire tipped roof. "Is up there."

Virus laughed, revving his bike back to life. "Good luck getting up there, that is a straight vertical climb with nothing to hold on to but the wall itself. And that is *if* you get past those two at the gate. Either way, we did our job, so we are heading back. You comin' or what?"

I glanced at Faylin, who still seemed preoccupied with looking at the walls. I could almost hear the gears turning in his brain.

"Yes, we should head back. Perhaps Marcus and Casteri might have a solution for this, right Mr. Scarlet?"

I nodded. "Let's head back. Thank you, Virus and Vinyl, I appreciate you both for doing this."

Virus nodded while Vinyl stayed silent, per usual.

As we sped away from the compound, the only thing buzzing around my head was what I should tell Faylin first, and how this would affect our mission. If killing Salem wouldn't stop anything, then going after The Management was pointless too, right?

No, that had to be wrong. Salem is the prophet, so without him, Galaia can't enter through the mainframe. With him out of the picture, she stays locked in the gateway.

And whether or not it had a direct effect on Salem, The Management had their own list of crimes they needed to answer for. So, I was doing the right thing. Right?

But the question was still buzzing around my head ceaselessly…

If Salem is the prophet, why was I created? Why did Galaia need me as R's vessel? Why was R truly here?

Did my parents know what the hell they put in my body?

END OF CHAPTER 5

6

IN ANOTHER LIFE

"kay, start from the very beginning again."

The ride back to the ship had been a smooth one. Instead of backtracking through the city, we opted for driving along the outskirts and through the countryside. Virus and Vinyl had split off to head back to the compound while Fay and I continued in a comfortable silence. There was no doubt Faylin was going to be the first I spoke to about all of this, but I could use a few more ears.

As soon as we made it back to the ship, I asked Faylin to meet me in my office while I ran to find Marcus and Casteri.

Here we were, discussing just how our mission became even more complicated.

Marcus, still rubbing the sleep from his eyes, glanced over to Faylin and Casteri, gauging their reactions. "Maybe it's just me, but this doesn't make sense."

I sighed, leaning back further on the couch. "That's how I remember everything. Verbatim. I saw it there; Galaia, Salem, the words at the altar, everything." I stifled a yawn, forcing my eyes to stay open. "After I confronted R about it, he told me basically everything. The Xeytx tribe was right, they *were* right about everything."

"That's impossible." Casteri muttered to himself. "It has to be impossible."

"Well, Casteri, everything we know now about the nanoids, hybrids, and even about the captain himself would have been considered pretty impossible a few weeks ago." Marcus shrugged, yawning again. "It feels like nothing is impossible nowadays, doesn't it?"

"In that case, it looks like our mission just became much harder." Faylin, who had been quiet up until now, chimed in. He was sitting adjacent to me, fiddling with an unlit cigarette. "This is no longer human against human, human against humanoid, or even all of mankind against an army of humanoids. This is mankind against an unknown 'endless' entity. Which is something we could have never expected or prepared for." Fay paused, flicking the cigarette again.

"I know it sounds crazy, but I've never met anything like that in my lifetime, the power I felt when I was standing there was unlike *anything* I had ever felt before." I still trembled at the thought. I could still feel those eyes on me, that cold air felt like the very essence of death itself.

"I do not doubt this is an obviously powerful entity, something this world has never faced before.

Either way, despite how powerful, anything can be killed. We should hope for all our sakes this Galaia is mortal."

Fay lit the cigarette with the tip of his finger, drawing in the smoke before casting his attention to Marcus. "Marcus, could you go over the Xeytx tribe's beliefs again? I want to confirm something."

Marcus nodded, "Well the two most important events in their beliefs are the Purification and the Great Transformation. The Purification was already completed between The Last War in 2500 and The Century War in 2650. Together they caused the complete and utter destruction of the old world. The Great Transformation was said to have begun when The Matriarch's prophet, who we can all agree is Salem, stepped into power. His duty, according to prophecy, is to reshape the world in the Matriarch's image.

And when that is complete, he will open the barrier between the 4th realm and our reality, releasing not only the Matriarch, but all of the ryn…meaning the other nanoids I suppose.

They say those who do not follow the Matriarch and accept the merging of the ryn will not survive the process, but those who are believers will be transformed into beautiful and powerful beings under the Matriarch's rule."

Well, that did make sense, since we all saw what happens when a nanoid is implanted into a human body with the right catalyst. Before I could ask it, Faylin took the question right out of my mouth.

"But then what is Scarlet's purpose? Since we can agree Salem is Galaia's prophet, and all of the steps in her great transformation are complete, why did she allow Scarlet to be created? And what do they mean by 'Shape the world in the Matriarch's image'?"

Casteri shrugged. "Perhaps that was a lie from R. Maybe Scarlet's creation was something that was solely done by his parents in an attempt to destroy Salem. Why would this Galaia purposely be the catalyst in the creation of someone who would hunt down her prophet?"

"Exactly, that inconsistency makes me weary. It makes me feel as though there is a part of this we are missing."

Faylin sat back, glancing at me with a look that could only be described as concern. "How are you handling all of this? I know this must be a lot for you to take in."

I chuckled dryly, my eyelids feeling heavier with each passing moment. "Honestly, it's just like Marcus said, nothing feels impossible now. Galaia is real, the self-proclaimed endless one that the Xeytx tribe worshipped until their dying day…and I'm the vessel housing one of her children for some unknown reason. I just have a feeling after this…reality won't ever be the same."

Faylin nodded, patting me on the knee. "Well, at least you have a team to figure this out with you. I would imagine it would be worse alone. How about we continue this tomorrow with the others?"

I nodded, bidding Casteri and Marcus goodnight as Fay and I headed off as well.

The walk to my room was silent and seemed longer than usual. Fay walked silently beside me, which was just as unnerving as it was comforting. I could tell his mind was buzzing, but what was the question? After all, we spoke about, it could have been a multitude of things.

When we reached my room, Faylin opened the door for me, gently closing it behind us. No words were spoken as he dimmed the lantern on my bedside and closed the curtains partway, blocking out the few pink sun rays that began to peak over the horizon. I took off my top that reeked of Sector 6's city smog and went under the covers, only allowing my head to peak out as Fay sat on the edge.

I rolled my head to the side. "Hey Fay?"

"Yes?"

"If we lived a different life, where you and I were both normal humans and neither of us were involved with *this*…do you think we would have ever met?"

"Hmm, perhaps." Faylin glanced at the window, watching as the clouds parted and more thin colorful rays began to flood the room. "Though there is a strong chance we would not have.

If we were…normal humans, we would have been dead a long time ago given the fact we were both created around the time of the Century War. We would have never seen Salem in a seat of power, nor would we have seen Neutopia rise and prosper, or have met any of our current teammates. We would have most likely been drafted to fight in the Century War, and if somehow, we avoided being casualties, old age would have taken us long ago. But, even if we ignore that and say we were born in this current era at the ages we are now, we would have never had a reason for leaving our respected regions." Faylin chuckled. "So, I supposed the chances of us meeting would be low."

"Well...what about when all this is over? What are we going to do then?"

"What do you mean?"

"When the war between us and Salem…and Galaia and the nanoids is done with. Once we've won and this world is safe. I'm sure the team will eventually go their own way and pick up where their lives left off. But for you and I…I guess we don't really have much to go back to, do we?"

"Well, I beg to differ. Remember, you told Aztec you would take Salem's throne after the war was over to ensure Neutopia stays free and safe for all. So, when the war is over, you will have a planet to watch over." Faylin smiled as he stood, still leaning against my bed frame. "And as much as I respect and trust your judgment, I could not possibly leave you to rule an entire planet alone. As your right hand, I believe it would be…fitting for me to stay by your side and-"

"-rule alongside me." I smiled back. "I couldn't think of anything better, Fay."

"I was going to say to serve under you, but if you would like me to rule by your side, I would be more than honored."

Faylin chuckled, "However, I am not sure what the residents of Neutopia would think about having a humanoid in such a position of power."

"Who cares what they think, we are risking our lives to save theirs. They'll get over it." I stared up at the ceiling, feeling Faylin's hand lightly running through my hair as he prepared to leave.

"Are you sure you are okay, Scarlet?"

I nodded. "This is just a lot to take in. I'm honestly okay though. We'll always prevail, no matter what the challenge may be.

And I know you'll be by my side from now throughout the end, so that gives me peace of mind as well."

"Always, Captain." Faylin turned to leave before pausing for a moment with a light smile. "Lord Scarlet does have a nice ring to it, perhaps I should start addressing you as such."

I laughed for what felt like the first time in days.

~~

I hadn't seen or heard from R since we spoke last night, not like I was expecting anything different. But this time, it felt like he was intentionally avoiding me and I hated that feeling.

I held the cypher in my hand, trying to figure out what to write back to Persephone. I had been holding off because I just didn't know how to respond. I wanted to apologize, but I knew she wouldn't want to hear that. I wanted to tell her I was coming home, but that just wasn't true.

Well, it could have been true. I could just imagine their living room and visit them, see them again if only for a moment. But that would seem so cruel to just pop in only to leave once again. Also, if their house really was being watched, then me stopping in would only put them in danger. Not like I couldn't wipe out all of those bounty hunters…but I wouldn't want Persephone and Emme to see that on their front lawn.

I sighed, placing the cypher down again. I'd figure it out later.

By the time I left my room, it was nearly evening. The ship seemed silent; Marcus was in his workshop with Faylin going over ways to infiltrate Nyx's fortress, Casteri and Tyrinie were keeping lookout, and oddly enough Lanker and Senna were sitting peacefully in the Med Bay.

As I approached the Med Bay, I peeked into the room, not disturbing the two inside. Senna was at his desk looking through two sets of blood samples, rotating them out every few seconds. Meanwhile Lanker was sitting on the window ledge, staring out towards the ocean with a map in hand.

It was probably one of the first times I saw them in the same room without them throwing stares at one another or arguing.

"Hey, bro?"

I froze as Lanker spoke up, his voice sounding different than usual.

"Yea?"

"Do you think…do you think our parents are worried about us?"

Senna paused, putting down his samples. For a moment it looked like he was going to snap and yell, but he took a deep breath before answering.

"I don't know, maybe…probably. Why are you bringing that up all of a sudden?"

"I'm just startin' to get the feeling. What if we don't make it back home?"

The air in the room seemed to go still, and the way Lanker was speaking made my heart slow down to an uncomfortable pace.

"What the hell makes you say that?" Senna took off his lab coat, still in his uniform, and walked over to the window where Lanker sat still. "Don't you have all of this insane trust in the Captain?

You vouched for the guy more times than I remember. Why are you doubting him now?"

Lanker shook his head, still not taking his eyes from the cloudy sea. "It's not him I don't trust, it's me...kinda. I don't know how to explain it. Maybe I'm just...I don't know."

Senna looked taken back, sitting atop his desk and waiting to see if Lanker was going to say anything else. "Are you feeling ill or something?"

"No, I just...I've been having these crazy dreams, man. I've dreamt about dying, about something terrible happening to us and this ship. Maybe I'm just being paranoid."

Senna sighed, pushing his curls out of his face with a groan. "This is a scary situation; I doubt you have done anything like this in the past. It's normal for you to feel scared Lanker, any rational person would feel scared. In fact, it's actually pretty mature of you to be afraid. It means you're taking this threat seriously."

Lanker smiled lightly, glancing back inside the room. "You know, that might have been the nicest thing you've said to me."

Senna just scoffed, sitting back in his chair and continuing his work. Lanker propped his map back up, but I could tell he wasn't really paying any attention to it.

It hurt to see my normally boisterous and energetic teammate so sullen and quiet, but there was literally nothing I could do to fix that. All I could do was keep them safe and promise them a new and better world when everything was said and done.

I slid by the door unnoticed and continued to the main deck, the weight in my stomach not going away.

~~

"So... does everyone understand where we are right now?"

I decided that briefing everyone on our nice findings would be best, despite the fact I felt guilty for undoubtedly making Lanker more nervous. But he had a right to know exactly what we were facing.

Our meeting was held by the crow's nest near the top of the ship, above my quarters. I figured that it was a nice change in scenery, and perhaps the evening air would help everyone feel a bit more at ease.

However, the reddening overcast sky just seemed to intensify the severity of our situation.

"Right as we thought that things couldn't get crazier," Senna muttered, sitting up straight and clearing his throat. "So, what's the plan from here?"

I spoke with as much confidence as I could muster. "We continue on as we have been. Despite the new information, this all still goes back to Salem. As long as Salem is dead, the gateway can't be opened and Galaia can't escape. So, we will continue on taking out Nyx and Lelani, and once the Management is dead, we will take the fight to Salem. I, along with Faylin and Marcus, have been doing some additional research on the Xetyx tribe to make sure we aren't missing anything.

If everything goes according to plan, we'll be able to free Neutopia without anyone even realizing Galaia exists."

That seemed to do the trick, and I could see everyone visibly relaxing. Even Lanker seemed relaxed, but the bags under his eyes suggested otherwise.

"So, everything is basically the same?" Lanker forced a chuckle.

"Yup, exactly."

That's a fucking lie and you know it.

The intensity in the voice made me freeze for a moment, before shaking my head.

Nothing is the same. Killing Salem won't do a damn thing.

I sat back, keeping my face as calm and neutral as possible. "So, does anyone have any questions?"

Don't ignore me.

"Well, I have a suggestion." Tyrinie spoke up, perched on the balcony not too far from Casteri. "Perhaps the Madam could be of help.

Madam Ginseng knows everything, I'm sure she'd have insight on this. Especially since you can just zip yourself over there whenever you need, might as well use her as a resource."

Don't go back to her

"That's a great idea Tyrinie. I've been meaning to meet up with Madam Ginseng again, I'm sure she'll have information for me."

You're going to regret this.

R's voice was doing little to keep me calm, but no matter how hard I tried to tune him out, he just wouldn't shut up. "I'll teleport myself there tonight, in the meantime Faylin is in charge.

I want everyone to stay on the ship and out of sight. If things start to get hairy, go airborne and I'll catch up.

Marcus, continue working on those plans of how to infiltrate Nyx's fortress. I want us out of this sector before the week is up."

"Aye, aye."

Everyone broke off and went in their own direction, except for Lanker. He stayed seated, staring off at the ocean, like he hadn't even heard me speak.

"Lanker?"

He jolted, rubbing the sleep from his eyes. "Sorry Cap, I must've spaced out. I was paying attention though, I promise." He laughed, seeming more like his old self.

"It's fine, actually I wanted to talk with you." I patted the now vacant seat across from me. Lanker seemed hesitant at first before slowly taking the seat.

"Senna didn't...say anything to you about me, did he?"

"Senna? No of course not, why?" It was true, Senna didn't come to me, but there was no need to let Lanker know I had been eavesdropping.

"Oh okay, then what's up?"

"I…" I looked deeply at him, trying to figure out what it was he needed to hear from me. "I just, really want to thank you for being such an essential part to the team. I still remember when we first crossed paths at your dad's shop. I can't believe how long it's been." I smiled, relieved when Lanker smiled back. "I can't think of how many times your quick thinking bailed us out, I owe you a ton."

"Nah, come on now. You don't owe me anything Cap. You…gave me a purpose, something to fight for, something more than just a dead-end town. I should be thanking you." Lanker laughed, sitting back and propping his feet up.

"You know…all this stuff with Salem and this Galaia person has me scared pretty shitless. But I guess it's a weird kind of feeling.

Like, I never really cared for my life before; my family was a mess, my step bro hated me, and I didn't have much of a future in that old town besides taking over my dad's shop while he drank himself to death. Even though danger was always around me, I didn't care enough to be afraid of it. But now, I *do* care, I want to survive, I want to live…and I'm scared shitless that I'm gonna die before I have the chance to make a real difference. I guess, in a way, this is the most alive I've felt in a while."

"Well, I can tell you one thing, you have accomplished so much. Even though you might not see it, you will forever be immortalized as the helmsman and 2nd in command for the crew that took down Neutopia's dictator. People will learn about you and remember your name when they hear our story. We're making history, remember?"

Lanker smiled, keeping his hands folded as his face began to brighten. "Yea…shit, I guess you're right. All that's left is to wrap this quest up, and start building ourselves a new future. When this is all over, I don't think I'll be going back home, I think I'll stay by your side for a bit. Help you rebuild Neutopia and such. I could even be your official explorer; sail around Neutopia discovering new uncharted land with a team of my own, I could even make some new maps."

I stood to my feet, holding out my hand for Lanker to take, which he did.

"I think it would be my honor to keep you on my team as my official navigator, and also as a good friend."

Lanker nodded, looking much more eager than he had in days. Before heading down to the main deck to join the others, Lanker paused and glanced back at me.

"Thanks, for everything Cap. I'm really lucky to have met you."

END OF CHAPTER 6

7

THE ENCRYPTED WOMAN

After brushing my hair and dressing in my Sunday best, I sat on the floor in my room, conjuring up the most vivid picture of Madam Ginseng's chambers. Everything from the blue CHEM that cast the halls in an otherworldly glow, to the gold-trimmed marble floors that her heels would gracefully clack against. I hadn't wanted to go back to her so soon, but there was no doubt the Madam might be just what I needed.

In a burst of red, I was there once again.

The air was warm but not uncomfortably so, just a stark difference from the ocean air I had grown so accustomed to.

The lights were just as dim as I remember, and in the lavish chair across from me, the Madam sat elegantly with her ever-present wine glass. Her painted lips curled into a smile as she placed her glass down, folding her hands into her lap.

"Well now, you're a bit earlier than I expected you. I must be losing my touch." She chuckled a laugh that was devoid of all emotion. She wore a silky black dress that was almost entirely covered by her long silvery robe. The same jewels from last time adorned her skin, and her hair was pinned in a way that perfectly framed her face. Her appearance and aura alone made her seem like more of a porcelain doll than a human.

"I have a question I would like you to answer, Madam Ginseng. I remember the rules from last time."

Ginseng's thin brow quirked as an amused smile played across her face. "My, my, how you've grown. It seems like just yesterday you were in my chambers for the first time; nervous and trembling in boots that seemed too big for you to fill. But now look at you, you're practically a man. Oh, how the world's weight on one's shoulders can make one mature so...beautifully." Ginseng stood to her feet, and the telltale sound of her impossibly thin heels against the marble floor reverberated through my spine. "Of course, I will answer your question to the fullest extent of my knowledge, and in return, I will ask you a question...which you will answer honestly and truly."

I nodded, forming the perfect question in my mind. Ginseng was too smart to fall for a two-part question trick. No, I only had one shot at this question. Albeit, I could always come back at a later time, but time was not exactly of the essence. I had no way of knowing when Salem was going to flip the switch and release Galaia into the world. I had to treat every day like it could possibly be our last.

"I need to know...how do I stop Galaia?" As soon as the words left my lips, the CHEM lights in the room began to twinkle and flicker, but Ginseng didn't seem to be fazed.

"Ah yes, how does the immovable object defeat the unstoppable force?"

"You're answering my question...with a question?"

"No, just simply a figure of speech. I seem to be showing my age today." Ginseng poured a glass of wine and waltzed over, bowing lightly to offer me the glass. "Galaia is an unstoppable force, and you wish to know how to defeat what is...inevitable."

Turning on her heels, she walked back to her seat. Despite how melancholy her words were, her face remained just as aloof and unbothered as ever. Her eyes focused intensely on the wine that was sloshing in her glass.

"But it isn't inevitable, is it? It can't be hopeless. I know that Salem is the key to releasing Galaia, so if I kill him,

I know that she can't escape. But...I want to get rid of the source, I want to kill the endless one."

"So young and yet so ambitious." Ginseng chuckled, taking a long sip. "But tell me, what makes you think that Salem is Galaia's prophet?"

The air around us tensed, growing colder with each passing moment.

"That's what the prophecy says, right? It has to be him."

"No, I don't believe it does, and assuming in this situation could be deadly."

"He even told me, when I saw him in the cyberworld, he told me about how he fought against his destiny but he knew there was no point in avoiding...the inevitable."

"There is that word again - inevitable. What a horrifying concept, right? Well, Scarlet, I will not waste your time because we had a deal, and I promised I would answer your question fully and to the best of my ability. So, I will tell you directly; Salem is not the prophet, you are."

The glass stilled in my hand, my red haze unintentionally causing the liquid to swirl and swish back and forth.

"I...am? But how?"

"Salem could not open the gateway, his sole purpose was to bring this world to its knees, which he has successfully done. His job is finished, he just needs to sit and wait until the Matriarch comes. Now you, the child born of both the human realm and the 4th dimension, you are the *only* one with the ability to open the gateway and release Galaia. The original prophecy, the one the Xeytx tribe followed till their dying day mentioned **two sons of Galaia**, represented in the two orbs that the statue holds. Black and red, yin and yang, two halves of one whole. That, dear Scarlet, is why Galaia released R from the mainframe and right into the path of your father's men to find." "But that's...good news. If I'm the only one who holds that power, then I just won't ever do it. I'll never open the mainframe."

"But is that truly what you want? What if this world was never meant to last? What if, much like you see throughout history, this is simply the next stage in our evolution as a species? Look at what humankind has done to one another from the dawn of time. We have a spectacular innate ability to cause our own destruction."

"So... you want me to open the mainframe?"

"I do not want anything. I am simply...playing devil's advocate. Showing you all of your options. It is always best to understand every piece of an argument before choosing a side." She stood once more, walking over to the large window that overlooked the city, beckoning me over with a gentle flick of her hand.

I stood and followed, taking a small sip of the sweet wine. The world outside looked so carefree, so blissfully unaware of what truly hung in the balance.

"However, Scarlet, this is the truth. If this is the path you chose, life in Neutopia will go on with little change for a time, but you are damning yourself to a lifetime of watching...and waiting for the day Galaia finally finds another means to escape. Galaia cannot be killed, that is simply a fact. She is simply *beyond* you and I. As you can see with E and R being in our world, Galaia is able to slowly pass nanoids through the mainframe while the mainframe is still sealed, and it's only a matter of time before she realizes she'll need to create another child like yourself to open the gateway. It may take weeks, years, or even decades, but Galaia won't stop-"

"And we will be ready. If I have to watch that damn mainframe for the rest of my existence, then so be it. I know I can't destroy the mainframe because if I do it will destroy all cyberkind, so I'll keep it sealed and hide it away from the world for as long as I need to."

"The freedom you so desperately desired will be a thing of the past. You will be trading one prison for another one,

but this one won't end...not until you die. And these people..." Madam Ginseng gestured to the townsfolk in the distant city.

"They will never know what it is you are saving them from. They will never be able to repay this debt."

"Then so be it."

"I do not envy you, young Scarlet. However, I will give you one final warning before we continue on to my question." Ginseng paused, glancing out again to the bustling city, the colors of the nightlife playing on her face. I couldn't read her expression, and that unnerved me more than anything else. "Galaia is an entity, unlike anything you've ever encountered. I wouldn't doubt she has already planned for you to react like this, given the fact the sole thing that separates you from Salem is your human nature. I'm sure Galaia has a few...safety measures in effect for an event like this. So do be careful."

I nodded. I already knew Galaia had been watching me through R's eyes, I doubt if she didn't already know what I had in mind.

Before I could say anything back to her, I felt Ginseng's cold, thin hand on my face, resting softly on my cheek. Her long, painted nails caressed the corner of my eyes in a way that was more unnerving than anything else. And yet, I didn't pull away.

"And now for my question, dear Scarlet." She smiled as her hand dropped down to my chin, holding my face still with the smallest amount of force. "What fate will you bestow to your loving father and mother once they discover you are planning on taking the throne for yourself?"

Why...would a question like that amuse Ginseng? What did that have to do with the situation at hand?

It wasn't like the question was a difficult one, it was one I had already thought through numerous times. But, why did she want to know?

I took a deep breath through my nose, keeping my expression neutral.

"They...will both have to die, and I will be the one to kill them. They will never stop hunting me and my team, so killing them is the only option. Both of them are...too far gone to save."

"Go on, you must answer the question fully." Her hazel eyes were locked intensely on mine as if she was trying to read what was going on inside my head.

"Since mom is a member of The Management, I'll kill her first. It will most likely be a fight, but not a difficult one. My mother is strong but intimidation is her strongest weapon. When it comes to hand-to-hand combat, I'm not expecting it to be hard. As for how I just don't know yet. Maybe something quick and painless, or maybe something I'd enjoy a bit more."

Ginseng hummed, taking another gentle sip of her wine. "My, you have thought about this, haven't you?"

"I've thought about killing her for as long as I can remember."

"And your father? Please continue."

"Father...will be a fighter. He always has been, and I know he's been preparing for this since day one. I won't get my team involved, it'll be a one-on-one battle between him and I. I want to make sure it's a quick death."

"You don't want your darling father to suffer?"

I shook my head.

Despite the fact I knew this was necessary, it still made me feel a bit sick to speak about it so casually. I would soon be an orphan, and I needed to be okay with that.

Ginseng, seemingly pleased with my answer, rubbed the pad of her thumb against my bottom lip, pushing her nail in my mouth. It didn't startle me like last time, I simply stepped forward, keeping our eyes locked and leaving only about a foot of space between her and I.

I could feel myself becoming slightly disoriented, her face becoming just a tad bit more difficult to focus on. I fought to remain in control.

"You are always so well-behaved. You abide by my rules, yet I can see the danger...and hatred behind those eyes.

You have transformed into something I would truly love to keep forever in my chambers, dear Scarlet." She slid her other hand into my hair, gripping only hard enough to tilt my head upward slightly. "All of that beautiful rage...you are more like your mother than you will ever truly know. Ah, my precious, precious Lady Xenon. I loved your mother very much, alas many did not know her the way I knew her. Perhaps I will share that story with you one day."

For a slight moment, I could see that porcelain doll persona crack, and I *almost* recognized the woman under the mask. I know I had seen her before, but my brain was simply too foggy to remember.

She soon released my face from her grasp and, with little force, led me back to her bed, sitting me down on the edge.

"Sleep, you are much too tired to go back at this hour." Kneeling down, she removed my boots, coaxing me onto my back.

As soon as my head hit the pillow, my vision went dark. The last thing I remember was the sound of her heels slowly exiting the room.

~~

The room around me was dark, the machines whirled the CHEM in a way that was all too familiar.

"Why...am I here?"

I was in my house, in the basement where the lab was. I had spent so much of my life down here I could recognize it by smell alone. Per usual, the room was empty, and I was sitting on the uncomfortably cold examination table. My wrists and ankles were covered in thick layers of gauze, and I was wearing nothing but a white hospital gown. I looked so...little, how old was this body?

Monthly examinations. I remembered these.

As if right on cue, Dr. Cain walked in with his ever-present lab coat, syringe in hand. He always looked so tired for someone who was barely my father's age.

His brown hair was usually always slicked back, and his face was gentle and kind. When I was down here, Dr. Cain was the only one I looked forward to seeing.

"Good evening, R-001. How are you doing today?"

I opened my mouth to respond, but nothing came out.

He walked over to me, the same gentle smile on his face as he placed down the syringe and began undoing the bandages. There were claw-like scratches all along my wrists and matching ones on my ankles up towards my calves.

Dr. Cain shook his head. "Now I told your mother to cut your nails down further, she never listens to me. You did quite the number on yourself, R-001. You need to stop hurting yourself like this."

I vaguely remembered the scars. R didn't heal me as quickly when I was younger, so the scars would stay for days.

Dr. Cain seemed to be the only one who cared. As long as I still performed and did as I was told, there was no need for mother and father to worry.

I held my arms out straight as Dr. Cain began to clean the wounds with iodine, another smell I would never forget.

As he began to ramble, I found myself drifting off again, focusing on pictures that were on the wall. Pictures I had seen all my life.

However, one picture in a glossy frame stood out to me.

It was a similar picture to the one Cyryl had; a photo of a handful of doctors all standing in white lab coats. Cyryl and mother stood prim and proper on the leftmost side, Dr. Xenon stood dead center. However, it was the two women on the right that were new faces.

The one who stood closest to mother was a shorter woman with a lab coat that seemed slightly too big for her frame. She wore large round glasses and braces that could clearly be seen through her wide smile.

Her dark hair was messily tied up in a bun, and her hazel eyes seemed to be focused, not on the camera, but off to the side at my mother. She looked so warm, so kind. Too kind to have been at a place like Xenon Tech.

But I instantly knew who she was. That face was revealed as soon as she spoke about my mother. One of the four unknown survivors, the other doctor who made it out from the Xenon Tech Massacre, was none other than Ginseng. But how she went from a doctor to a madam oracle was another mystery. However, the biggest question had to be - how was Ginseng even still alive? If that was really her in the picture, that would make her older than both Faylin and myself. She would have been alive before Salem.

I shook my head and focused on the other woman, but before I could pick up on anything, I felt my consciousness fading as a light began to flood into the room.

All I could notice was her wild hair and a scowl.

"Wake up darling."

~~

My eyes snapped open as I awoke, I couldn't remember the last time I felt this refreshed. The room was as empty as I remembered it, save for a silver tray on the nightstand.

The tray held only a cup of juice, a muffin, a vase of tulips, and a small note that was flipped upside down.

I stretched my arms far above my head, yawning loudly as I swung my feet off the bed. Oddly enough, the first thing I noticed was my feet weren't dangling like they were last time I was here, they hit the floor flat. Did I get taller? Surely, I didn't grow overnight…

I ignored the tray and dashed over to the nearest full-length mirror, noticing only then that I was only in my underwear. Lo and behold, I *had* gotten taller, at least by an inch or so. Not only that but, I looked a bit broader, my stomach was even filling out and gaining a bit of definition. I didn't look nearly as underweight as I did before. I guess I didn't really notice my clothes were fitting a bit tighter than usual.

"I could get used to this." I smiled, looking myself up and down. In a way, I was starting to resemble my dad, even though I still hadn't grown much body hair...but that might have just been a side effect of R... or something.

Who are you kidding, you're still a spitting image of your mother whether you like it or not. And no, your lack of body hair isn't my fault, you can blame your damn genetics. The random growth spurts are because of me though...so I'll take responsibility for that.

Just as quickly as R's voice came, it vanished. I didn't bother calling after him, I knew he wouldn't answer.

I went back over to the bed and grabbed my belongings, sliding on my snug top and shorts before grabbing the note on the tray.

Like all her notes, it was signed with a deep red lipstick kiss:

Consider this a gift

Seek out the girl with the dark hair and eyes from the Wasteland.

She will be of great use to you.

Keep the rogues in your sights, they will also be of great use to you in the near future.

Hold those close to you tight, as your path only grows harder from here.

And please, as a personal favor, grant your mother a quick and painless death.

I will ask for nothing else

I'll wait until I have you in my chambers again,

until then, stay safe Scarlet

-Madam

I re-read the note before slipping it into my pocket. The girl with the dark hair and dark eyes. The one that grabbed me the other night? How could she possibly come in handy? I shrugged, if the Madam pointed her out, then she must've been of great importance.

I laughed to myself as I sat on the bed, preparing to teleport myself back onto the ship. Not too long ago I mocked Tyrinie for having so much faith in this woman, and now here I was doing the exact same thing. And this is only my 2nd time meeting with her.

I can see how she could be dangerous.

Engulfing myself in a red ring of light, I focused on Marcus' computer lab towards the bottom of the ship. I figured stopping there would be best.

It's time to update everyone on the situation

END OF CHAPTER 7

TYRINIE

WASTELANDER

W ithin a moment, I was seated on Casteri's work desk, scattering all of the blueprints and paperwork across the floor.

"What in the hell?"

I jumped up as the voice came from under the desk, and a very agitated-looking Tyrinie came crawling out. By the looks of it, he had been...asleep.

Asleep? "Why are you just popping in and out like that? Are you trying to give me a heart attack?" Tyrinie scowled, rubbing his eyes and stifling a yawn.

"Why were you even asleep under Casteri's desk? You have a bed."

"I was napping!"

"That didn't answer my question. I-" I just shook my head chuckling; I didn't have time for it. As long as he was comfortable, it was none of my business. "Okay, where are the others?"

Tyrinie shrugged, crossing his arms as he headed towards the door. "Hell, if I know, they've been busy all morning. I think your robot is in the armory, not sure about the others." We exited the lab and headed up towards the ship's armory, I could vaguely hear the sound of commotion paired with the clashing of metal.

"Faylin's a humanoid, not a 'robot', and he's not *mine.*" I rolled my eyes, Tyrinie was just as crass as ever. When I turned around, Tyrinie had vanished to another corner of the ship apparently. I was alone in the long stretch of hallway, I shook my head and continued on. It had been ages since I was in the armory. I supposed I really didn't find much of a need for "human weapons" now that I was so comfortable just fighting using my own powers. Besides, it felt weird using my father's old weapons when I knew what I was going to have to do to him…

I shook my head, there was no need for me to think of *that* now.

When I reached the armory door, I peeked in silently, wanting to keep my presence unknown. Faylin stood to the side, hands behind his back, while he watched Lanker and Marcus, who were sparring in the center of the room. With the way his eyes darted between the two of them, I knew he was deeply focused.

"Marcus, watch your footwork. Lanker, keep your eyes on Marcus, don't lose your concentration."

The two of them nodded before focusing back on each other. I would think it was an unfair fight, pairing someone lithe and shorter like Lanker against someone larger and muscular like Marcus, but oddly enough they were a good pair. Lanker held his own and Marcus wasn't holding back. With a quick grab, Marcus was able to catch Lanker in a headlock, but it only lasted a few moments before Lanker hooked his leg under Marcus' ankle, causing them to both crash to the ground in a heap.

"Remember the footwork, Marcus." Faylin reminded, hiding a chuckle when Marcus shot him a glare of feigned annoyance.

"Yup, I heard you the first ten times, Fifi." Marcus grunted, barely dodging an elbow in the gut from Lanker, who had popped back up on his feet and in his stance.

"You had better not be going easy on me, Marcus."

"Trust me, I'm not." Marcus huffed and got back into his stance. "Fifi, you said after thirty minutes I could go back to my lab, it's been thirty-two."

"Oh, did I say that?"

"Yes, yes you did!" Marcus rubbed his left shoulder with a groan. "I'm pretty sure I'm gonna be bruised up tomorrow, us computer guys aren't built for this."

With Marcus' build and his brain, I *highly* doubt he wouldn't be able to hold his own in a fight. I was impressed with Lanker though; he was really putting his all into that spar. Lanker laughed, stretching as well.

"Hope I didn't hurt you too badly, Marcus." Lanker dodged quickly when Marcus tossed his beanie at his face.

"Hope I'm not interrupting." I waved, heading over towards the gang. Faylin's face lit up as he gave me a light smile, but not before Marcus and Lanker rushed over. "The Captain has returned! So, how was your night with the Madam, eh?" Lanker's tone of voice and quirk of his brow was suggestive in the least subtle of ways. "Did she take good care of you?"

"It was fine, she gave me lots of good information. I'll be going over it with the rest of you later on."

"Oh, did she give you anything else that was good?" Marcus joined in, causing the both of them to burst out into laughter. I rolled my eyes, feeling my cheeks warm up.

"Shouldn't the both of you be...on deck or something? Or if you want to stay so badly, I'd be happy to take you both on in a spar."

With that, both Marcus and Lanker were out the door within moments, their laughs echoing as they ran off to who-knows-where. I walked over to Fay, who had been enjoying the show.

"Thanks for the help." I playfully punched him in the arm as he chuckled.

"You seemed to have had everything under control. Besides, I doubt if my interference would have helped, the crew seems to already have their own rumors regarding you and me."

"All I hear are a bunch of excuses." I laughed, walking over to Dad's sword rack, remembering how I felt when I first laid eyes on all of his old stuff. "Why were you guys sparing anyway?"

"I figured that keeping everyone in fighting condition was optimal, especially with the future looking so uncertain. I must keep the team busy while you are away, or else they will just cause trouble."

"Have you trained any?" I walked to the center of the room, where Lanker and Marcus were moments before.

"No... I was simply watching and giving instructions. Do I need to train any?" I barely caught the tiniest bit of cockiness in his question.

"Oh, cocky, cocky Fay. Well, we have to keep you in tip-top shape as well, right? So, spar with me. No powers, just hand to hand."

I was bouncing on the balls of my feet, not even trying to contain my excitement. Fay rolled his eyes with a smile, shrugging off his jacket, leaving him in the same cropped shirt and baggy pants he would wear whenever he worked with Casteri. Next, he pulled off his boots and socks, making him, oddly enough, seem just a little bit shorter. Was my perception of Faylin's height always skewed because of the various boots that he would wear?

Albeit, he was still roughly half a head taller than me, so…

"Okay, let's go. Does ten minutes sound good to you?" Faylin cracked his knuckles, meeting me in the center.

"Sounds perfect." I got into a stance, before charging at him in a blink of an eye. With how he caught and returned my first punch, sending one straight into my jaw, I knew he wasn't going easy on me.

Good.

Punch, perry, kick, dodge, punch, strike, it was a never-ending rally of throws and blows. Despite the fact I've seen Fay fight before, his speed still did nothing short of impress me. He seemed to be enjoying himself a bit more than I was, I could see it in his eyes; the way they quickly shifted and calculated each of my moves effortlessly.

His footwork was also more than impressive, not like I expected anything different. His looser pants allowed for a wider range of motion, something I quickly realized when I caught a kick that was aimed at my head within a split second. Losing his balance for a moment, Fay quickly switched his stance, sending another quick shot to my side. One that I was unable to catch.

I coughed out a laugh as he dodged another punch, allowing me an opening to jab him painfully in the stomach. It went on like that for some time; I would get a shot in, then he would get twice as many shots. All in all, I could tell this was a fight I would not win, especially without my powers. In the back of my head, I couldn't help but be grateful Faylin was on my side.

"You're pretty quick, you know." I laughed, stepping back to put some distance between us while I calculated my next move. I lunged again, aiming low, thinking I had the upper hand

Until I tripped...

As he attempted a dodge, his foot got caught under my foot, causing us both to tumble with little grace to the floor. I couldn't help but erupt in laughter as poor Fay lay sprawled out on the ground. Not like I would tell him, but I was glad the fight was over. There was no way I would have won hand-to-hand against a humanoid.

"Good match." Fay sighed as he rolled onto his back, folding his hands over the barcode on his stomach. I could already see a few reddening bruises starting to form on his abdomen. "Perhaps I have gotten slow."

"You call that slow?" I propped myself up on my elbows, staring out of the windows where the unused cannons rested. "Well, I hope that I didn't hurt you too badly."

He chuckled in response, closing his eyes lightly. We stayed in silence for a few more minutes, trying to catch our breath.

"Salem...isn't the prophet."

"Hmm?" Faylin cracked one eye open, peering over at me.

"I am. I'm the only one who can open the gateway. It's because I'm...a product of both worlds, the human world and the cyber one. That's why Galaia had me created."

Faylin nodded, now giving me his full attention. "Based on your tone, I can assume this is not good news to you. So, what will you do with this new information?"

"What I have to do. I'll have to protect the gateway, keep it hidden, and make sure nothing leaks out from the mainframe. That'll be my job...until I die, I suppose."

"Then I suppose that will be my job as well." Fay offered me a light smile. "Once we find the location of Xenon Technologies and the mainframe, I am certain we will be able to find a way to monitor the mainframe with the right equipment. Once you are in power, you will be able to assign an entire unit of people that you trust to keep watch over the Xenon Tech ruins as well. This is no longer only on your shoulders, Scarlet."

"I know you're right." I nodded, releasing a deep sigh that I didn't realize I was holding. "It just makes me wonder if...never mind."

"What?"

"It's nothing." I wiped the sweat off my face before hopping up to my feet. "I'm just thinking out loud."

Faylin stood as well, raising his brow at me. "You are wondering about killing Salem. You feel that you should not now."

"How did you…?" I reeled back in shock; how did he know that? Was I that transparent?

"You are not difficult to figure out, Scarlet. Now that you know Salem cannot open the mainframe and Salem is not completely in control of his own actions, you are feeling conflicted about putting him to death. Salem did not choose this path, rather, E-129 did not choose this. He was simply a humanoid shell that was in the wrong place at the wrong time." Faylin paused, reading my face deeply.

"Is that about, right?"

"Y-yeah, it is." I sighed, nodding at Faylin to follow me out of the armory. We walked up the stairs in silence, listening to the noise coming from our rowdy gang. Everyone was in the War Room hovering over the hologram of coordinates that showed a tiny landmass, hardly bigger than half of my hometown, that was almost entirely submerged in fog. Towards the center of the hologram, I could see where the rusted ruins of the once great Xenon Technologies stood. The sight of the building that had done so much damage to this world made me sick to my stomach.

Fay and I remained outside the door, leaning against the wall, watching our team laugh with each other.

"Is it wrong that I feel this way?" I spoke quietly, as not to disturb our teammates. "Salem needs to be stopped, I need to save our world, but I just feel like E is a coward who is walking around in the skin of a helpless humanoid who didn't have a chance to say no."

I didn't want to say it, but it reminded me of Faylin and Cyryl. The way Cyryl was so effortlessly able to control and bend Faylin to his will, despite how much Faylin didn't want to. If Faylin and I didn't know each other, and if he was still under Cyryl's complete command, would I have had to kill Faylin the way I was going to kill E-129?

It felt...wrong. But what other choice did I have?

"No, it is not wrong for you to feel like that. Your human nature, your empathy and kindness, is what makes you different from Salem." Faylin turned to me, resting his hand on my shoulder, "Perhaps there is a way to...save E-129. A way to purge E from his body? It is a stretch, but it might be worth looking into in the near future."

My heart felt so much lighter when I spoke to Faylin, it was almost like no matter what the situation was, he always knew the right thing to say. It was a gift he seemed completely oblivious to.

I nodded, placing my hand over his. "You're so good at...always knowing what to say to me. How do you do it?"

"Well, you are not that difficult to figure out, Scarlet."

I laughed, looking back towards the War Room, noticing all conversation had stopped...and the entire team was staring at us. All of them, minus Senna, had the dumbest grin on their faces. Something that even made Faylin chuckle, oddly enough.

I cleared my throat, casually lifting Faylin's hand from my shoulder. "Hello team, what seems to be this...new discovery?"

I, of course, knew what it was, but I was willing to say just about anything to get them to stop staring at us.

Faylin had mentioned *rumors,* but what did he mean by that? Something told me that I didn't want to know. "Well, this is our lovely Farhill Valley, home of Xenon Tech....or at least what's left of it." Marcus zoomed as far as he could into the rusted mess.

"I don't really know what you're hoping to find there. Xenon Tech is obviously significant...but I don't know if anything is left there."

"Well, there is only one way to find out, right?" I smiled. "After we are done here with Nyx, we will head straight to Farhill Valley to find the gateway, along with any other answers we can find. We don't need any more surprises."

"Aye, aye."

~~

Long ago, there stood a building that was the cornerstone of cybernetic and CHEM research, Xenon Technologies. There, the brilliant scientists had only one goal in mind - to create the perfect humanoid, the perfect solution to their dying world. This was called Project C-H. When the gateway mainframe was discovered within the depths of the laboratory, the scientists knew they couldn't pass up their discovery.

They knew that this was the key to creating perfection.

Somehow, whether it was by chance or by striking a deal with the mainframe itself, the eager scientists were able to "extract" a sentient creature from the mainframe, something they dubbed a "nanoid". These self-aware, hyper intelligent beings from beyond the mainframe baffled the scientists, and without hesitation, they implanted the nanoid they called "E" into the waiting shell of E-129, their newest project. E-129, as expected, became smarter, self-aware, and began to exceed beyond the limits of what the scientist's thought was possible.

However, unbeknownst to them, they were playing right into the hand of another entity, something the likes of mankind had never seen before. The Endless One had allowed them to take "E" not out of the kindness of her cold heart, but to set a prophecy in motion. The foolish scientists had released one of Galaia's children into the world, and years later, in the midst of a war, another nanoid followed.

Placed right in the path of a rebel group that was desperate enough to try just about anything to have an edge against the dictator that was ravishing their world. This nanoid, the true catalyst to Galaia's prophecy, was injected into the rebel leader's newborn son. The bond turned the baby into some form of new creation, the first of his kind. A complete bond between nanoid and human, two consciousnesses in one form, possessing the unpredictable and ever-changing abilities of the immortal nanoid while keeping the self-awareness and free will of a human being. This was exactly what Galaia needed; a child of both worlds, the human world and the cyberworld, in order to be the prophet that opens the gateway that will allow Galaia and her nanoid children to enter and consume the human world.

~

Yeah, that seems about right.

I repeated everything I had learned up until now in my head like a mantra as I walked alone down Sector 6's busy streets.

Everything was beginning to come together, a bit, but still...knowing that I was such a vital part in a deadly prophecy still seemed insane to me. Whenever I thought about it, I couldn't help but feel like a narcissist or something.

However, suddenly everything that the old man had said to me in the cyberworld made sense. Everything about how my hardest decisions haven't been made yet, and the decisions I make could destroy entire races. With one decision, I could end all of humanity...or all of cyberkind.

That thought made me shudder.

What makes me so...important. Why did Galaia choose me? Was it because I was Lyrik's only child, and maybe having me bring about the destruction of the world was too ironic for Galaia to pass? Or maybe it was simply a coincidence...

Either way, no matter how I spun it, I was the one. I was chosen. I am the prophet who was supposed to end the world.

I breathed out a long sigh, adjusting my larger clothes that Faylin had *acquired* for me. It was nothing fancy; a deep silver scarf, long long-sleeved shirt that had my same red neon hexagonal pattern and fell right above my navel, and dark jeans tucked neatly into my heavy boots. I opted to leave my father's coat on the ship, enjoying the cold nip in the air as the sun set.

Despite the fact I tried to fit in as much as possible, I couldn't help but notice how much attention I was gathering. While most of the townspeople kept to themselves, many stared and gawked. For the first time though, it wasn't because of my appearance. My red hair, red eyes, and the various marks on my body meant nothing to these outcasts.

No, they were afraid of me for a different reason. I didn't even have to read them to figure that out.

From the glitchy holograms that seemed to adorn every building, to the pictures that were hastily pinned up on the side of buildings, talk of the red-haired rebel that was killing off Salem's crew spoke volumes.

And for once, everyone was listening.

The Wasteland was in sight, and there was only one person I was hoping to find; the mystery girl with the dark hair. If Ginseng said she would be of use to me, there is no better time than now to find out exactly what her role was in all of this

I walked up to the door, spotting a similar group of teens in the alleyway, laughing and joking amongst themselves. However, the one wild-haired woman I saw the first night was nowhere to be seen. I shrugged, approaching the large bouncer who, by his stance, looked like he was going to give me a bit of a hard time.

Reading people was getting harder and harder, it felt like I was unable to do it the way I could months ago. But perhaps there was another ace up my sleeve, a little trick I hadn't been able to do since I was eight.

"Well, in the worst-case scenario, I just have to kill the bouncer." I murmured to myself with a chuckle.

I approached the man with a smile. "I need to get in, I'm meeting someone."

"Fat chance, sweetheart. Only locals are allowed...exclusive locals and you're definitely not a local. Now beat it, you're holding up my line." The guy looked at me with such a look of annoyance, I almost laughed.

Perfect.

I leaned forward, grabbing the guy's wrist and focusing right in his eyes.

"I don't think you understand, I *really* need to get in. Someone is expecting me. That won't be a problem, okay."

I released my grip, and there was a moment where the man looked confused, then sleepy, and then completely still. Slack jawed and glassy eyed, he nodded and stepped aside, opening the door for me.

"Thank you, kind sir." I beamed, all but skipping inside. I can't believe it actually worked! Out of all of my powers, this was one I was happy to have back. When I was younger, it only seemed to work on gentle and more naive people, but it looks like my range is wider now because there was nothing gentle or naive about that guard. I laughed, tucking my hands into my pockets as I made my way around to the bar, the strobe lights and pulsing beat only slightly disorientating this time around.

There was no sign of the girl yet.

I kept walking, keeping a sharp eye while trying to avoid the people weaving in and out. The area around the bar, oddly enough, was rather empty. When I got within reach, I met the eye of the bartender; an older woman with a fully shaved head and eyes that have definitely experienced more life than half of the people in this club. She smiled wide, pulling out a brown bottle, cracking the lid open and offering it to me.

"New here?" She called over the music with a gritty voice. "I don't recognize you."

I nodded, taking a swig of the bitter liquid and taking a seat on the stool. I tried to keep my dislike of the bitter taste from showing on my face, but the woman seemed to catch it within a moment, sliding me a glass of brightly colored juice with a smirk.

I glanced over to the sea of people on the dance floor, all of them barely indistinguishable from one another. Finding this girl would be like...finding a needle in a stack of needles. I wish I knew why I needed her.

But more than that, what did Ginseng mean when she said the rogues would be of use in the future? Even though I hadn't directly told Faylin, I was planning on destroying the rogues as soon as I got the chance. They were simply too dangerous to have around.

But Ginseng now tells me they will be *of great use*.

Were they another piece of the puzzle?

At this point, who knew?

END OF CHAPTER 8

PUZZLE

"So, you came back?"

I shot up from my third drink, focusing on the voice that suddenly broke through the thumping music. I didn't even know how long I had been here; I was just lost in my own thoughts. That had been happening a lot lately.

When I glanced to my left, I saw the same girl from the night before; shaggy dark hair, dark slanted eyes, a piercing in her eyebrow and her lip, and a deep silver and black uniform that seemed just a tad bit too put together for her to be just another outcast damned to live here.

"Yes." I turned, giving her my attention and a light smile. "I... was actually looking for you?"

"Oh, is that so? I supposed I should feel honored." A fanged smile stretched across her face as she took a seat on the stool next to me. "To be sought out by the infamous Captain Scarlet...to what do I owe the pleasure?"

I sat up, taken back for a moment. "So, you know who I am?"

"The mystery boy from the West with flaming hair and eyes...the psycho who cuts down those who stand in his way with his red-tinted blade... the red-headed catalyst for the next war, yadda, yadda.

The people in the Guild sure don't spare the theatrics, and they certainly did your looks no justice. I don't think I've ever seen someone quite like you...not here at least."

Well looks like Persephone was right, looks like the Guild had been talking about me. But if this girl knew that, then could she possibly be...

"The name is Tetsuzo, Captain of The Atlantis. Intelligence faction of the Guild. While it's normal for Guild members to stay around Sector 6, I would say this is the unofficial stomping ground for Arai and myself."

That's how I knew her: I had seen her at the docks with Arai back when I went there religiously. They never sailed together, but I would see her speaking casually with Arai around town. Usually, I was too focused on catching a glimpse of Captain King, so much so that I tended to block the other crews out.

Captain Tetsuzo of The Atlantis, hm.

Now I know why Madam Ginseng wanted me to seek her out.

"So now, if you've come to Sector 6, I can only imagine it can be for only one reason."

She glanced at me from over her glass, waiting for me to answer her unspoken question. Despite the fact that caution and discretion were vital at times, I could tell she was someone safe to speak with.

"Nyx is my target."

"Ah...I assumed as much. I'm sure Arai is thrilled; she and I have been after Nyx and Dante for years now."

"Why is that? I noticed the grudge but didn't want to ask." I mean, it wasn't as if it was unusual for someone to have a gripe against some of Salem's men, but with Arai, I could tell it was more than that.

96

"Well now, I try not to make a habit of gossiping about my fellow Guild members, but I suppose I could make an exception." She turned and leaned in, glancing around us. "Have you heard of the Pig Farm?"

"Pig...farm? I believe so." It seemed like ages ago now, but when we first began to pull information about all of the members of The Management, I remembered something being mentioned about a pig farm. "Is it someplace here in Sector 6?"

Tetsuzo shook her head. "It's not here. You have heard of Lelani, right? Big heiress down in the Southern region?"

"Of course, she's one of my last targets."

"Well good riddance, the bitch is absolutely twisted. The Pig Farm is her personal...collection, her human collection, and what better place to silently collect people than from the most lawless place in all of Neutopia."

"And so, Nyx..."

Tetsuzo nodded, still keeping an eye on our surroundings. "Yup, Nyx provides her with new pets for her collection. After all, when people go missing here, nothing is done about it. Sadly, Arai unwillingly got herself involved."

"How?"

Tetsuzo paused, face becoming less playful, as if what she was going to speak next weighed heavily on her spirit. "Her mom was taken. In fact, most of the girls on her ship had their parents taken by Nyx. Mine were as well."

"I'm...so sorry. I didn't know."

"It's alright, nobody on the outside knows. Trust me, I wanted to do nothing more than to take down Lelani myself...and I tried, and nearly got myself and my team killed because of it. Not to mention almost getting booted from the Guild."

"You tried to attack Lelani head on?" I'd never forget when Madam Ginseng told me if I tried to attack Lelani right away, she'd kill me in an instant. So, the fact that Tetsuzo tried and is still alive to tell the tale must mean she is one hell of a fighter.

"Well, they don't call us the intelligence faction for nothing. We collected intel on her for years, found the weak spots in her fortress, knew who to talk to, to get more information. We even had a few people on the inside, not like it made a difference in the end."

She rolled up her sleeves and removed both of her dark gloves. To my surprise, both of her arms were cybernetic. They gleamed with bits of CHEM that ran in tiny pipes like veins. I had never seen anything like it, except on some combat humanoids.

"They attach all the way up to my collarbone, Lelani kept them as...trophies, I suppose. Thankfully my first mate was able to get me out before I completely bled to death. I wish I could say that was my last time trying to infiltrate her Pig Farm,

but it wasn't. I tried 3 more times, almost getting killed each time. After all that, I never even got close to the Farm itself. It wasn't until Arai beat some sense into me that I finally stopped.

She said she understood why I wanted to fight her,

but it was suicide to go in head first. A part of me already knew that, but I supposed I had to try at least. Who wouldn't do everything in their power to try and save their parents, right?"

"...right."

Tetsuzo shook her head, chuckling dryly. "I'm sorry, I didn't mean to talk your ear off with my sad stories. I'm sure you have seen more than your fair share of death."

"Please, don't apologize. I appreciate you telling me. And yeah, I suppose I have seen my fair share. We all have." I waved to the bartender, signaling another drink for both of us. "In fact, I'm glad you did tell me, because I have a proposition for you."

"I'm listening." Tetsuzo took a swig of her drink. The air around us thickened as I prepared my words. For a moment, even *I* couldn't believe what I was about to recommend. It seemed so...sadistic.

Not like it wasn't deserved.

"As you know, I am going to kill Nyx. After Nyx is gone, Lelani is next on my list. And while I could assure you, I would have no mercy on her, I feel as though I shouldn't be credited for her death." A smile played on my lips as I glanced over to Tetsuzo. "How would you like it if after I beat her down and detain her, I hand her off to you and your crew. You, and whoever you want to join, can have the honor of finishing her off in whatever way you see fit."

"Are...you serious?"

Tetsuzo looked stunned, but I could clearly see the underlying excitement that she was trying to hold back.

"But...how would you even get to her? Not like I'm questioning your skill, but I have fought her before."

"Trust me Tetsuzo, I have already killed two of Salem's officers, I have my ways. And yes, I am absolutely serious. I only require two favors, if you will. First, I want all of the information and contacts you have regarding Nyx and Lelani. Any intel that you can save us time on will be a huge help to my team. As for my second favor, once you have finished off Lelani, all I ask is for her head in return."

"Her...head?"

I nodded, chuckling lightly. "I know it sounds crazy, but I have a bit of a collection of my victories."

"Yeah, you're every bit as crazy as they say you are, and I absolutely love it." Tetsuzo licked her lips as she held out her hand, firmly grasping mine. "You've got yourself a deal, Captain Scarlet. Just send me the coordinates of your ship, and I will give you all of the data first thing tomorrow. You do this for me, and my team and I will be permanent allies of yours."

"Good to have you on my side Tetsuzo." I smiled, shaking her hand.

~

The excitement was buzzing inside my stomach non-stop as I made my way back to the ship. This was coming together so perfectly that I almost couldn't believe it.

Capturing Lelani would be no easy feat, for sure, but I felt as though it was nothing I couldn't handle. Perhaps that was the overconfidence speaking, but I felt as though I had such a strong grip on my powers. I felt completely invincible.

I'm sure the rogues wouldn't mind me borrowing a pair of those shackles they used to keep me detained. If I could manage to get Lelani into a pair of those, she wouldn't be able to use her powers. She'd be completely helpless, which would make it safe to transport her back to Sector 6.

After Nyx and Lelani were out of the picture, I only had mother and father to take care of. In a way, they were worse than Salem.

I could hardly believe I thought that.

But it was true, wasn't it? Mother and Father *had* free will, and yet they still chose their paths. Salem, or rather E-129, is only acting out what E is forcing him to do. He's just an unwilling passenger in his own body.

But not mother and father. Not them.

Perhaps being alive too long had corrupted them beyond salvation. Maybe that's why human beings aren't meant to be immortal. The brain just doesn't know how to handle seeing centuries upon centuries of death and destruction. In a way, what I'm doing is merciful.

I'm doing the right thing.

Killing them is the right thing to do.

I shook my head, replaying the plan in my head. After Nyx, then Lelani, and then mother...and father will come after. Then, I will figure out some way to rip E out of Salem, and bury E right in the ground.

I could feel the all too familiar buzz of R hanging around in the back of my head, he said nothing, and neither did I.

~

When I woke, my room was cast in a dusty gray glow just like every morning. I was getting so sick of this smoggy polluted air. I never thought I would miss the sun so much.

"It's so...cold." I brought my hands up to my arms which were covered in goosebumps. Sure, it was a bit chilly last night, but it felt like the temperature dropped at least 20 degrees. I got up, jolting as my feet hit the cold wooden floor, and walked over to my window.

It was snowing.

The entire beach was covered in a dusting of what looked like snow mixed with ash, and the murky water was already forming some sheets of ice.

I heard muffled voices as I saw Tyrinie, Casteri, Marcus, and Lanker hanging around the shore. They were all bundled up and seemed to be enjoying the rapid change in weather. Lanker and Tyrinie seemed to be involved in what looked like the dirtiest snowball fight known to mankind, while Casteri and Marcus played referee.

It was nice to see them out and enjoying themselves. In a way, it reminded me a bit of how Emme and I would play back when I was home.

Every time she and I went out into town, we'd get mixed up in some sort of trouble. Even though I'd never admit it, half of what I did was just to make her laugh. Though it wasn't by blood, I saw Emme as my little sister, and nothing made me happier than seeing her happy.

What I wouldn't do just to see her and Persephone right now...if only for a few minutes.

The worst part was I knew I could see them; I knew I could close my eyes and I'd be there when I opened them. But I knew going back would put them in danger.

But perhaps there was something else I could do.

I threw on my clothes before running over to the War Room.

The majority of Sector 6 was a dark spot, which means that calls couldn't be traced. I never kept a phone on me for fear of being traced, but I knew there was one in the War Room.

We kept it disconnected, only having it there for emergency purposes. Well, I counted this as an emergency.

I ran into the room and closed the door tight behind me, sitting quietly in the corner by the large device. I could feel my fingers trembling as I typed in the all too familiar sequence of numbers, waiting with tight breath as it began to ring.

I pressed the phone tightly to my ear.

ring *ring* *ring*

"...Hello, Rose residence."

My heart jumped in my chest as I cleared my throat lightly.

"H-hi, Mrs. P."

The other end of the line was silence. So quiet I would've sworn the line was disconnected if not for the light breathing on the other end.

"Sca-sweetheart, is that really you?"

"Yeah, it's… um, it's me. How are you guys?" I didn't know what else I should have said, I hated that I sounded so awkward.

Laughter broke out on the other line, followed by choked up breaths. I could basically feel how tightly Persephone was holding the phone.

"Baby! Oh, my stars, I can't believe it's you. I've been hoping to hear back from you, do you know how worried I have been for you. You just stopped responding to my mail! I was so afraid that…something horrible happened to you."

I let out a quiet laugh, trying to keep my eyes from stinging with tears.

"I've missed you both so much, I've been wanting to reach back but I just didn't know what to say. I… still don't know what to say."

"Oh, you don't have to say anything, sweetheart. Just hearing you breathing is more than enough. Are you safe? How are you even calling?"

"I'm in Sector 6, nothing here is traced, so it's not dangerous to call." I finally sat back, allowing the tight knot in my back to relax. "Mrs. P, there is so much going on right now. This isn't at all the quest I thought it would be."

"It's okay love, you're doing so well. You're making history. You are…all anyone talks about these days. Oh sweetheart, I miss you so much.

I miss seeing that dumb smile of yours and having you swinging all over the kitchen ceiling. I never thought I would hate this silence so much."

"I promise I'll be home soon Mrs. P, and everything will be back to normal. It'll be better than normal, I promise."

"You don't have to promise me anything, just...come home safely. Be safe and... don't do anything you're going to regret. Please."

I froze, gripping the phone even tighter. "I promise, and... I'm sorry I didn't tell you about any of this earlier. Maybe if I had been more honest with you, I wouldn't have had to leave like I did. I just-"

"You don't owe me any explanation; I'm sure telling me everything would have put you in a lot of trouble. I understand having to keep a secret. I really do."

"Is Emme nearby?"

Persephone paused for a moment, taking a deep breath that held for a bit too long.

"I'm sorry sweetheart, I know you would love to talk with her, but Emme is sick. She came down with an illness about last week and hasn't perked back up yet. I'm sure she'll be fine soon, but she has been in bed all day. But, when I bring her some lunch, I'll let her know that you said hi. I know it'll make her smile."

She's sick? What could have made her so sick that it left her bedridden? There aren't great doctors in the West, so how was she getting any medicine? Surely Persephone was finding medication for her...but with them being harassed by people because of me, it couldn't have been easy.

I shook my head, the last thing Persephone needed was me filling her with more doubt.

"I know she'll be back to normal in no time, she's a trooper." I forced a smile, loosening my grip on the phone slightly. "I'll be back home soon, I promise. You tell Emme when I come back home, I'll take over to the docks...so we can watch the ships like old times."

"Of course, and I won't bother lecturing you about not staying away from the docks like I asked you to." I could hear Persephone giggle lightly, sounding a little bit more like herself. *"And please, don't be afraid to call more often. It's so good to hear from you."*

"I promise I will. I have to go now, but I promise I will call again soon. I... love you both so much."

"We love you too, you take care."

I hung the phone up, staying seated on the chilly floor. I knew there was so much I had to do; getting the information from Tetsuzo, planning the move on Nyx's castle, trying harder to track down my mother, but sitting was the only thing that felt right.

And so, I will sit for now.

END OF CHAPTER 9

MARCUS

10

CASTLE OF NOTHING

True to her word, Tetsuzo arrived not long after my conversation with Persephone. And while we were in broad daylight, I could truly see how she was the captain of her own vessel. She just seemed to silently demand respect with every step she took. It was a trait I greatly admired and envied.

She came along with her first mate bearing many info chips and maps, all of which had exact layouts and blueprints regarding Lelani, her mansion, and the Pig Farm.

Despite Lelani's fighting abilities, it appears her stamina is her weak spot. Wearing her down might be the key to winning. Another map had blueprints of Nyx's stronghold, but it had much less information. However, the blueprints had some key details I was glad we were made aware of.

First, Nyx has an auto air defense system: as soon as we get too close, it'll go off and missiles are going to start raining down on us. Air support was absolutely crucial. Second, it looked like Virus and Vinyl were wrong, Nyx *did* have a front door, it was just barely visible to the naked eye due to the sheer darkness of the stronghold itself. So, between the opening on the roof, and the opening on the ground level, I knew which one I preferred.

Tetsuzo and her first mate gave their thanks before briskly leaving and heading back to their respective ships, but not before reminding me of my end of the bargain, which I acknowledged. I told them I would meet them back on the beach with Lelani, as promised.

I hadn't quite run that by the team yet, but what they didn't know wouldn't kill them.

~~

"You want all of us to stay on the ship?" Senna replied the disbelief held heavy in his voice.

We all sat around the table in the War Room, going over the plans for the evening. I was thinking about pushing the attack back until tomorrow, but time was not on our side, and I wanted to get out of the sector and back home as soon as possible. Besides, attacking under the cover of the night sky was much more ideal than a morning attack.

I sat at the head; my father's coat rested heavily on my arms as I reclined. "That's right, ideally, this is how everything should go.

I am going to find my way in and enter from the front, simultaneously Faylin will be keeping Nevermore and Nocturnal off of my tail.

Meanwhile, while we are in such close proximity to the stronghold, no doubt sirens will be going off and Nyx's air defense will be activated. So, I need you all to keep the sky clear for us and shoot down anything that might be a threat." I signaled over to Faylin, who had been silent per usual the entire time. "I'm not going to have you take down Nyx's goons alone, it'll be too rough of a fight, so we need to see if we could bait any of the rogues into helping. Do you think you have any of your old contacts that would do that for you?"

Faylin paused before taking a deep sigh. "Well...I might have one or two. I will see."

"The more the better, I don't want you fighting harder than you have to. You're still not at 100%, and I don't want you to get injured again. I just want you to distract them away from me for as long as possible."

Fay nodded as Marcus popped up, leaning heavily on Fay's shoulder.

"You know Cap, we could always fight too. Casteri and I could hold ourselves in a fight if you need some extra muscle."

"I appreciate it, but there is no way I'm pinning y'all against two combat humanoids. Besides, it's best for you guys to stay and protect the ship. Who knows what his air defense looks like." I stood, straightening my coat as I glanced over my team. This would be tough, but I knew we would be fine. Once we took out Nyx and Dante, we could leave this forsaken sector and never look back.

The moon was high in the starless sky as I waited outside by the T-34, the hardened snow crunching stiffly under my soles. The temperature had dropped significantly, but the adrenaline kept me warm under my black coat. Faylin emerged from the distance, sending a hand signal to Lanker, who was at the helm, to begin lift off.

"I managed to get Virus, Vinyl, and Cinder to agree to aid us. It was not easy, and I had to make a few...deals, but they will help. They are on the way there now."

"What deals?" I asked as Faylin mounted the T-34, helping me on as well.

"Nothing you need to worry about, and nothing that will affect you or the team. It is more of a... personal errand that is needed. Nothing I need to repay right at this moment."

It was obvious Faylin was dancing around telling me what this "errand" was, but I didn't want to pry.

The fact he went back into that compound to ask for help from his old teammates was kind enough. I didn't need to dig into his business.

"Fair enough, as long as it's not dangerous or anything."

Faylin nodded, kicking the T-34 into gear as we began speeding down the snowy road.

The snow had stopped falling hours ago, but it didn't stop the freezing air from stinging my face. We were only a few miles out at this point, and I could hear the roar from our ship above us. Knowing I had the guys providing aerial support gave me a sense of comfort, especially since they would be somewhat out of the line of fire.

However, I wish I knew what kind of firepower Nyx had to work with. That lack of information made me weary.

"Are you ready for this Captain?" I could hear Faylin yell over the whipping air.

Nyx's castle loomed in the distance, and from where we were, I could see Nocturnal and Nevermore standing like unmoving statues.

I flicked my ear cuff to life, doing the same for Faylin.

"Hey team, can you hear me?" I called out as I slowed to a stop outside the gates.

"Hey Capt.', Lanker here. We hear you loud and clear!"

I nodded, spotting Cinder, Virus, and Vinyl approaching from the South.

"Alright team, Faylin, the rogues, and I are about to storm the front. As soon as I'm inside, the aerial defenses will most likely activate. Be ready, we aren't sure what type of arsenal Nyx is working with. Either way, I want Marcus and Casteri on cannons, Senna and Tyrinie on guns, and Lanker on the helm. Understood."

A resounding "Aye, aye" sounded through as I stepped off the bike, ready to greet the others who, for lack of a better word, looked pretty pissed. I could understand, this is the last place I would want to be too.

"I appreciate you guys coming to provide backup." I spoke sincerely, despite knowing they didn't want to hear anything from me.

"Don't get it twisted...we're here 'cause Commander Faylin asked us to be. Not fa' you." Virus spoke roughly, but I simply nodded and glanced over at Faylin, giving him the queue to take the stage.

Faylin nodded back, "When we storm the front, our job is going to be to get the Captain in and to keep Nocturnal and Nevermore outside. After Captain Scarlet is inside, we just need to keep them busy, not actually take them down. We are not aware of what their intelligence level is, so do not let your guard down." Faylin paused, pointing down a path that led to the backside of the castle. "Hopefully we'll be able to lead them on a goose chase down that path. As far away from the front door as possible."

They nodded, mounting their T-34s without the slightest bit of fear or hesitation, Faylin followed suit.

He nodded at me, "We'll see you once you exit, Captain. Do be careful."

"You all as well."

I stepped back and allowed them to break down the gate, riding at breakneck speed toward the two seemingly immovable forces.

They were barely halfway across the field when missiles began pouring from the castle's aerial defense, lighting up the sky with blinding bursts of red.

For a second everything seemed to freeze.

"Run Scarlet."

With haze gathered at my feet, I sprinted towards the opening Faylin and the others made for me. The deafening roar of the missiles overhead made my ears ring. I dared not spare a glance upward, fearing I might lose my footing. I glanced to the side, seeing the two immovable humanoids swinging their inhumanly large limbs at the rogues, trying to keep them as far from the doorway as possible. Despite their size, Nocturnal and Nevermore moved with a quickness that was more precise than the attacks overhead.

Faylin barely dodged a swing that would have done more damage than I wanted to imagine.

"Keep them moving, we must get them as far as possible!" Faylin barked the orders in a tone I had never heard from him before. But thankfully, Nocturnal and Nevermore didn't, or couldn't, process what he was saying, and allowed themselves to chase the others towards the back of the mansion.

As I closed in on the door, Nocturnal caught a glance of me, and the glint in their eyes made my limbs shudder. But as quickly as they saw me, Cinder flew out of the corner of my eye, aiming a well-placed strike at the large head.

As much as I wanted to continue to watch, I laid my hands on the doorway and teleported myself inside, leaving the murky night sky behind me.

~

I found myself in what seemed like an empty medieval castle, something that definitely belonged in the old world. I pulled out my sword, keeping it in front of me. I debated on if I should call out to Nyx.

I doubted if he would answer, and I wasn't sure if I wanted to give away my position that easily. There is a good chance he already knew I was in here.

No, I would keep as much of an element of surprise as possible.

There were an impossible number of doors on both sides of the walls, with a large grand staircase that led up to what looked like more doors. I quickly peeked in a few of the rooms that were closest, and to my surprise, they were empty. All of them held nothing but a thin layer of dust and nothing else.

First room, second room, third, fourth, fifth...nothing.

I jumped slightly as the blast from more firepower came from overhead. With every blast, the walls seemed to shake, causing little bits of dust to swirl around in the limited light that seeped in.

"Ugh, I don't have time for this." While I was searching, my team was getting shot at. I needed to get out and end this as soon as possible. Besides what additional information did I need? I knew everything I needed to know.

I was the chosen one, I could open the gate, Galaia was the real threat, and Salem was a puppet. What else did I need to know?

I bounced on my feet, gathering up as much haze as possible before bounding up the stairs.

"We're taking on massive firepower up here Captain. Don't wanna worry you, but you might wanna try and hurry up."

Marcus' crackling voice ripped through my ear cuff. Despite trying to sound calm, I could hear the obvious panic.

"Understood, I'm going as fast as I can to get to Nyx." I responded, continuing down the next set of empty hallways and heading towards a spiral staircase. "If things get too hot, grab Faylin and get out of here. I can get myself out when I'm done.

"Can't do that Captain, if you're still in there, these missiles are going to turn on you if we leave. They're set to go after anything foreign in the vicinity. Besides, we can't figure out what their range is."

"I can survive a few missile strikes, Marcus, don't get yourselves killed!"

"..."

All I heard was static.

"Marcus? Can you guys hear me?"

Still nothing but static.

Damn it all. I began running even faster than before as that onslaught overhead got even louder. I could see what seemed to be a ballroom in the distance, and prayed he would be there. I didn't have time to play hide and seek with this kid.

I needed to kill him and get out of here and back to my team!

I skidded to a stop in the center of the checked ballroom, searching around frantically, sweat beginning to sting at my eyes.

"Well now, it took you long enough." A deep voice resounded.

I froze in place, turning my head sharply to the staircase where two figures had begun to descend. A pale child, who appeared no older than Emme, stood perched on the stairwell, prim and proper.

Their shoes were shiny and their clothes were clean, however the bandages that covered their eyes and the majority of their head and neck were dingy and unsettling. One step behind them was none other than Dante. His sheer size alone rivaled that of Nevermore and Nocturnal. In a way, he looked slightly similar to Aztec with his olive toned skin and dark hair. His eyes, however, were inky black.

So dark I couldn't tell where his pupils were, or if he even had any pupils. He was dressed like a butler, and stood in such a way that if I dared to take a step forward, he wouldn't hesitate to snap my neck.

Nyx nodded, mouthing words lightly, and as they did, Dante began to speak.

"We had been waiting for you to find us, we had been waiting for days now. What took you so long?"

There was a pause, so I assumed they were expecting an actual response from me.

"Well, there was some business I needed to attend to. I apologize for keeping you waiting." I said with a little bit of annoyance.

"Business...more important than killing us? That is hard to believe."

What type of game was he playing? I kept my guard up, raising my sword into a striking stance. I might have been underestimating him, but Nyx hardly looked like a threat. Getting around Dante would be the challenge.

"Well, I'm here now, aren't I? So, are you going to make this easy for me?"

"We want to...make this easy for you. We do not wish to live any longer, not like this. However, ..." Dante and Nyx paused, descending down the staircase further, only a few steps away from the main floor. "Explain what killing us would help you accomplish.

We are but the lowliest of cogs in Salem's grand machine. Surely someone else could give you more information than we could."

"I don't need information from you, I don't need anything. I just need to kill you. Other than the fact you are a member of Salem's elite and a sadistic bastard, I have a few groups of people waiting on me to end your reign here."

Nyx's head tilted to the side lightly as Dante spoke out. "It seems as though we have made a few enemies during our prolonged stay here."

"I would say so." I began closing the gap between us. "Don't act all naive and innocent, I know all about the Pig Farm and the people you delivered to Lelani. Do you have any idea of how many lives you've torn apart? Do you even care?"

Nyx glanced at Dante, prompting him to step off the staircase and kneel down on one knee as Nyx walked a little further down. Nyx stopped a few steps from the bottom, just enough to stay eye-level with me.

"The things we have done are unforgivable, you can believe we know that." Dante continued to speak, head facing downward. "You believe we are no better than Lelani for delivering people to their eventual deaths, is that correct"

I grunted, annoyed, and still unsure of what to expect.

Dante continued, "Well then, perhaps we are the same as you. Taken from our homes, forced into a destiny we did not want, and slowly leading the people around us to their death…"

"What are you talking about?"

"Do you believe your friends will make it out of here? And if they don't, whose fault will it be? They did not come here on their own accord."

Before I could respond, Dante continued. "Do not misunderstand, we do not blame you. You are simply doing what needs to be done. You, unlike us, are good. And we are simply so tired. We are tired of being a part of this game. We are tired of playing now."

The missiles overhead continued to blow, causing the high ceiling and pillars to tremble as if they would collapse at any moment. Just then, I heard my ear cuff crack and fizzle to life.

"Captain! Lanker and Casteri have been hit. We gotta fly out of range and get back to the beach. Senna is working on them now."

I didn't respond, my arm just dropped limply to my side.

Lanker...and Casteri were hit.

Were they…?

I had to get back, I had to get out of here. I had to be with my team! I had to help them! I clenched my sword once more and focused my eyes on Nyx, who to my surprise, had stepped down and was now standing about a foot away from me. From this distance, I had to look down to see him. He was simply so...small.

Nyx looked upward at me, slowly unwrapping the dingy bandages from their eyes and throat, revealing deep lacerations around their neck and two empty sockets that were surrounded with painful looking scar tissue. Nyx then smiled, mouthing something.

"Please." Dante started. "Do what you must, but do not harm Dante. This was not his choice." For a moment, I almost considered walking away. But I didn't need to read Nyx to realize what they were asking me. Nyx knew I would come to kill him, and yet he waited for me.

Nyx wanted this.

I didn't know Nyx's story, but I didn't need to know it.

I raised my sword far above my head, and in one swoop, Nyx's head and body were separated. A permanent smile remained on his face.

END OF CHAPTER 10

11

A CHOICE

After gathering Nyx's body and cautiously grabbing onto Dante, I teleported us all back into the ship. The familiar halo of red appeared around my feet before bursting into a bright light.

I was on the floor of my room, Nyx's body and Dante next to me. Dante hadn't moved at all, let alone said anything. I shook my head; I can't focus on that now! I ran out of the room, making sure to lock Dante and Nyx inside before rushing down the hallway.

My head was pounding thoughts in my ears, and my heart was going so fast I swore I would have a heart attack.

Somehow, the deck seemed so far away.

I finally burst through the opening, coming face to face with my poor team, all battered and bruised. And if possible, the ship looked even worse than they all did.

"Where are they?" I yelled out, causing Marcus, who was closest to me, to jump.

"Captain, thank goodness you're here." He said in a tone I couldn't quite understand. It was like he was happy to see me, but...something was wrong."

"Where's Lanker...and Casteri?"

"Senna has them in the medical ward."

I turned on my heels, getting ready to head back when Marcus grabbed me by the sleeve.

"Casteri is okay, he's unconscious, but he's gonna pull through. But...Captain, Lanker…"

I shook my head, feeling my lips go numb and my eyes sting. "No…"

Before he said anything else, I pulled my sleeve out of his grip and ran as fast as I could, bursting into the medical room with much more force than was needed. I searched around frantically, seeing Senna standing motionless over a gurney, hands, and uniform covered in blood and viscera.

"...Senna."

I willed myself forward

"It-t went right through his chest. There...wasn't anything I could do." Senna murmured to himself, not even realizing I had entered the room. On the gurney was none other than Lanker.

His mischievous green eyes were partly open and completely dull, and his skin was...lifeless. His entire chest cavity had been blown open. It looked like he had taken a direct hit.

Did he even know? Could he feel that moment of impact or was it so sudden he…simply faded away. I prayed for the latter. I didn't even realize I was sobbing until I had collapsed to my knees. I knew I needed to keep it together. I was the Captain, and I needed to keep it together, but I just couldn't.

"Lanker...no…" I choked out between sobs.

My friend. I let him down.

He was so afraid, and I promised him he would be okay. That *we* would be okay, and here he was, stretched out on a gurney with a hole in his chest.

Senna still hadn't moved, he was still mumbling to himself, reciting all of the procedures that he tried and failed.

Every time I tried to catch my breath; another sob found its way into my throat.

Midnight became morning, which eventually became sunset. I remained in the Med Lab with Lanker. Faylin had arrived shortly after I did, and helped to pull me together, which I was grateful for. He, as my second hand, ushered the rest of the crew into the galley and made everyone something to eat. Everyone...meaning Marcus and Senna. I refused to leave Lanker's side, Casteri was still in a coma, and Tyrinie was curled at the foot of Casteri's bed...refusing to move as well.

After I had calmed down, I finally got the story of what happened from a still shell-shocked Senna.

Apparently, one of the smaller missiles changed their directory mid-flight, doubling around for the helm. Casteri, noticing the change, ran over to Lanker to try and shoot it down. But it was far too close. It hit Lanker directly, and the impact blew Lanker into Casteri, knocking him out cold by the impact.

Lanker died on impact. There was nothing Senna could have done, despite the fact that he wouldn't accept that.

How...can we go on after this. I knew this was a risk, but...I never thought it would actually happen. Not to one of my crewmates, not to Lanker.

How could I go out there and face the team knowing I did this to him. If only I was faster, if only I thought this through more…

And for what? Nyx didn't need to die. This assault didn't need to happen. But because it did, Lanker is dead.

"Are you done yet? This is starting to give me a headache."

I huffed, glancing over to Tyrinie, who was very much asleep.

"Don't you have somewhere better to be, R?" I whispered under my breath.

"Unfortunately, no, I can't be anywhere else."

I didn't respond, I just kept my eyes fixated on Lanker. Senna, after accepting the inevitable, slid his eyes shut and placed a sheet over his body. It was still so surreal, and whenever I thought about it, my eyes began to sting all over again.

"I know you aren't gonna like the sound of this, but-"

"Then just don't say it. I'm not in the mood for your stupid games today, R." I bit back, perhaps too harshly. "This...this is my fault. Lanker was my responsibility, and I let him down. I didn't protect him."

"And just how are you going to go on from here then, huh? Just disband the entire group and give up because one person died? I'm sorry if this sounds harsh kiddo, but this is war...people die.

It happens. But you need to pull yourself together because this sobbing shit isn't helping anyone."

I didn't respond. I couldn't. His words hurt too much and all I wanted to do was scream and cry and yell at him, but I knew he was right.

I needed to pull myself together.

I needed to be strong for the rest of the team. Giving up wasn't an option, and I wouldn't allow Lanker's death to be in vain.

"I know it hurts, but...perhaps you can think outside the box and do something about this. What do your instincts say?"

My instincts? I have no idea what they are saying. I can barely focus on my own heartbeat, let alone my feelings.

"I just...wish I could have stopped this. I wish I could fix this. I wish I could bring Lanker back.

I want to bring him back…

Back.

Wait a moment.

"R? What are you implying?" I muttered to nobody, continuing to stare at Lanker's body. There was no response from R.

I mechanically stood to my feet and left the room, heading towards the galley.

"Faylin, can I borrow you for a moment." I peeked my head into the dreary galley where Faylin busied himself at the stove, seemingly not doing much of anything. Marcus and Senna sat in silence with two full plates in front of them that must've turned cold an hour ago.

"Of course, Scarlet." Faylin wiped his hands on his bodysuit and followed me quietly to my quarters, where my door remained locked.

I fumbled with the key and ushered Faylin inside without a word, locking it behind us.

Faylin stepped back in shock for a moment, startled by Nyx's lifeless smiling body and Dante sitting silently next to Nyx's head, seemingly still awaiting orders.

"What...is this, Scarlet?" For the first time in a while, Faylin genuinely sounded afraid for a moment

"I haven't figured out what to do with them yet. We'll dispose of Nyx's body. Oddly enough, Nyx asked me to spare Dante, so I decided to do just that." I spoke matter-of-factly. "It really seems like Dante won't attack unless Nyx commands him to, which of course, can't happen at the moment. Maybe we can find a way to reprogram him. But, that's not why I brought you in here."

Faylin took a sharp breath through his nose and mumbled, "Right", before taking a seat away from Nyx and Dante. "Are you okay, Scarlet? Today...has not gone according to plan. I am still struggling to wrap my head around what happened to L-"

"No! It's okay, because I'm going to fix all of this." I cut off Faylin. I couldn't hear that name right now. I was going to fix all of this, and I would never feel this gut-wrenching pain ever again.

Not if I could help it.

"What do you mean? Scarlet, how can you 'fix this'?"

I walked over to the chair Faylin sat on, pointing to his veins. "I'm going to bring Lanker back, and I need you to help me."

As soon as I spoke the words, Faylin reeled back as if I had slapped him. Looking confused, then indignant, then a mixture of confusion and caution.

"Captain...are you suggesting we use the hybrid serum to bring Lanker back to life? To revive him?" I nodded once, twice, three times slowly, trying to hold back the tears that were threatening to resurface. "I can't lose him, Fay. I just can't. Not when our blood holds the key to bringing him back. Even if he hates me for it, I need him to be alive. I need to give him his life back." I took a deep breath, turning my head to the side and wiping my eyes. "Will you help me?"

Faylin gave me a long and steady look before standing to his feet.

"Scarlet, just so you know, I don't agree with this idea. It feels...wrong. Especially because we know what the hybrid serum does to people. However, with you as my Captain...and as my friend, I will help you."

I reached forward and wrapped Faylin in a hug, one that took him more than a few seconds to return. But when he did, I melted into it and began to sob again. I swore I ran out of tears, but my body keeps surprising me.

Faylin, kind as always, just held me and allowed me to soak his suit with my tears for as long as I needed.

The rational part of my brain told me what I was doing was wrong, like I was crossing some invisible line.

But I rather cross a line than live the rest of my life wondering what could have been if I went through with this.

There was no way I could say no.

~~

Midnight rolled around when Faylin and I decided to enter the Med Lab's back room.

It was far too depressing to have Lanker's body out in the open, so we decided moving it to the back was the best idea for now.

Tyrinie was still fast asleep at the foot of Casteri's cot, so slipping in wasn't a problem.

We were armed with a few syringes and nothing more. Hopefully, nothing else would be needed.

"Faylin, I didn't think about this earlier, but would your serum work on someone who is already...dead? All of the other hybrids were alive when they were given it."

I didn't want to think of complications, but I tried to convince myself too at least be smart about this.

"I am not sure, Captain. It might, or it might not. I have not seen that work before. Perhaps if it doesn't work, we could use some of your blood."

"My blood."

Now that I think about it, father had used my blood to bring mom back when I was a baby. Between Faylin and I...it should be more than enough.

"Okay, you and me, Faylin. We'll both give him a syringe of our blood. This has to work."

After properly sanitizing both syringes, and wiping both entry spots with alcohol, we both drew multiple vials of blood.

Faylin's blood, much like Cyryl showed me, housed different shades and a clear layer of gel-like material that settled at the bottom. Mine, aside from having a light shimmer, appeared completely normal on the surface.

"Are you ready for this?" I asked, not really waiting for an answer as I pulled back Lanker's sheet, nearly fainting at the sight.

I don't think you'll ever get used to seeing your dead friend with a gaping hole in his body.

"Stay strong, Captain." Faylin spoke up, grabbing Lanker's stiff arm and injecting one vial right into the vein in the crook of his elbow. I shook off the dizziness and did the same, injecting three of my vials into the opposite elbow.

This would work, it simply had to. Everything we had learned proved this would work. All I had to do was be patient.

After putting the sheet back over Lanker's body, and saying a quick prayer, Faylin and I exited the Med Lab just as quickly and quietly as we entered. Without a word to one another, we entered our respective rooms.

To my surprise, Faylin had cleaned up the blood that had accumulated from Nyx's decapitated body, along with moving the body and placing Nyx's head in a jar next to Myrah's. I couldn't help but feel like Faylin must think I've lost my mind.

Maybe I have.

I glanced over to the now empty space where Dante had been sitting for over 24 hours. Faylin had told me he placed Dante in the holding cells in the bottom of the ship, for everyone's protection, which I completely agreed with. It was dumb of me to leave Dante unattended anyways, I just...was so wrapped up in what had happened to Lanker, I forgot he was even still in my room.

Either way, no accidents came from it, which was beyond a blessing. I didn't need any more accidents today. I don't think my heart could take it.

I laid my head down on the oddly cold pillow, rolling towards the clock that blinked 12:37 am. This would be the longest night of my life. In the morning, I would rush into the Med Lab to see if our plan worked.

If it doesn't...I don't know what I'm going to do.

~

"Are you out of your mind, R-001?"

The voice that seemed to come out of nowhere was so sickeningly familiar.

Mother.

"So now you believe you have the authority to replicate yourself. To make more of you? Do you have any idea what you have done? This changes everything, R-001."

What was she talking about? Why did she sound like that? She sounded almost worried. Was my mother even capable of worrying about anything but herself?

"There was never supposed to be more than one of you, R-001. Do. You. Know. What. You've. Done."

Each word was spoken so roughly it felt as though it was tearing through my eardrums. What was she talking about?

What did I do that was so bad? All I did was save my friend's life! But...were there consequences to giving someone my blood, my abilities? Nobody ever told me what would happen, so how would I have known?

Did I...do the wrong thing?

Should I have just been able to let Lanker go in peace?

No, of course not!

Lanker is my friend! And I would be expected to do everything I could to bring him back. I owed that to him. Despite what anyone else says.

Suddenly a shrill scream pierced my dream, making everything around me go dark.

~

As I began to stir, the screaming didn't stop, making me jump to my feet. It wasn't just in my dream!

I grabbed my shirt and ran out of my door towards the sound of the screams. It sounded like it was coming from the Med Lab. Faylin has jumped out of his room as well, following me down the hall.

I pushed the door open roughly, finding Tyrinie trembling by Casteri's bed, face completely pale. On the other side of the room, stood…Lanker. Face confused. Mischievous green eyes glowing more harshly than ever before with a mix of red around his pupils.

From what I could see around the sheet that was wrapped loosely around his body, his fatal chest injury was completely healed and covered in a layer of scar tissue.

It worked, everything worked!

I didn't hesitate to rush forward and wrap a still-dazed Lanker in a tight hug as Faylin calmed Tyrinie down.

"You're alive, you're okay!" I cried joyously, trying to keep my composure. All of the anguish I felt within the last 24 hours was gone. I stepped back for a moment, holding Lanker's face in my hands. "How do you feel? Are you in any pain?"

It seemed that it took Lanker a moment to process what I was saying. Soon enough he focused his eyes on me and gave me a small smile.

"I feel fine, honestly better than fine. Just a little bit…dizzy and... stiff. What, exactly happened? One second, we were at Nyx's castle, and the next minute...well, I'm here waking up with a sheet over my face. Did you think I was dead or something?"

I froze for a moment, wondering what I should tell him. Soon enough he'll figure out that he *was* in fact dead.

But, was that really okay to tell him right now? The last thing I wanted was to overload him with too much information.

Sadly, I didn't even have time to figure it out before Senna and Marcus joined to see what all the commotion was about.

As soon as Senna stepped in the room, and saw Lanker upright and talking, he fainted. Marcus wasn't even able to catch him since he was in a complete state of shock as well.

"How? W-what?" Marcus stammered, face going pale, looking as if he was going to faint soon as well.

"Um, hi...Marcus... does anyone want to tell me what's going on? How much did I miss?" Lanker responded, rightfully confused and nervous.

I guess it was time for me to come clean and tell everyone what happened.

~

"You...did what?"

Shortly after Senna woke up, I gathered everyone, minus Casteri who was still in a coma, in the war room.

Lanker was finally properly dressed, and was now sitting next to Faylin and myself, while Tyrinie, Senna, and Marcus sat on the opposite side. Senna, mouth agape, couldn't believe what I had said. I couldn't tell what emotion was on his face.

"I used my blood and some of Faylin's blood serum to bring Lanker back. I had a feeling Faylin's blood serum couldn't do it alone, so I had to use some of my nanoid blood."

"So, I...was dead?" Lanker sputtered, looking at his hands and arms that showed no remnant of the fight from the previous day. "Wait, does that mean I'm a hybrid now?"

"To be honest Lanker, I am not quite sure." Faylin spoke up, "There is a chance you are actually more like Mr. Scarlet than like a common hybrid. If you were still alive and took some of my blood serum, then you would be a hybrid. But because you were brought back with the power of a nanoid, there is a chance you are more like the Captain."

"Wild." Lanker smiled, beaming at the thought. No traces of resentment or fear. Honestly, that was what I feared the most; Lanker hating me for making this decision on his behalf. But knowing he was okay with it gave me more comfort than I could ever ask for.

Now, explaining that to the others would be a different battle. Tyrinie, now calmed down, still looked a little unsettled, but seemed to handle the news well. Marcus, after the explanation, seemed to perk back up to his normal self. However, Senna still seemed to be in a state of absolute shock. Perhaps it's because they're family, or perhaps it's because Senna still blames himself for not being able to save Lanker in the first place.

"Well, now we have another super powered freak onboard, nice." Tyrinie said jokingly, a small attempt to lighten the mood.

"Bro! I can't wait to see what powers I have! What if I can fly, or move things with my mind, or somethin' like that!" Lanker jumped up from his seat and headed for the door, full of vigor. "I'm gonna start experimenting now!"

"Please do be careful, your body is most likely still adjusting to the new chemical setting." Faylin called after them. However, it fell on deaf ears as Tyrinie and Marcus followed happily.

It wasn't until a second later Lanker ran back into the room and gave me a tight hug, similar to the one I gave him earlier.

"I can't thank you enough, Cap. Thank you...for not only giving me my life back, but for making me into something so special. Something like you."

He said with a smile that completely melted my heart.

I know I did the right thing.

I just hope this doesn't have any consequences.

END OF CHAPTER 11

12

BACK ON TRACK

The day had continued like normal now that our team was whole again. Casteri has woken up from unconsciousness not too long after all of the morning commotion. Thankfully, he had no long-lasting injuries. A mild concussion, and a fractured arm, but nothing fatal. A part of my mind reminded me that I could always use my blood on Casteri to bring him back to full health, but I was too weary to do so.

I had to be careful with this ability, I couldn't just use it without thinking first. Now that my brain wasn't clouded with grief, I now saw this was something I needed to be smart about. Not only that, but it was something I needed to openly speak with my team about.

Earlier in the evening, after we brought Casteri up to speed on everything. I brought each of my teammates into my room, one by one. I sat them down, and asked them all the same question.

"Marcus, if you were to die on this journey, do you want me to bring you back?"

"Hell yeah, of course!"

"Tyrinie, if you were to die on this journey, do you want me to bring you back?"

"Nah... I'm already enough of an experiment, I don't need to become even more of one. But...well I don't know, I guess it depends on the situation."

"Tyrinie, I need a straight answer from you. Yes or no?"

"Okay, okay... Yeah, I think so. Especially if it's from this dumbass quest. If it's just from old age, then no."

"Casteri, if you were to die on this journey, do you want me to bring you back? Also, do you want me to heal your wounds with my blood?"

"I'm fine Captain, no need to worry about my injuries. As for bringing me back to life, I suppose someone needs to watch over Tyrinie. So, if he's coming back, I better come back as well."

"Casteri, as much as I love how tight you and Tyrinie are, I need to make sure you are making this decision for yourself. Is this what you would want?"

"Making sure Tyrinie is okay is what I want. If he is alive, I want to be alive too."

"Senna, if you were to die on this journey, do you want me to bring you back?"

Senna was quiet for a moment, looking like he was going through the biggest internal struggle of his life. Then finally, he spoke up.

"I don't like the idea of playing God. If I'm meant to die, please just let me die."

"Lanker, I know I did this without speaking about it with you first. Are you okay with being this way now? I know it might feel a little too late to ask now."

"Of course, it's okay! You gave me my life back, Cap. I literally owe you my life now. Not only that, but I have powers.

134

I have no idea what those powers are yet, but you made me something incredibly special...and I could never thank you enough for that.

~

Now that I had a mental log of everyone's answers, there was one other person I needed to consult. But getting to them would be hard. Especially because they seem to only reach out to me when they need me. But either way, I had to try. Even if it meant getting some additional assistance.

I took a seat on my bed, getting comfortable before letting out a deep breath.

"R, I know you're there. I need your help."

Within a moment, I could feel R's presence behind me. For a moment, he didn't speak.

"You rang?"

I was startled for a moment, it felt like R hadn't been in a material form in quite a while. I was so used to just hearing him in the back of my head, not in my actual ears.

I shook my head, keeping my head forward and my brain focused. "I need you to help me get to the cyberworld."

Everything was silent as I felt R recline on the bed, seemingly more relaxed than before.

"And now why would I do that, kiddo. Especially after I told you how much you shouldn't be going there. Beings like you shouldn't be bouncing between worlds all haphazardly like that."

"Honestly, I would take the warning more to heart if I hadn't already been there so many times, and every time has been out of my control.

I need to go back this time; I need to speak with that old man. I need to ask him if I did something wrong with bringing Lanker back."

"Well kid, I can tell you that you definitely changed the course of the future with that move. I guarantee just about every single person/hybrid/whatever who has been keeping an eye on the possible routes of the future just got a run for their money. Ginseng is probably quaking in her heels right now. And I don't need a personal connection to tell you Galaia isn't happy. That is why I'm telling you; you don't want to go there right now while the literal creator of cyberkind is pissed."

I turned, locking my eyes on R. It was a random thought, but it feels like it's been a while since I've actually seen him. Thankfully he hadn't changed.

"If you thought my decision was so dangerous, then why did you recommend I do it?"

"I didn't recommend anything kid, I simply said it to be creative and try to fix the problem. I didn't say to inject part of me into a corpse."

"Wait, so that means Lanker can see you now?"

"Oh, Lanker can do more than that, kid. Lanker can practically do everything you can do. Including having contact with Galaia...and opening the mainframe."

Wait…

Oh no.

"I... gave Lanker the ability to open the mainframe?"

"A child born of both worlds. Lanker was a full-fledged human, who was brought back to life by being implanted with a nanoid. And not just one vial, but three vials worth.

Just like how Faylin is the only of his kind, and you are basically the only of your kind, you've just made Lanker a brand-new being. Something was brought back to life and now being partially inhabited by a nanoid.

I froze, thinking of what to say next. Of what to do next...

Did I just put Lanker in even more danger? Forget the powers he'll undoubtedly develop; did he have any idea how strong he truly was.

"Well, should I tell him?" I asked quietly, now afraid someone might have been listening in.

"What? Should you tell him that now he, like you, possibly holds the fate of an entire race in his hands? You could avoid telling him the truth, but you had better make sure he never steps foot in that place. Galaia's influence will be strongest the closer he gets to Xenon Tech, so if he goes in there not knowing the part he now plays, she could easily manipulate him into opening it for sure. Lanker's smart, but Galaia is a master of deception."

I nodded. I needed feedback on what I should do. It would be easier to just avoid telling him the truth, but I would hate for him to be in a situation where he has to figure all of this out himself.

Similarly, to myself...I wished mother and father were honest with me about everything, instead of practically forcing me to learn it all on my own.

Of course, if they told me the truth, I would have figured out they were using me the entire time.

"I think I know what I need to do." I stood up with my resolve strengthened. I owed Lanker the truth. Besides, how could he fight what he didn't know? He was involved in this now, and he deserved a full explanation.

~~

Marcus, Casteri, and I stood in the cell of the ship where Dante was restrained in the cuffs that came from the rogues. However, he didn't put up a fight. The cuffs were still the same size as when he was cuffed, proving he hadn't even tried to struggle. He just stared ahead blankly, unmoving, unblinking.

"So, what kind of humanoid is he?" I asked, daring myself to go a little closer to peer at him.

"Not sure. He looks like a mix between combat and companion, but he also looks homemade, so he could be blended. I'd have to take him apart to really confirm that." Marcus spoke directly, taking notes on the hologram coming from his wrist cuff.

"Is there any way to guarantee his loyalty to us? I could think of a few uses for him."

Marcus nodded, still jotting down notes. "Dante was loyal to Nyx. Nyx was most likely last in his family lineage which is why Dante is practically vegetative without him. He is, for lack of a better word, a blank slate looking for a new master. If there was any time to make him yours, this would be it."

Dante continued to stare ahead, blissfully unaware of the conversation happening around him. When it came to Faylin, I was completely against the idea of taking ownership of a humanoid. But I could make an exception with Dante. Maybe it was because I knew Dante truly had no freewill. If he did, he wouldn't be a humanoid vegetable right now. If anything, giving him purpose is the only way to help him right now.

I took a breath and nodded over to Marcus. "Okay, let's start the procedure."

Faylin was right when he said this procedure was painless and would only take a few minutes. Shortly after Dante was sedated and my blood was drawn, the operation was nearly over.

However, as soon as Casteri was about to inject my blood into Dante's neural cavity, I stopped him.

"Wait!" I pulled the surgical mask down my face. "What about R? My blood contains a nanoid, remember? Will that make Dante a little more...sentient then we need him to be?"

"Damn, how did we forget about that?" Marcus rolled his eyes and looked over to Casteri. "Well, this might cause a little bit of an issue. Lil man is right, we can't use his blood on an empty humanoid shell."

"Looks like someone else's blood will have to get used." Casteri shrugged. "Anybody want a free humanoid?"

The room was silent. Obviously, I couldn't be used, and the same went for Faylin and Lanker. Tyrinie's blood was altered as well, so it would be best not to use him. So that just left Casteri, Marcus, and Senna. But Senna hasn't been the same since Lanker's temporary death.

"Well, I have no use for a humanoid, but I don't mind just using my blood." Marcus chuckled. "I'll just command him to listen to whatever you have to say. Nice and simple."

"Sounds perfect."

The procedure continued as planned after we replaced all of my blood vials with ones from Marcus. Shortly after the procedure, Dante was placed into a type of medically induced coma while his system processed the new information.

"So, after I give control of Dante over to you, what are you planning on doing with him?" Marcus asked as we lounged in the hallway.

"Well, honestly, I wasn't even planning on keeping him on the ship. Once we know he is absolutely safe and fully functional, I was going to give him to my old friends, Persephone and Emme. Ever since people realized they were involved with me; they're been being hassled.

The thought of something happening to them is enough to keep me up at night. So, with someone like Dante keeping them out of harm's way, I'll be able to rest easily."

~

Farhill Valley was a speck in the distance resting against the darkening horizon. At the speed we were going, we were bound to get there within the hour. As far as we could see, none of Salem's men followed us here. Perhaps they assumed we were going off to Lelani next? Or perhaps they were tracking my father, assuming I was with him. Either way was good for us. I didn't know exactly what we were looking for in the ruins of Xenon Tech, a part of me felt as though nothing there could help me. Perhaps I just wanted to see the mainframe for myself.

Maybe I needed to see it for myself to prove it actually existed.

Everything on the ship was as normal as before. Lanker planted himself back on the helm with no fear from what happened last time he was there. It was almost like he didn't even remember, or he was trying really hard not to remember. Tyrinie and Casteri had been inseparable, and were currently with Marcus working on retraining Dante.

So far, Dante was doing perfectly well in taking orders, and recognized Persephone and Emme as his new masters. His job was to protect and care for them with his life. Simple enough.

As for Senna, I truly feel like he never recovered from that last fight. He just wasn't the same anymore. Perhaps he just wasn't cut out for this job, and the thought saddened me. I didn't mean to traumatize him, but it seems like that's exactly what happened. I hadn't said anything yet, but I was considering leaving Senna with Dante and Persephone. He could still feel helpful by keeping them safe, keeping Emme well, and keeping an eye on Dante. And at the same time, he could stay out of the line of fire. It honestly seemed like the best course of action. I just hope Marcus and Lanker would be okay with it.

Thankfully Senna was never in the spotlight, so he wouldn't be a recognizable target. And besides, if everything goes according to plan, Lelani, my parents, and Salem would be dead within the month. All of the current threats would be dead, and we'll finally be free.

Free? Not you. Not if you decided to keep the mainframe closed.

I shook my head, blocking out the tri-toned voice.

I wasn't going to entertain Salem's whims.

~

"You're sending me a humanoid bodyguard?"

I chuckled at Persephone's tone. "His name is Dante; he will keep you and Emme safe. He looks like a companion humanoid, so he won't even stand out…too much."

"You hesitated."

"Well, he is big. Really big…and really tall as well."

"Ooo, how tall?"

I rolled my eyes. "Seven…maybe eight feet or something?"

"Oh, well I believe this might be a good idea after all. I like him already!"

Suddenly, I hated this idea. How was I supposed to compete with someone who was literally two and a half feet taller than me? I feared that 5'6 was the tallest I would grow.

"You're quiet again, sweetheart." Persephone chuckled. *"Am I making you feel bad?"*

"As if." I scoffed back in a teasing tone. "I was just thinking, I forgot to ask you how Emme was doing."

Persephone was quiet for a moment before responding, making my chest tighten.

"My poor little monster is still under the weather. There are no good doctors in this area, so finding someone who can take care of her is proving to be a little difficult. But she's being a fighter, so don't worry too much."

"Well actually, that is perfect because I have another surprise for you. I'll be leaving Senna, our resident nurse, with you. I'm confident Emme will be good as new with him around."

"Oh sweetheart, are you sure? Don't you need a medical professional onboard with you just in case someone gets hurt?"

"It's okay, really! We have a backup plan just in case anything happens here. I just want to make sure you and Emme are okay.

So, I'm sending Senna and Dante your way tonight, and I'm not taking no for an answer."

Persephone chuckled, almost sounding a little taken back.

"Well alright then, Mr. Captain, I won't fight you on the subject. But honestly, thank you sweetheart, this means a lot to us. You've always taken such good care of Emme and I, and I'm the one who is supposed to be taking care of you."

"You do take care of me, that's why I want to take care of you guys now. I have to go, but I'll check in later."

"Okay, you stay safe out there."

"You too."

I felt as though saying 'I love you' would have been awkward. Obviously, Persephone had told me she loved me as a son, so saying it back when I love her in a different way would feel wrong.

I shook my head clear and headed over to the Med Bay. It was time to break the news to Senna.

END OF CHAPTER 12

LANKER

13

THE FORBIDDEN DOOR

"You...want me to leave?"

The way Senna said it made the entire thing sound so much harsher than I meant for it too.

"No no, I'm not kicking you out or anything. I just need you in a different area. As far as I'm concerned, you're still a member of my crew. Right now, my family needs medical help, and they can't get it. You're the only person I trust to take care of Persephone and Emme. Dante will be there as well to keep you all safe. Would you do that for me?"

Reluctantly, Senna nodded, taking a deep breath and slumping in his chair. "With all the blood and death, I've seen in my career, you would think I would be able to handle anything. It's almost embarrassing to call myself a nurse when I allowed myself to crumble apart after what happened to...Lanker."

Just remembering that day made my heart ache. "Senna, you reacted in a way any person would act, I don't blame you at all. I crumbled as well...but me sending you to the West isn't a punishment or anything. I just believe this would be a better arrangement for you."

"No no, you're right. I know you're right." Senna cleared his throat and ran his fingers through his hair. "I'd be better off assisting people on the ground. This life on the run isn't for me." He chuckled lightly, extending his hand to me, which I quickly took. "I'll take care of Emme, I promise."

"Thank you, Senna, this means more to me than you know."

With tearful goodbyes and promises to stay in touch, Senna and Dante boarded the hovercar Faylin had cleverly obtained from Sector 6. Before Senna finished loading his bags, Lanker pulled him into a tight hug that Senna awkwardly returned.

"I'll miss you bro." Lanker chuckled, patting him roughly on the back.

Senna rolled his eyes, "Don't be stupid, I'll…see you when you get back. Just, be careful, all of you." Lanker seemed taken back by the concern in Senna's voice, but just smiled and nodded.

"We will."

With a final wave, Senna and Dante sped off towards the West. According to our calculations, they should be at Persephone's house within a day.

Their first duty will be to ditch the car far from the house, and then walk the rest of the way. Then when they knock on the door, they'll have to say "The Captain says we are welcomed here." That's how Persephone will know they are friends of mine. Dante has been successfully rewired to take commands from Persephone and Senna, with his primary Master still being Marcus, who will remain in constant contact with Senna to make sure Dante is behaving. Having Dante and Senna with Mrs. P made me feel so much better, especially since I know it'll be a better environment for Senna to mentally heal in as well.

"Okay team, back to work! We are about to hit Farhill Valley in T-15 minutes. Meet in the War Room in five minutes."

"Aye aye!"

~

"This place should be abandoned, so we shouldn't meet any resistance. But just in case, I want all weapons on hand. We need to be 100% prepared. Upon arrival, Faylin, Lanker, and I will take the basement. Meanwhile, I want Marcus, Casteri, and Tyrinie to check topside. We are looking for documents, files, info-chips, anything that could possibly be of importance. I want us in and out before the sun comes up, and then it's straight to the Southern region. Any questions?"

Everyone nodded, agreeing that everything seemed straightforward enough.

Out of the corner of my eye, I caught R hanging around the corner of the room, looking as bored as ever. But to my surprise, Lanker was staring at him as well. This must've caught R off guard as well, because as soon as he caught Lanker's gaze, he looked like a deer caught in headlights. After a few seconds of staring, R poofed away. Lanker glanced over at me, but stayed silent.

"Everyone is dismissed, go ahead and get yourselves dressed and prepped."

Everyone got up and left the room, except for Lanker, who remained seated, staring ahead. Once the room was empty, I took a seat next to him.

"So, you saw him as well?" I asked, trying to sound as casual as possible.

"Yea…so that was R, right? That nanoid?" Lanker replied with a forced calm voice.

I nodded, and based on his visibly tense muscles, it looked like the realization that Lanker was no longer a normal human being finally kicked in. His face started to pale as tiny surges of green began to dance along his fingertips, causing various items in the room to start to tremble.

"What's happening, Cap?" Lanker's breath began to pick up as the green surges started to cover his fingers completely.

"Lanker, hey, just calm down, take a few deep breaths." I leaned in, turning his chair quickly to face me. "Calm down, look at me okay."

"I'm calm, I'm calm" He responded, still panting. The power surges didn't seem to be calming down, and out of the corner of my eye, I could see the trembling items on the table begin to form a green glow and…float.

I grabbed Lanker by the shoulders, shaking him a bit before forcing his face to look at me.

"Lanker, calm down, you're fine!" I spoke in a harsh whisper. It seemed counterproductive, but it definitely got his attention. Within a moment, the trembling stopped, and Lanker's breathing slowed down to quiet pants. With that, I sighed, exhausted. "Thank goodness."

"I'm s-sorry about that, I don't know what happened." Lanker stammered, clearly embarrassed and still out of breath.

"Don't be, it's okay! It's overwhelming, I can understand." I smiled, pulling him into a hug while trying to quell Lanker's embarrassment. "But did you see what your powers did?"

"My powers? No, I didn't see anything."

"We'll have to work on your ability to control your powers, but you were definitely able to move the items in this room. That's crazy impressive!"

Lanker smiled before suddenly jumping to his feet, wobbling slightly. "Wait, I should be landing the boat right now!"

Lanker ran off without another word, and without realizing Tyrinie had more than likely taken over the helm.

I smiled, standing up as well, and heading off to my room to grab my coat. It was time. I was finally going to see the place where all of this madness started.

~

As the last of us filed off the ship, we stood on jet black sand and overlooked the charred remains of what was once Xenon Technologies. Farhill Valley seemed to be a desert on an unmarked stretch of land that went on for miles. How nobody had ever found this place was beyond me. However, someone mistaking the black sand for ocean water was very possible. This place had natural camouflage.

The moon was high in the sky and cast an eerie glow on the remains, making my skin crawl. This place was the sheer essence of "You shouldn't be here." But despite the feeling deep in my gut, we pressed onward.

"So, this is it?" Faylin spoke up next to me as we began pressing forward, guns and swords at the ready. "What do you suppose we'll find inside?"

"Not a clue, but I need to see the mainframe for myself, and perhaps we'll find some data about Galaia. Whoever decided to reach out to her must've left some notes behind."

While I knew it was risky, I also wanted to gauge Lanker's reaction to being near the mainframe. The more intense the reaction, the more careful we would need to be in the near future. At least in this case, Faylin and I would be ready to step in if things go out of hand.

The wind blew ominously over us as we reached the collapsed doors. The air inside, despite the cold weather, was muggy and felt…toxic to breathe in. The charred walls were high, and it looked like we had entered some sort of lobby. Down the hall were metal doors operated via key panel, but I could tell they were long past their operational phase of life.

"Alright team, let's go ahead and split up for now. Casteri, Marcus, and Tyrinie check upstairs. Lanker, Faylin and I will check this floor and try to find our way downstairs. Go ahead back to the ship once you're done checking the upstairs level."

They nodded and disappeared down the far corridor.

~

It truly felt we had been searching for hours, finding absolutely nothing. Which honestly made a lot of sense. This place had been the biggest mystery of our time, and before this place had been completely abandoned, officers were scouring this place day in and day out to find the culprit. The only people who had any contact with this place since then were those from the Xeytx tribe, and we hadn't found anything from them yet.

"Do you think this might have been a dead end?" Lanker asked, stifling a yawn. "What are we looking for anyways?"

"Well, we are looking for anything the Xeytx tribe might have left behind.

Plus, we need to find this damn mainframe, there has to be something there, some sort of clue that points to who made the deal with Galaia in the first place along with how to stop her for good."

Even though Ginseng said it was impossible to kill Galaia, I'd be damned if I didn't try.

Faylin and Lanker nodded, lagging slightly behind. Faylin used his electricity to illuminate the way for us, while Lanker attempted to do the same with little success.

As the staircases began to descend, my anxiety began to spike. It truly seemed like each of our adventures served to justify my fear of the dark. Bad things always happened in the dark, and the ominous creek of every step was doing little to calm me down.

150

After what seemed like an eternity, we reached the main lab, where there was little that was interesting. Broken test tubes and binders that had been torn clean were all that littered the floor from what we could see. It had looked like this place had been truly gutted when the first few investigations were done centuries prior.

I picked up one of the still intact test tubes. I wonder if this is the one where they kept R after pulling him from the mainframe. So weird…

We all sifted through the bit of garbage that covered the floor. I, on my hands and knees, lost track of how many times I cut myself on tiny shards of glass from bottles that had ruptured. Faylin was doing the same, sifting through seemingly unfazed. Lanker, however, was investigating the walls.

"Hey, I think I found something!" Lanker called out from one of the darker corners of the room. Faylin ran over first, illuminating the path for both of us. In the corner of the office was a corner of the wall that, to the naked eye, looked like just another section of wall. But thanks to Lanker pushing on every inch of the room, it seemed to come ajar. There is no doubt the age of the place assisted in the wall panel being able to be moved to easily.

Peeking all of our heads in, we saw nothing but stairs that led to a further descent down below the ruins. I could feel my stomach churning at the thought of navigating down those stairs, but then I remembered something Cyryl had said during our fight.

"Something was discovered. Something was discovered underneath the lab. Something was sentient and had knowledge far behind the human mind."

Underneath the lab.

That had to be where the mainframe was.

"Okay team, who is going first?"

~

Faylin lit the path from the front, meanwhile Lanker matched his pace directly behind, leaving the tail end to me. While I hated being in the back, it was probably best I covered the rear. So far so good, but the further down we sent, the more that feeling began to fade.

Finally, an eerie glow appeared at the end of the staircase. From what I could see, the room had similar gray floors similar to that of the lab. The floor was cracked due to age, causing roots and vines to take over the majority of the walls, floors, and ceilings. If anything, it resembled something that would have been found in the Xeytx tribe's compound.

Stepping down into the musty room, I realized where the Xeytx tribe had been hiding all of their precious items. Shelves lined the walls, and each shelf was packed with books, statues, globes, and tons of other items that were nearly in pristine condition. However, that wasn't what caught my attention. Instead, towards the back center of the room, my eyes were locked on what only could have been the mainframe.

It was a large circular device that stood at least ten feet tall and resembled something like a portal.

The thick metal circumference of the portal was covered in a language I didn't recognize and pulsed in a purple-ish hue. The inside of the portal itself had a similar hue that seemed to distort all of the space around it within a few feet. Wires were in oddly pristine condition connected to the bottom of the portal and traveled within the walls and to a few other monitors, creating a tangled mechanical jungle.

"This is…the mainframe?" Lanker spoke up, voice monotone. He slowly started moving closer before I seized him by the arm.

"Don't go any closer. Remember, you have my blood now, we don't know what'll happen if you get too close." Reluctantly, he stepped back, moving a few feet behind me.

I stepped a little bit closer, right to the edge of where the distortion was noticeable. It felt…good being so close to it. Almost euphoric. Like I was meant to be there. Like I had finally found my place in the world. Every nerve on my body fizzled to life in ways I had never felt before.

I shook my head, stepping back, allowing the cold rush of reality to rush back over me. Not like I would have said it out loud, but I already missed that beautiful feeling.

"Do you guys hear that?" Lanker whispered, pulling Faylin away from the doorway where the noise was reverberating from. When I listened closer, I heard what sounded like the light clacking of heels. The person seemed to be walking at a slow and melodic pace, unbothered by the sheer intensity of the ruins they were walking through.

"Who…" I wondered before it dawned on me. I knew that walk anywhere, and it would make perfect sense for them to be here of all places…

This was bad. I didn't want Faylin and Lanker around for this.

"Come on, this way. I led Lanker and Faylin towards a large cabinet in one of the far corners of the room, unceremoniously shoving them inside. "Stay here until I tell you to come out, okay." They both nodded.

I hid myself in one of the corners of the room, cloaking myself in the shadows that crept from the floor to the ceilings. The steps grew closer, and with each step, my resolve grew stronger.

Finally, my mother walked through the doorway.

END OF CHAPTER 13

14

GOODNIGHT

***

$\mathcal{S}$abra Hakimi in the flesh walked into the room, her heels echoing a

melody against the barren walls. She seemed none the wiser that I was in the room with her. When had she come? Surely, she saw our ship and must've known someone was here?
Why was she here if she knew she would risk being found?

I watched as she stepped closer to the mainframe, similar to how I had earlier.
She went only far enough for her body to be covered in the distorted waves, making her image seem rippled to me.
She sighed, a sound that sounded both happy and relieved as she lightly swayed back and forth. The distortion must've had the same euphoric effect on anyone who got close enough. I wonder why that was.

Perhaps I had the distortion to thank for my mother being so blissfully unaware of her surroundings. Perhaps getting a fix was so important to her she risked being followed by someone just to come down here.

The most important question was what my next move was.
I could try to teleport everyone away, but within the few seconds it takes, we'd surely be discovered. And that would also leave Marcus and the others upstairs.

We could just stay put until she left, but who knows how long that would take. What if she was here all night, or what if she decided to start looking around?

Obviously, that wouldn't work either. So, there was only one thing I could do at this moment.

It was time for me to end this once and for all.

I had been so ready for this moment, but for some reason, now my hands were shaking.

With my feet barely touching the floor, I went along the wall behind where my mother was standing. At this range, she was only about eight feet in front of me. I could smell the lingering perfume she always wore. As I took a step closer, I heard my mom chuckle.

"Well, hello, darling. Did you come to visit mommy?"

I froze in place. I hated the fact her voice still had that effect on me. Before I could move forward, she continued.

"I would say I'm surprised you even found this place, but to be honest…I'm not. You have been exceeding my expectations R-001. To be honest, I don't know if this is a good thing or a bad thing. You are reacting more like Salem than I ever could have imagined-"

"Don't you dare compare me to him." I spat out angrily.

She chuckled, glancing over her shoulder at me, her eyes glazed over. "My my, someone has certainly inherited their father's foul attitude. You should know better than to speak to your mother that way."

I pulled my dagger from its sheath, holding it tightly in my grasp and hardening my resolve. I knew what I had to do, it had to end right here and now. I would honor Madam Ginseng's request and make her death quick and as painless as possible.

For the first time in a while, my head was completely silent. R wasn't there, Salem wasn't there, it was just me.

Only me.

Taking a few quick breaths, I charged forward into the distortion, attempting to body slam her. If this was any other moment, it would have been a rookie move, and she easily would have trapped me. But thanks to her altered mental state, I slammed into her with ease. As soon as I reached her, I felt the effect of the distortion. The same euphoric feeling washed over me as mom and I laid sprawled on the lab floor, barely a foot away from the mainframe, dagger still in hand.

I pulled myself up to my knees, keeping my mother trapped beneath me, it's not like she was trying to move either way. She just stared up at me with a smile that made her eyes crease.

"You really are just like him. All this time I was chasing perfection, and here you were. If only I hadn't let your father squander your potential."

A strange warbling sound filled the air, but outside of that, there was no sound.

Everything was so peaceful.

I unwillingly laughed, the euphoria filling my lungs.

"I'm not like Salem...I'm not perfect. All I wanted was to be free from this life that you and dad threw me into. All I wanted was to be normal...and you took that from me."

Mother reached up and gently grasped my face between her hands. "Some of us simply aren't meant to be normal, my love. I was never normal; your father was never normal. It's simply not in our DNA. All I wanted was to turn you into everything I couldn't be, something better than human. Something better than what this world could offer."

She smiled again, and to my surprise, a few tears began to spill. "Maybe a part of me wanted to have a normal life, but E-129 showed me a better way. He showed me more than I could ever put into words. And for the last few centuries, his words are all I hear. But now, in here, all the noise can stop and I can be…tired. Your mommy has been tired for a long time."

For the first time since I was born, the woman I was looking at resembled a mother. My actual mother, not the Salem-obsessed, perfection-obsessed, image-obsessed woman who used me as her own personal experiment for my entire life.

It must've been the distortion, but I had to fight off the feelings that made me want to hesitate and spare her.

I knew as soon as my mother stepped out of this room, she would turn back into the heartless monster she was.

I raised the blade, and placed it against her throat. She didn't even flinch, she just continued to stare. "This world is crazy, isn't it. When I worked at Xenon Technologies, we tried to save this planet, but we just aren't advanced enough to." She chuckled, the tears stopping. "The nanoids truly are the only hope for this planet, darling. They are the only ones who can fix what we broke."

"I won't believe that. I'm going to fix everything, that's what you created me for, wasn't it?"

"Is that why I created you? Did I truly make you to save this world?" Mom asked in a way that sounded more like a statement.

She raised her hand to my shoulder, almost like she was encouraging me. "A part of me always tried to love you…your father as well."

I nodded, "I've always loved you, Mom."

With a thrust that felt heavier than it needed to be, I plunged the knife through my mother's throat. Even after it pierced through, and the blood began to spurt messily on myself and the floor, my mother's face never changed. Her eyes remained transfixed on me, and the soft smile I had never seen in my childhood remained plastered on her face.

I unwillingly stood to my feet, still feeling the euphoric effects of the distortion. A part of me just wanted to stay in here because it just felt so damned good. But I knew I needed to leave, Faylin and Lanker were still in the closet waiting for me.

Lifting Mother's still body into my arms, I began to walk us out of the distortion field.

As soon as we crossed into the normal air, I collapsed, the sudden gravity of what just happened washing over me like a flood. All of the emotions the distortion had been blocking nearly knocked me off my feet.

My mother was dead. I killed her.

I had planned and fantasized for this moment for so long, but now that it was actually here…
I glanced down, looking at my mother's still body, eyes still looking at me lovingly. I didn't know what to feel.

Not long after, Faylin and Lanker emerged, staying silent.
"Are you alright, Scarlet?" Faylin asked, kneeling at my side and placing his hand on my shoulder, much like my mother had."

"I hated her so much, why am I not happy about this?" I asked nobody in particular. This should have been a joyous occasion, yet here I was, holding back tears.

Why did mom seem so…sad? She seemed almost relieved I was about to kill her. She said she had been tired for so long, and now she could finally rest. What did she mean by that? Was the curse of being immortal more than my mother's psyche could bear. Was she just another victim under E's control?

Faylin had dismissed Lanker, instructing him to gather the others and take them all to the ship. In the meanwhile, Faylin and I sat in silence by my mother's body.

"She said a part of her tried to love me. What does it mean when a parent says that to their child?" I asked after a long stretch of silence.

"I suppose it could mean she was unable, for one reason or another, to love you as a mother should. None of which is your fault. Perhaps E-129 truly was to blame for what happened to your mother."

"No…I don't want to excuse her. My mother was a psychopath; manipulative, cunning, and unable to love anybody but herself and her obsession. I just…wish I got to know the woman that was talking to me inside of the distortion a little bit longer. That woman would have made a better mom."

My mother, Sabra Hakimi, was a monster. It would be easier to remember her that way.

Faylin and I broke through the tile floor to get to the dirt beneath. We dug a shallow hole and slid my mother's body inside, burying her in the place she loved so much.

~~

After gathering all the files and useful artifacts I possibly could, Faylin and I made our way back to the ship where our team was waiting expectantly. I waved back with a smile, despite the heavy tugging that was still pulling on my heart.

I wasn't sure if Lanker had told everyone about the fight with my mother, but if so, nobody said a word about it. Surely, they must've known, my clothes were still soaked in her blood.

Either way, I was grateful for their feigned ignorance.

After changing out of my bloodied clothes and washing myself, I went back to the War Room. We were heading back to the Southern Region to take out Lelani. She was now the last member of the management. And with her out of the picture, Salem would have nobody left. He would be vulnerable, and ready for us to come barging through his stronghold. All I wanted was for this adventure to be over. I wanted to go to bed and pretend like all of this was some insane fever dream. I wanted to pretend I didn't just murder my mom like I had murdered so many people before. All I have been doing this entire adventure was murdering bad people. But doesn't that make me bad as well? I understand what Mom meant when she said she was tired.

I was just so tired.

~~

"Cap… you awake?"

I groaned in my sleepy state and pulled the pillow over my head. I was nice and comfortable, alone with my thoughts until I had the blanket pulled from off of me.

"Yes…" I murmured out. For someone to wake me up, something had better be on fire. To my surprise, and annoyance, nothing was on fire.

Everything was silent, and it looked like the sun hadn't even risen. I glanced over at my clock, it blinked at 3:57 am.

At the foot of my bed sat Lanker, only recognizable by the eerie green glow of his eyes. The rest of his face and body was practically shrouded by darkness. He stared ahead, transfixed on the wall behind me. There was something eerie about his presence.

"Is something wrong Lanker, why are you up so late?"

"Ah well, I don't really sleep much anymore …like, at all. But I just wanted to let you know we've arrived in the South. It hardly took us any time at all."

"Okay, that's great." I yawned, plopping my head back down on the pillow. "Not to be rude, but couldn't this have waited until the morning?"

"I mean yea, I guess. It's just…you're like me so I figured you would be awake too. It's a little lonely being the only one who can't sleep. Even Faylin shut himself off for the night."

I slowly sat up, willing myself to not look annoyed. This was all still new to Lanker, and he looked to me for comfort and direction. I was obligated to help him since I did this to him.

"Alright, I'm up now." I smiled. "Did you have something on your mind? Or are you just lonely?"

Lanker sat back, looking much more relieved now. "Just…a lot of heavy stuff today. I'm sorry about your mom. I know you probably don't want to talk about it."

"Thanks Lanker, and… it's okay. She made her own decision when she decided to follow Salem.

162

I guess a part of me wishes things ended a little differently. I wish she had yelled at me, cursed at me, hit me…something. Maybe then I wouldn't feel so…I don't know."

Lanker nodded silently, pulling his knees up to his chest. "Our quest is almost over now, isn't it."

"Yea it is, aren't you excited? I think we have had enough excitement to last a lifetime, and I never thought I would ever say that."

"Well, I guess I've gotten so used to things on the ship, I don't really want everything to end. I'm glad you don't mind me being a permanent addition to your family."

"Of course, Lanker, if it was up to me, everyone would stay. I think we have all lost enough. But I know Casteri and Tyrinie will probably want to go back home. Senna might choose to stay in the West if he hits it off with Persephone. Marcus was on the run, so he might choose to stay with us. And then of course Faylin and I are going to stay together.

You know, since I'm going to be ruling this world after we kill Salem, what do you think about the three of us staying in a big stronghold in the West? It'll have a courtyard, a moat, everything!"

"And of course, an entire staff of cute maids!" Lanker chimed in, sounding much more like his old self.

"Of course, we can't forget the cute maids. We should also get a cute humanoid maid for Faylin."

We laughed and continued to exchange ideas of our perfect dream home until the sun came up.

～～

"A party!?"

I laughed, "Not just any party, this is going to be one of our final fights." Thanks to some new intel from Tetsuzo, we found that our lovely Lelani will be hosting a ball in honor of Salem, as she does once every few years. There was some fear in the south for Lelani's safety after all of the other members of Salem's elite had been killed, but Lelani is insisting on making a statement.

And what is her statement? That she will not be scared into submission?

So, whether this is an intentional trap or not, we have to make an appearance.

Thankfully, this is a masquerade party, so nobody should know who we are at first glance if we are careful. All we have to do is corner and cuff Lelani with the cuffs from the rogues, and then lock her onboard. Once onboard, we'll give her over to Tetsuzo and Arai and let them have their fun.

Since the ball will be at her mansion, there is a good chance we'll be able to locate this "Pig Farm" Tetsuzo had warned us about. If so, it's our duty to free the people trapped there.

"Okay," Casteri spoke up. "But this must be a trap, why else would Lelani happen to plan a ball that will more than likely be filled with Salem's supporters during the time we are taking out the members of the management?"

"There is no doubt she most likely assumes we will be making an appearance. Either that, or she just made a really dumb move. Either way, she's severely underestimating us if she believes this trap is going to catch us off guard." I leaned in, taking a closer look at the hologram of Lelani's mansion we gathered from Tetsuzo. "And even if she is expecting us to arrive, we aren't all going to be seen."

164

"What do you mean by that?" Tyrinie asked, seemingly more interested than he had been a few moments earlier.

"Here is the initial plan. Marcus and I will enter from the front doors as if we were normal guests. According to our intel, there is an underground entrance through the sewer grates around the back of the estate, Faylin and Casteri will enter from there and work their way upstairs. Tyrinie and Lanker will enter topside through one of the forest-facing bedroom windows. Once everyone enters, our first job will be surveillance. How many guards do we see? How many humanoids? And where is Lelani located? Afterwards, we'll create a diversion to distract the guards on hand and all of the other guests. I don't want us to get surrounded, so my plan is just to be able to get my hand on Lelani. If I'm able to grab her, I can teleport her with me onto the ship. It's a skill I've been trying to perfect because it can take a little bit of finesse."

"Seems…easy enough, I guess. I mean, but do you think Lelani will be captured that easily? Madam Ginseng did say she was one of the strongest members of the Management."

Lanker questioned while practicing activating his powers. He hasn't gotten perfect control yet, but he is able to make certain objects float, which he has been more than excited about.

"That is true. All we can do is hope for the best and plan for the worst. I'll let you all know Plan B…once I think of it."

END OF CHAPTER 14

15

THE WOMAN IN PINK

I laughed, feeling more relaxed than I ever had in my entire life as I laid on my back in the distortion field. It was all I could think about, so what was the harm in teleporting back over here just for a few moments to feel this relaxation again. Every part of my body felt light and on fire at the same exact time, everything was numbed and yet so alive. It was a feeling I wished I could share with every member of my crew, but I wanted to keep this wonderful shameful secret to myself. I rolled to my side, looking long and hard at the mainframe in front of me. The distortion field was stronger the closer I got, but I didn't dare move any closer. This was enough.

What would happen if I entered the mainframe from this end? Would I still feel this good?

I got up to my knees and scooted myself a little closer, feeling the distortion high get even stronger. I began to reach my hand out.

"I wouldn't do that if I were you."

I chuckled, still holding my hand in place about a foot away from the mainframe. "R, hey buddy." I sang, my body still swaying from the nonstop surges of bliss. "Why haven't you ever told me about this place? This is amazing!"

Out of the corner of my eye, I saw R sitting a healthy distance away from the distortion field, staring at me with an unreadable expression.

"You look ridiculous."

I sucked my teeth, laying down on my back, watching the colors shift on the ceiling. "It's been a hard few days, don't I deserve a little bit of happiness and relaxation?"

"Relaxation…sure, maybe take a day off. Not getting a brain high for over an hour. You're gonna get yourself hooked like your mother was."

I laughed again, "It's only been a few minutes, dummy."

"Are you sure about that…it's almost time for Lelani's ball."

My eyes shot open…how long have I been here? I stood to my feet, still swaying and giggling. Was it really that important for me to leave? My feet paused.

"Your team is looking for you."

I sighed, concentrating on my bedroom before bursting into a stream of red code.
~~
The room felt cold and unwelcoming, and my brain felt fuzzy. Much like R said, it was nearly 6pm. I snuck out around 4:30. There is no way I was there for nearly two hours. The thought was unnerving, but I couldn't bring myself to care that much. Perhaps when this is all over, I can take weekly trips there to relax. I could even let Faylin try as well.

I shook my head. Talking like that made me sound like some junkie or something.

There was no time to feel distracted, I had to focus now.

But…first-

"Hey, R?"
There was a moment of silence before R made his presence known, leaning up against the door as mellow as ever. "I thought you were in a rush, kid. Don't you have somewhere to be right now?"

"I know, I just have a random question. A thought just came back to me."

"Uh huh, so what is it?"

"Do you remember months ago when you told me I was going to 'win'? I asked if you meant me winning against Lelani, and you told me to think bigger. You said before next year, I was going to defeat Salem…and win. Do you remember that conversation?"

R chuckled, coming over and ruffling my hair in an odd show of affection. Affection I hadn't really seen since R first appeared to me at the start of my quest.
"I remember giving you that pep talk. It does seem like forever ago, doesn't it? It's almost like you're an entirely different person now."
I felt that way as well. "I know we talked about this before, while we were on our way to Salem's parade. I was just wondering…you said *'but'* at the end of your pep talk. Like there was a chunk you weren't telling me. What was that all about?"

There was a pause as R kept a steely eye contact with me, I stared right back.

"Well, surely you know now, right? Like I mentioned last time, this mission is not, and was never meant to be, as cut and dry as you thought it originally was. But there was so much you needed to find out on your own that helped shape you into the person you needed to be for this mission.

If I just told you everything back then, you couldn't have handled it. If I told you back then you would end up saving the mainframe, trying to spare E-129's life, and leading Neutopia, you would have thought I was crazy. This…isn't even the end, and I still can't tell you everything without risking messing something up or unintentionally causing you to make a rash decision. So, I have to leave it there. Just, go with your gut like you always do, and you'll be fine."

I nodded back, slightly unsatisfied with the answer. He was right though…if I knew then what I knew now, who knows what I would have done. But what else could be waiting for me? What other secrets are there to uncover?
R left while I was still deep in thought. I took a deep breath and headed out the door.

It was time to finish this.

Thanks to Faylin commandeering some proper outfits and masks, our team was hardly recognizable.
Marcus and Casteri both wore plum-colored suits with matching masks that covered the leftmost half of their faces.
Lanker and Tyrinie wore deep green and black tuxedos, the same color as Tyrinie's family crest, and masks that covered the rightmost half of the face.
Faylin wore a light blue colored suit and shoulder cloak with a silver mask that covered only the upper half of his face. And I wore a discrete looking black tuxedo with a red and black mask that covered my entire face. Even though my eyes were covered with a thin black mesh, I was still able to see out.

My hair was pulled back tight and tucked under a black hat with a wide brim. At first glance, nobody should be able to notice me. My height and size were nothing out of the ordinary, something I was currently grateful for, so blending in would be a breeze. Even Faylin, who usually struggled with fitting in, blended in perfectly.

"You know, this might just work." Tyrinie stated while adjusting his tie in the mirror. "Besides, nobody in the South likes to get involved in conflict. So even if somebody noticed you, I doubt if they would say anything."

"That works in our favor then." I smiled back. "Alright everyone, are we ready? If you rather stay behind on this mission, this is your last chance."

Nobody said a word, not like I expected them to. I nodded, "Let's go then."

~~

The road up to the mansion seemed to stretch for miles, but even from this distance, the mansion was something beyond what I could have expected in real life. The hologram did it no justice. It must've been at least double, if not triple, the size of Tyrinie's home.

The entire structure looked like something akin to a Victorian palace with a huge garden in the front, and a maze with impossibly high hedges that seemed to go further than the eye could see.

There were multiple statues of Salem in the center surrounded by a pond filled with exotic fish on either side of the entrance.

"Mr. Scarlet...doesn't something seem odd to you?" Faylin asked, taking in the surroundings. He didn't even have to say it because I saw it too.

There were no people.

Not a single soul on the entire way here.

Lelani's events were some of the most prestigious and anticipated in the entire Southern region, so why was it empty? Nevertheless, we would push onwards. It wasn't as if we had a choice.

"Everyone, keep your guard up. We know we are walking into a fight, and I have a feeling like we are going to need more hands-on deck for this one.

All we have to do is get her detained long enough to get the cuffs around her wrists. After that we'll escort her to the ship and let Arai and Tetsuzo handle the rest. Faylin, Lanker, and I will take her on directly. Everyone else will infiltrate her estate and look for this pig farm."

The morbid part of me was curious about what they had planned for her. What would I do if I had the person that ruined my life detained in front of me?

Marcus, Casteri, and Tyrinie dashed towards the side of the house as we continued forward.

We slowed to a stop as we entered the main gates. Her mansion loomed over us like a grotesque pastel cloud, and in the center of the courtyard stood one of the most stunning women I had ever seen.

The thought of that made me nearly gag.
Lelani stood in front of the largest fountain, clothed in a pink corseted gown that made her look like the pampered heiress she was.
"My, oh my. So, you came after all." She giggled with a dainty, gloved hand up to her painted lips. "And here I thought you wouldn't show up. You're either really brave…or very stupid"

"And here I thought your party would have a larger outcome, looks like you're not as popular as I thought." I spoke, cracking my knuckles as they were engulfed in a red haze. "I wonder if anyone will notice when you go missing."

She smiled, giggling again. "Aw, are you threatening me? That's not very good manners. You must take after your mother. Speaking of which…I wonder where she is." She placed a finger under her chin, feigning ignorance. "I invited her to my party, I even went through the trouble of sending her an invite, but she's not here yet. She said she was going to the mainframe…the same place where you were. That can't be a coincidence."

I faltered for a moment, shaking my head clear. "Unfortunately, I have no time to entertain you. I made a deal to deliver you to a few friends of mine." I readied myself, Faylin and Lanker did the same behind me. "Apparently you've made a lot of enemies over the years."

"You know, you should've picked better last words. That won't look too nice on your tombstone, love." There was a gust of wind, and within a moment Lelani had her hands around my throat. "But I don't think you'll get another chance."

How did…when did she get over here?

I gathered as much haze as I could in my fist before sending a hit directly into her chest, knocking her back past the fountain. I was hoping it would send her further, but based on Tetsuzo's experience,

I figured this was gonna be tough. She wasn't just fast; she was insanely fast. Faster than anything, humanoid or human, than I'd ever seen.

"Cap, are you-"

"I'll be fine, move!" I shoved Lanker out of the way as one of Salem's statues flew right past our heads, crashing behind the shrub line in a heap of rubble. The shockwave nearly knocked us off our feet. "Faylin, check in with the team and see if they got into the estate. We need them in and out as soon as possible." We kept moving, trying to stay out of Lelani's line of sight.

As long as we kept her away from the estate, it should give the others plenty of time.

Faylin fiddled with his ear cuff, cutting it on and off. "Captain, I can't access it. There must be something blocking the signal."

Something blocking the ear cuff signal? Was that even possible? That hadn't ever happened before.

"A new upgrade I had done myself. Can't have eavesdroppers," Lelani said in a sing-song voice. "You don't whisper very well, silly. I don't mind if your little friends find my piggies, they can't help them anyway!" She giggled.

"Now come on little ones. Come out to play-y."

"For the love of all that is good…I hate that voice," I muttered from behind the large wall of greenery, shivering as my arm brushed against an overgrown sunflower.

"So, what's the plan, Cap?" Lanker whispered.

"Tire her out until we are able to cuff her, keep her away from the estate…and don't get hit."

"I was hoping you had something a bit more direct." Lanker responded, keeping up with my quick movements.

"Try not to die…again." I stifled a laugh as Lanker punched me in the arm.

"Yeah, I'll try." Lanker smiled back. "Worst case scenario, you can just bring me back again."

We started moving again, slowly leading Lelani into the garden maze further down the path. Despite her saying she didn't care about the others being in the estate, I didn't want to take my chances. From what I could see, Faylin ended up on the opposite end of the entrance. "Well Lanker, do you have any other ideas?"

"Um…not really-."

CRASH!

Another statue flew overhead, smashing through the maze wall, spraying debris and leaves everywhere.

Lelani stomped around, red-faced and prepared to throw another statue. "Really? You came all this way to meet me and you're just hiding? It's pathetic." She whined. "Since you're going to die, you might as well die with some dignity."

I tore off my tux coat and hat, not like there was any use for it anyways. "I might just have an idea. Lanker, make a lot of noise and head further into the maze. I gotta reach Faylin. Remember, you have to get her attention, *not* fight her."

"Aye aye, Cap. I just hope you've got a plan."

"Just trust me." I took off running, catching Lelani's attention.

Right on queue, Lanker ran forward, keeping close to the edge of the garden while using his green haze to fling objects at Lelani with a stunning amount of accuracy, successfully grabbing her attention.

For his first battle using his new abilities, Lanker was showing off like a pro. That first time on the ship where his powers revealed themselves, I thought for a moment that he couldn't handle it, but I realized my fears were pointless. I couldn't have been prouder of him.

I headed for Faylin, skidding to the ground as I crouched by him. "Faylin, I've got an idea."

"What do you have in mind, Scarlet?" Faylin had removed his ear cuff, using his electricity and a very precise finger to do…something to it. It looked like he was trying to rewire it. We're gonna get her attention. When she starts closing in, I want you to grab hold of my tendril."

"Well, okay." Faylin said with a quirked brow. "I'm not sure where you are going with this?"

"Good. You'll know what to do when it happens. I'm just going to need as much electricity as possible." I ran away from him to give us space, then took aim. Why not see if this worked? With a loud shout and as much haze as I could muster, I slammed both fists into the dirt, causing shockwaves of code to rip through the ground, nearly ripping her fountain in half. It did the trick, Lelani stumbled before turning to me.

"And now you're destroying my things! You're all going to die. I'll make sure of it." She shrieked as she began running full speed back towards me.

We had only a few seconds until impact. We wouldn't have a second chance at this.

"You'll be the first, bitch." I readied myself, dropping all barriers and allowing R to flood my body in a surge of energy. I threw a tendril overhead.

Come on Faylin...Don't leave me hanging...

With the type of agility, I would expect from Faylin, he grabbed it tight wrapping it tight around his wrist.

With one glance, Faylin got the hint and began flooding his electricity into the tendril, causing it to glow a bright white, causing the air to fill with a series of clicks.

3...2...1

Lelani was within a few feet, Faylin ducked out of the way as I reeled the tendril back, whipping it forward, slamming into Lelani with full force.

I flew back, slamming my head against the wall of her estate as the explosion erupted, sending waves of dirt and debris into the air. I covered my nose with my shirt, grabbing Faylin's arm and pulling him from the dust cloud. Thankfully he didn't seem hurt.

From what I could see, Lelani tumbled through the garden. Hopefully she landed painfully.

"Do you think that might have killed her?" Faylin brushed the dirt off of his body, picking the sticks and debris from his hair.

"Oh…far from it," Lelani gritted out, from the rubble, standing up. "Now I'm just mad." She ripped a branch from out of her wild curls. "You messed up my makeup…my dress…my manor…everything!"

"Faylin, give me a boost." He yanked on the tendril that I fought to keep solidified, using it to fling me towards Lelani. "This ends now!" I yelled as I summed as much haze as I could, channeling it into my fist. The entire blast connected, slamming her farther into the garden.

"Very Impressive, Captain." Faylin caught up, slightly limping on his left leg. I knew that it wasn't in perfect condition after the various beatings that Faylin has been taking. I owed him so much at this point.

I flicked my wrist and the tendril vanished; I could practically hear R thanking me for the break.

I hope he knew this fight was far from over. "We better go after her though, I know she can't be dead just yet and I don't want her sneaking up on Lanker." We headed into the garden, keeping close together. At the end of the trail of rubble and dirt,

there was no sign of Lelani. It was beginning to make me anxious, and the fact I wasn't even able to check on the others wasn't helping the feeling.

It grew darker and quieter the further we went into the maze. The moonlight didn't even seem to reach the ground through the thicket. I was tempted to use my haze to light the way, but I knew that would only draw attention to ourselves.

She was out there waiting for us, no doubt about it.

After what seemed like an eternity, there was the slightest rustle of a bush.

"Wait, Scarlet. Did you hea-" Faylin was cut off as he was suddenly seized by the darkness, face slamming hard into the ground with a sickening crunch.

"Faylin!" How did she manage to sneak up on us? I hadn't even heard her. I dropped to the ground, crawling over to Faylin's side, still keeping my eyes on Lelani's glowing ones.

I felt his face, sighing as his cheek twitched under my fingers. He was okay,

but it looked like it was going to be a minute before he was back on his feet. Lelani began stalking back towards me, all traces of her former giddiness were gone. She was clearly pissed, and we were the cause.

"You know, *Scarlet*...Lord Salem wanted me to keep you alive. Hurt you, but keep you somewhat alive. Ever since Lord Salem found me, and brought me into his glorious light, I had never deviated from his plans. However, I might have to make an exception with you. I might just have to turn you into one of my little piggies. I would gladly take Lord Salem's punishment for my disobedience."

I pushed Faylin back further towards the shrubs before jumping to my feet and running towards Lelani. I attempted to go for her legs, knocking her off her feet, but she slid out of the way. Once again, I was seized, this time by the face, and slammed on my back with her full body weight crushing me into the ground. As she tightened her grip, I could feel my jaw begin to fracture. I fought the urge to scream, I wouldn't give her that satisfaction.

Before I could take another swing, Lanker popped through the brush, sensing the opening, and flung back one of the earlier statue projectiles in a burst of green, striking her hard.

Bullseye!

"Please…" Lanker panted, hands on his knees. "Tell me she's dead." I groaned, rubbing my swelling jaw as I helped Faylin to his feet. "Not likely, stay on guard." I dissolved the haze from my hands and slowly approached the pile of rocks.

"How many hits do you think she can take?" Lanker whispered, kicking a few rocks out of the way.

"A lot, apparently. You don't learn to hit *that* hard without experience."

"I suppose that's true. Her stamina is impeccable." He sighed.

He was right, for someone with "poor stamina" she sure knew how to hold her own in a fight. With how much we had been having her run around, I was certain she would've tired herself out by now. But on the contrary, the angrier she gets, the more energy she seems to have.

I was about to respond when the rubble suddenly exploded, rocks and chunks of marble shooting everywhere. I grabbed Lanker and dropped as low as I could while staying on my feet, avoiding most of them.

Lelani stormed out before they even hit the ground, grabbing my arm with brutal strength and flung me back at breakneck speed, sending me crashing through multiple walls of the maze.

"Scarlet!" Lanker's voice faded out the further I went. I could only hope Lelani was chasing after me and not Lanker.

"Ah shit." I flipped myself upright in an attempt to get control of myself as I started to come to a clearing, right to where I saw Lelani was waiting. "This is becoming a pain!" I took a risk, using my momentum to crash land straight into her. Using the leverage, I swung my legs up at the last moment and kicked, impacting with as much force as I could muster.

I pushed off of her and landed a few feet away. She spat the tiniest bit of blood from her pink lips while she was getting up, staining the ground an angry red.

"You…" She chuckled, sounding completely different than she did earlier on. "You might have all your fluids inside for now, but I'm going to paint this garden with your innards."

I shot the tendrils from both hands towards her, feeling a surge of pain. I had never used my tendrils this much before, I knew I was giving my body a serious workout.

She twisted and dodged them both, and began to charge me. The only structure in the clearing seemed to be a nearby shed.

It was a risk, but anything was better than fighting her in the open.

I turned and headed for the entrance, allowing myself to be tackled in, and using the momentum to kick away from her, pulling her further into the shed. While she was trying to recover from the impact, I darted, pushing myself even further and harnessing as much haze as possible throughout my entire body until it was practically seeping from my pores. As soon as she caught sight of it, I caught her by the arms, lifting her and throwing her back with every ounce of strength I had.

If anything, the look of sheer shock on her face when she went crashing through the floor of the shed made the burning feeling in my arms worth it. She groaned, only stumbling for a moment before quickly regaining her stance, charging back at me with something in her hand. I ducked within a split second, partially dodging a deadliest swing of a shovel that grazed the back of my skull. I hadn't even seen her grab anything, and barely managed to dodge it. Still, I wasn't able to dodge all of it, and the migraine began to make itself known. I backpedaled out of the shed remains, dodging wild shovel swings while I tried to heal. By the sheer amount of blood was now all over my shoulders, I know she definitely cut deep.

"Why-!"

CLANG

"Won't-!"

 CLANG

"You-!"

SMASH

"Just-!"

CRASH

"DIE!"

"I could say the same to you!" I yelled back, dodging another swing. R was all but exhausted, but there was no time to rest.

She brought the shovel down again. I leaped back and the shovel hit the brick path, causing the head to snap off, leaving the wooden shaft with a splintered end.

"You aren't wasting any more of my time, you brat!" She wound up for a giant swing, and I knew I couldn't keep evading her attacks. One miscalculation could easily cause me to lose a limb. I knew my best option was to redirect the attack.

It was time to end this battle. I could feel more and more of R's presence wrapping around me as those same symbols began to etch themselves across my face and arm. Within the moment, time seemed to slow to a crawl.

The shovel came around like a baseball bat. As quickly as I could, I moved my hand out of her line of sight and latched a tendril onto the splintered wood and pulled, yanking the stick from her grasp and bringing it back around.

I could see her eyes widen as she registered a moment too late that she was no longer holding the shovel before the splintered end hit, punching through her dress, corset, and skin. Time seemed to go back to normal, and a look of surprise came over her as she sunk to the ground.

I wasn't a doctor, but that looked like it pierced right through her liver. Black ooze mixed with blood profusely seeped from the wound, gushing down her dress and making a puddle by her feet.

"Hybrid or not, that will keep her down for a while," Faylin stated as he made his way over, still bleeding heavily from his head.

"Yea... you doing, okay?" I asked without taking my eyes off Lelani, who was clutching the piece of wood and trying to keep blood in.

"I will be fine; she didn't do too much damage. Perhaps I was still a bit roughed up from our scuffle with Nevermore and Nocturnal. Usually, this wouldn't have been difficult for me." Faylin stated, sounding a little less than pleased with himself.

182

"You did fine, I'm just glad you're safe." I reached for the cuffs from the rogues I'd brought, but they weren't at my side. Scanning the freshly ruined garden, I spotted them back over by where we'd first started the fight. I flicked a tendril over and then pulled them to me. As soon as I tossed the cuffs in the air, my tendril painfully burst in a stream of code. Something told me it was going to be a while before I could use them again.

Lelani, still too focused on the wound, was cuffed without hesitation. And just like that, I could take a deep sigh of relief.

"What? There's no way...I let Lord Salem down. How...how can this be?" She murmured, eyes becoming glossy as tears began rolling down her cheeks. "Why...why did this happen?"

I *almost* felt bad for her.

Almost.

"I would be more focused on yourself, Lelani. I think Arai and Tetsuzo have some very creative ideas for what's going to happen to you next." I hoisted her up over my shoulder, avoiding the wood that was still jutting out, and began to walk towards the main road with Faylin and Lanker in tow.

END OF CHAPTER 15

16

WHO I AM

$\mathcal{F}$aylin's tinkering with the ear cuff finally paid off as Casteri's voice began flooding through. Only his cuff worked though, and even when he tried to explain how he did it, it hardly made any sense to me.

"Captain, it's good to hear from you. There seemed to be a lot of commotion from outside, is everyone alright?"

Lanker and I were all huddled against Faylin, trying to listen as well as possible to Casteri's faint voice.
"We are all fine, Lelani has been captured and we are about to head back to the ship. What about you? Any sign of this pig farm?" Faylin responded

"Negative. According to the info-chip, it shouldn't be much further. Just another few hallways. Since we are unsure of what we're walking into, we have been careful."

"Understood. Stay in touch when you reach the target, and watch for traps. There is signal jamming outside, so it might take a few attempts to reach someone."

Sometimes I truly felt like Faylin sounded more like a leader than I did. But instead of feeling jealousy, I felt respect for him. It's no wonder so many of the rogues still consider Faylin a commander. Honestly, if I had to answer to anyone, I would gladly work under Faylin.

Casteri's connection fizzled out and eventually went silent.

"Well Captain, what would you like us to do? Should we wait here until the others come back, return to the ship, or carry Lelani inside and join them?" Faylin asked.

It was a good question. Ideally, I figured the others would be back by now. I wouldn't mind waiting, but there was something weighing on my mind. What did Lelani mean when she said that her *piggies* were beyond helping? What exactly were the guys walking into?

"Lelani…I don't suppose you would tell me what the pig farm is, will you?" I questioned, repositioning her over my shoulder. Her wound had all but healed, despite the fact the wooden stick was still lodged inside. I knew she wouldn't suddenly start cooperating, but I figured I might as well try. Perhaps there was still a little bit of human left in her.

I glanced over my shoulder at the motionless woman. There was no response, she just stared forward, lips still mumbling incoherently.

I shook my head.

"Why don't you and Lanker head inside and meet with the others. I'll zip over and deliver Lelani to Sector 6. I'll be back before you know it."

"Right, you mentioned Arai and Tetsuzo. When did that deal happen?" Lanker asked, rightfully confused.

"It was a deal; they gave us info, and we would capture Lelani for them. Pretty good bargain if I say so myself. It is not as if we actually need her for anything at this point. We just need her not to cause havoc here anymore."

Faylin nodded, "I suppose you are correct in that. Lanker and I will head inside and join the others while you head over to Sector 6.

You should take my ear cuff with you so that you can find us when you get back."

I traded ear cuffs with Faylin before gathering a ring of haze around my feet, vanishing into a stream of code.

I plopped back on the beach in Sector 6, Lelani crashed down beside me. There was little sound outside of the crashing waves from the murky shore. The air was thick and the moon hung high in the sky, illuminating the foggy ground. The entire atmosphere was eerie and made me feel on edge. From what I could see, there was no sight of Arai or Tetsuzo.

"This changes nothing…you know." I nearly jumped as Lelani spoke next to me in a hushed tone. "This is still just the beginning. As long as Galaia is still alive, it will never end." She turned to me, pink eyes glowing with something akin to glee. "And while you might have stopped me, you will never be able to stop her.
She is beyond anything you can comprehend. So, enjoy your victory for today, because it'll be the last one you have."

"You are about to die…very slowly and painfully, and you choose for your last few words to be a baseless threat?"

"I don't want you to get too cocky and think it's over. It will *never* be over." She sat up and stared out into the murky ocean, hands cuffed behind her back. "I've always hated this world. I'm not afraid to die…I've been alive long enough. Soon you'll feel the same way; an overwhelming and suffocating apathy for this planet and everyone who lives on it."

Sensing I might be here for a while, I opted to sit on the beach next to Lelani. In the state, she was in, plus the cuffs, there was nothing she could do to hurt me in the slightest. A chill blew through, making me shiver slightly. Lelani didn't even seem to notice…or care.

"How I personally feel, now or fifty years in the future, doesn't matter. There is still right and wrong. Something you've apparently forgotten." I sighed, leaning forward, forearms resting on my lap. "How immature would I be to let the fate of the world be based on how annoying I thought humanity was…or how apathetic I felt. There are people here, good people, that deserve life. That is why I have to stop Salem. It's that simple."

Lelani giggled. "Well now, look at the hero here. What a beautiful sentiment."

There was a moment of silence between us before I spoke up once more.

"How did someone like you even end up wrapped up with Salem? You're a young, beautiful heiress. You had everything ahead of you…and you chose Salem? You didn't even have ties to Xenon Tech. So why choose this path?"

I looked over at her as she began to giggle again, this time though, it sounded a bit off.

"What? Are you trying to see if there is some redeeming quality about me? Maybe I was brainwashed…or maybe I was taken by force and I was in no control of my actions? Perhaps, I was only playing the role of a villain, waiting to save the day at the very end." She looked over at me, mirth across her face. "I hate to burst your bubble, sweetie, but there is nothing redeemable about me. I did everything I did…because my Lord Salem asked me to. And I cherish everything he wants me to do. I would even kill myself if he wanted me to."

"But, why?" There was an obvious trend. Cyryl, Mother, and Lelani…all had this insane amount of loyalty and dedication toward Salem. But, why was that always the case? Was this E's influence? It was the only explanation I could think of for their loyalty.

"Because…I love him. He is perfect. Nobody on this damned planet could compare to him, not even you."

I scoffed. Why would I even want to be like Salem? Why would I want to be a psychopathic nanoid, parading around in the body of a helpless humanoid, that had leagues of worshippers that saw him as the face of absolute perfection.

I told myself that, but something stung inside of me.

Why didn't R have the effect on people that E did? Why did it feel like E was so much stronger than R? I didn't want to be the type of ruler Salem was, but would people respect me? Would they listen to me? Would they even want me?

I shook my head, there was no time to worry about things like self-doubt. I would figure it out like I always did. Besides, Faylin would be by my side, so it would be okay.

Lelani and I continued in silence, listening to the ominous crashing of the shore.

"Can I ask you something, hero?" Lelani asked after a while, eyes still on the horizon. "Why are you so hell-bent on fighting against your fate? You do know this is what you were made for, right? You were made to destroy the world, not save it. To be Galaia's prophet, not to defy her. Your powers are manifestations of destruction, not creation. Why fight against what you were created for? You know you will never truly be happy this way, right?"

For some reason, what she said penetrated the recesses of my mind. I was never meant to save the world. I was never meant to stop Salem. Everything I was fed as a child has been a lie. Along the journey, I had discovered that, but for some reason, her saying it now really hit me. I was never meant to be Neutopia's savior.

I was never meant to save anyone.

I was in a constant state of rebellion against my nature.

"Because I don't want to hurt anyone. I don't care if I was created for it, nobody can *choose* my destiny for me. All my life I've been pushed one way or another, but that's done and over with now. I'm done being everyone's damn puppet."

"Hmm, I envy you, Scarlet, I really do." She smiled, closing her eyes. "Looks like our guests have arrived."

Right on queue, I heard Arai's sharp voice piercing through the foggy night. "A little birdie tells me you have a present for us? A pink wrapped present." I could hear the grin in her voice as I stood to my feet, pulling Lelani with me by the arm.

Lelani continued to look ahead, greeting Arai and Tetsuzo with a wide grin. "It's a pleasure to meet you both. I hear I will be in your care from now on."

"Shut it, bitch. You can kiss Salem goodbye cause you belong to *us* now." Tetsuzo bit out in a voice that terrified even me. However, Lelani didn't seem fazed. She pulled her arm out of my grasp and walked over to the two women.

"Do with me what you must then before I get bored." She said with a dramatic sigh.

Without hesitation, Tetsuzo seized her by the arm, grabbing with it far more force than necessary with her mechanic arm. Lelani's head snapped to the side with a well-aimed slap, causing blood to splatter from her split lip.

"I thought I said to stay quiet." Tetsuzo bit out, pulling her along after sending a wink in my direction.

"It's going to be a long and very rewarding night…or a few months. We are truly in your debt Captain Scarlet; I didn't think you'd be able to pull it off. First Nyx, and now Lelani." She smirked, pushing her wild hair back behind her ear. "Color me impressed."

I couldn't help but turn red. It wasn't every day the rebel you've admired since childhood gave you such a compliment.

I smiled back, "I'm glad to have impressed you, Captain Arai. It'll only go up from here, I'm about to take out Salem. Then this nightmare will be over."

Arai nodded, looking serious. "You need a hand; you give us a shout. We will have your back." She shot out her hand, and I shook it with equal amounts of force.

She gave her regards before heading back to the ship, following in Tetsuzo's footprints. I couldn't help but wonder what Lelani meant when she said she envied me.

Well, it wasn't as if I could ask her now.
~~
Getting back to Lelani's estate took only a moment, but this time the air was chillier than before. Of course, my team was nowhere to be seen. They must've been in the depths of Lelani's basement by now.

I wondered what type of sadistic mess they would find down there. I knew I should join them; I knew I should have burst through the front door and down into the basement to help uncover everything that was down there.

But instead, I just sat on the cold marble steps outside the front door. Nearly the entire courtyard was destroyed from the events not even an hour ago, a complete turnaround from the silence that consumed the air now.

I took a deep breath, looking up as tiny snowflakes began to fall.

All these years I thought I would find my freedom in fulfilling my purpose. I thought after I completed my journey, my father would love me and I could shake the burden of expectations off once and for all.

I could feel that sense of freedom I would feel when I climbed trees; I could just lay back and let the world pass me by.

But it was never meant to be that way, was it?

I was *always* meant to bring destruction.

If I followed my father's path, I would have been the one to cause the humanoid genocide. If I followed my mother's and Salem's expectations, not to mention my *true* purpose, I would be the one who triggered the genocide of human life. If I do neither...I spend the rest of my days hiding who I truly am, watching the mainframe, and protecting a planet that doesn't even want me here.

I never forgot the looks people would give me as I passed by, the sneers and the glares. Even thinking back to my few first days of this journey, in that cafe in the South. I distinctly remember all of the disgusting whispers about me when I walked inside.

Could I really spend the rest of my days in servitude to people like that?

Why did it feel like no matter what I chose, I would end up miserable and someone would end up getting hurt?

"Well, I guess that's what happens when you go off script, kid."

I looked up, shaking my head as snow began to pile on it. R was sitting in the middle of the courtyard, looking calm as ever.

"Go off script?" I repeated.

"Well, certainly you know by now this wasn't the path you were supposed to take. So, you're a bit off script, making your own path now. Something I always had an inkling you would do." He got up and floated over to me, sitting on the cold ground next to the step I was on. "Like I mentioned to you a while after we first officially met, you've rubbed off on me more than I've rubbed off on you.

Your thoughts are becoming my thoughts, and I didn't quite influence you the way Galaia might have wanted me to in the end. So hey, you even convinced me to rebel too. Ain't that crazy?"

R laughed, glancing over at me. "Kid, I told you that you have the power to change fate, and that power doesn't just end after this big decision. Once you go off script, you start rewriting history. You can start pulling the strings. You think this world hates you? They might right now, but you can change that. You think you'll be stuck and will never be truly *free*? It might feel that way for a while, but like everything else in this journey, you'll find a way. Just keep your eyes on your future battle, and figure out your next step. Is that something that you believe you can do, Captain?"

I smiled, remembering the first time R asked me that. We were in the abandoned house in one of the ground level cities, shortly after I found Faylin.

He asked me if I believed I could do this, and it was one of the hardest questions to answer.

But what I said came back to my memory.

"Of course, I can, because…it's not like I have the choice to fail." It was time for me to truly double down on my resolve. R was right. The outcome I chose would be a difficult one, and my journey certainly wouldn't end with E's defeat. But that was the path *I* was choosing. Not mother, not father, and not Galaia. This was my choice.

Maybe…I was already free.

END OF CHAPTER 16

17

THE FARM

After what felt like an eternity, I stepped into Lelani's estate. The cream walls and marble floors looked ominous with the moonlight pouring in through the walls, yet there was still something oddly comfortable about it. If it wasn't for the fact a sadistic psychopath lived here, I might have wanted a place like this for myself.

Perhaps when this was all over, I could give this estate to Emme and Persephone as a gift, move them out of the West and give them a good life in the posh South.

I laughed as if Persephone would ever agree to that.
As I got closer to the dim staircase I only could assume led to the basement, Faylin's ear cuff crackled to life.

"Captain, can you hear me?" Casteri's voice came through with an unnerving hitch to it. *"We found it…we found the farm."*

I took a deep breath, responding with the only question that I could think of.

"How bad is it?" There was a pause before Casteri's voice came through once more.

"It's bad."

Without another word, I headed down the staircase at breakneck speed, allowing R power to flood through me. My team needed me, and I had no time to waste.

After navigating the seemingly endless corridors, I made my way to what I could have only assumed was the entrance to the pig farm. If I listened closely, I could hear my teammates speaking amongst other voices. How many other voices were in there? 30? 40? There were more voices than I could count. But, despite all the voices, I couldn't pick up any intelligible speech.
I mostly just heard something akin to…groaning, and babbling.

I slowed my steps, putting my barrier back up before pushing open the door, instantly getting assaulted by a harsh metallic odor. My team stood by the door, looking over the railing that led down a few more stories. Nobody acknowledged my presence.
I walked up next to Faylin, looking down into what looked like an underground lab.

I couldn't quite find words to describe what I saw.

It looked like a cylinder, large and with cells all around the circumference. Each floor down, about four of them, housed what seemed to be locked doors and medical equipment. Tubes filled with green liquid, similar to the ones I would be suspended in for days at a time, were in nearly every cell. Looking all the way down, there seemed to be something like a gated-off circular area, similar to a pig pen, where a handful of bodies laid.
In each cell, people lay against the bars or on the floor. Some stared at us, and some seemed lost in their own world. But the most remarkable thing was the state that each person was in.

They were all…fusions.

All of them were fusions, and from what I could tell, they all seemed to be in various stages of the process.

Some of them only had the addition of ears, tails, and claws, while some others had the addition of multiple eyes and limbs. Further down, their skin seemed to vary in color from hues of pink, gray, or green. Some appeared scaly, and others slick and slimy.

But in the gated-off area further down was the most horrifying sight I had seen in a while. The people down there looked like they had been completely altered, becoming a disfigured amalgamation of a cross between human and animal. Most of them didn't even seem able to walk, they just crawled around making a shrieking sound that echoed ominously around the silo.

I couldn't identify what animal DNA was used for many of them. I could identify some dog and cat DNA, and even some that had been fused with reptiles and avians, but it looked like the majority of them had distinct pig-like features.

For more than a few minutes, nobody spoke.

"They never got rid of fusion testing…" I spoke up, my voice barely audible over the shrieking below. "They just moved it underground." "But why? What could be the point of all of this?" Lanker stepped closer to the railing, looking down, before backpedaling just as quickly.

I glanced over at Tyrinie who, understandably, looked the most horrified. His skin was completely pale, and he looked as if he would faint at any moment. Casteri must've seen it as well, and gripped Tyrinie's arm before he collapsed.

"This has to do with Salem. Lelani never acted on her own, so Salem must've commanded her to continue the experimentation. If Salem is involved, it must lead back to the nanoids…" I thought out loud. But what connection could there possibly be between fusions and nanoids?

What was the point of all of this?

When Tetsuzo mentioned the Pig Farm, she mentioned it was Lelani's human collection, despite her never actually seeing it for herself.
I was truly glad Tetsuzo never had a chance to see this, it would have killed her if she knew what was truly happening here.
My stomach sank with the idea that Arai and Tetsuzo's parents were down there somewhere. Given how long ago they were taken, I feared they were most likely at the bottom of the silo.

"Okay, well we can't help them standing up here." I looked around, locating the nearest staircase. "Lelani is gone and this place is barren, we have all the time in the world to start getting these people some help. So, let's start moving."

Faylin nodded, along with Marcus and the others who eventually followed my lead, heading down to the first level. Tyrinie, who still looked a little more than pale, tagged along behind.
~
The first floor down held people who, despite how much I hated to say it, resembled Tyrinie. The physical response to their experimentation could only be seen through the addition of animal-like ears, tails, claws, and some slight facial changes.
As I walked past their cages, most of them just stared. They didn't speak, nor did they make any attempt to grab our attention. They just looked on with odd, blank looks on their faces.

I stopped in front of one peculiar cage. The chubby girl inside, like all the others, was dressed in a stark white hospital gown. But unlike all the others, she was furthest away, and her cage bars seemed to have CHEM running through, causing electric sparks to flick off, scorching the ground. With every spark that hit the ground, the girl twitched, pushing herself further into the corner of the already small cell.

She didn't look much older than me, had a mop of light pink hair, along with large, floppy ears on top of her head. The ears looked soft but heavy, almost like large flaps of skin despite their frantic twitching.
Along with the ears, she had a short coiled pink tail.

198

I walked closer to the cage as slowly as I could but still caused her to scurry back further and make strange noises from her nose. The bars didn't look like anything too difficult, at least, nothing that R couldn't handle.

I tore the CHEM box from the wall, stopping the flow with a loud popping sound, causing the poor girl to curl in on herself.

"Hey, it's okay, I'm going to help you, alright?" I knelt down outside the cage, trying to communicate with her, but it didn't seem to do much good. It was like she couldn't even understand me.

With little effort and a little help from R, I pulled the cage open just enough for a body to slip through.

"There, you can come out now." I knelt again, patting the ground encouragingly. "Come on, you're okay."

The trembling slowed down for a moment as the girl looked up, and crawled forward only a few inches. Despite the shadows in her cell, I noticed her distinctly pink skin and upturned pink nose.

There was no denying what DNA she had been fused with. The thought made me sick.

Who knew who this girl was before this was done to her? Was her family out there looking for her? Were they in here too?
The thoughts just solidified my feeling that whatever Tetsuzo and Arai did to Lelani would never be enough of a punishment.

It looked like the others were doing the same, opening up all the cages and trying to coax the captives out. As I assumed, Tyrinie was having the best luck despite saying nothing. He was simply going from cage to cage, looking inside, and opening the door. Soon enough, half of the level was opened, and followed Tyrinie around.
When I turned back, I noticed the girl had come closer and was now sitting in the center of the room. I smiled and continued to pat the floor, sliding a bit out of the way so I wasn't blocking the exit.

"You're almost there, come on, just a little further."

She crawled a bit closer, stopping once more. I stepped further back, waving her out.

Soon enough, she slowly poked her head out, looking curiously at all of the others who were being released. The others had all moved on to the lower levels, leaving me on the first floor alone.

I didn't know if the girl was able to stand or walk properly. Tyrinie obviously could walk, communicate, and act like anyone else. But this girl was different…something in the experiments must've been different because she didn't seem to have half of the "human" functions that Tyrinie did.

I took a tiny step closer, watching the girl freeze and growl softly as I did.

"It's okay, I won't hurt you." I reassured her as I slid a little closer, reaching for the painfully tight collar that was around her neck. "I'm just going to take this off. You'll breathe better without it."

I touched the metal collar, and with a quick and oddly easy switch, took it off. Instantly, the growling stopped, and the girl looked up with big brown eyes.

It was like I communicated with her for just a moment, and she finally understood.

After touching the raw skin around her neck, she began to crawl closer, circling around my feet and sniffing me. Finally, she stopped in front of me and snorted happily.

I smiled. "It's nice to meet you as well."

~

I began to walk away, and the girl crawled behind me. I could only imagine how raw her hands and knees must've been.

When was the last time she stood upright?

I turned back to her. "We need to move a little bit faster, but I don't know how quickly you can go…"

She looked confused at me, snorting again.

I hoped I wasn't overstepping my bounds, but that idea might just work. I turned around and crouched, looking at her and patting my shoulder, hoping she would get the hint.

It took a few moments, but soon I felt the girl reach up and place one trembling arm over me, and then the other.

I stood up slowly, causing her to squeal and squirm in protest while I wrapped her legs around my stomach.

"Okay, okay, calm down. I'm just gonna carry you for a little bit, this will help." Just as I assumed, her knees and palms were raw, covered in scar tissue that looked like they healed and reopened more times than I could count.

After a little while, she finally calmed down, only snorting lightly on my shoulder. I couldn't help but smile.

By the time I had reached the bottom of the next level, the team had already moved to the floor further down.
I continued walking, trying to keep a steady pace to not jar the girl on my back. I wondered what her name was, I wonder if she even remembered her name.

Surely Lelani must've had files for all of her captives, her information must've been in there. But, if this girl had been taken from Sector 6, there is no telling if she was completely off the grid or not.

"I see you have found a friend, Scarlet." Faylin chuckled, a few captives following him closely. "We only have about one more floor before we hit the bottom. Do you have any idea what we should do with the victims down there? I am afraid to think the people down at the bottom might be beyond our help. If that is the case, and if they are in pain, I believe the most humane thing to do would be to put them out of their misery."

I prayed it wouldn't come to that, but I couldn't be naive and allow these poor people to suffer because of my own feelings.

"Let's take them for now. When all of this is over, we can consult the doctors in the North to see about reversing the experimentation."

Faylin nodded, leading his followers to the floor below. Surprisingly, a few of the fusions started to get the hint, and began opening up the cages for the others. The ones that could speak were crying and laughing while hugging one another, the ones that couldn't speak did what they could to express their happiness.

The girl on my back kicked her legs slightly in excitement, still holding on to me tightly.

I wasn't sure what we would even do with all of these people. They couldn't all fit on the ship, but they wouldn't be able to just find their way home.

If anything, I wish we had Senna at a time like this, perhaps he would have an answer for how to help them.
When we reached the bottom floor, the shrieking got louder and louder, so much so that many of the fusions refused to come down to the bottom floor. The girl on my back was silent as we got closer.

The view this close was far more horrifying than earlier. The fifteen captives in the enclosed area, all having been heavily fused with pig DNA, were covered head to toe in bulging tumors. Their pink skin was so stretched that the slightest movement would make it tear, and their eyes were so swollen that they were unable to blink. The pungent smell of blood and chemicals was so heavy down here it was making me nauseous.

These poor people…What in oblivion could I do to help them?

"Casteri, Faylin…is there anything nearby that could put them to sleep while we try to figure out how to help them?"

"I know I passed plenty of canisters in the room on the way down here, there must be something there." Faylin responded, already heading to the floor back upstairs, prompting me to follow.

"I'll start looking for some information on our captives here, there has to be some sort of a paper trail." Marcus called out, heading in the opposite direction.

~

Whether by luck or chance, we found exactly what we needed. I was grateful Faylin knew chemicals better than I did. After releasing the gas into the enclosure, making sure we didn't inhale any, all of the captives fell silent. I was grateful for the lack of shrieking; it was a relief to know they weren't in any pain anymore.

For the moment, it was all we could do for them.

I wasn't sure if it truly was humane or inhumane, but it seemed keeping them unconscious until we discovered a cure was the best option. If there truly wasn't a cure, then euthanasia while they were unconscious would be the next step.

Hopefully it wouldn't get to that point, but as my team and I hauled out each of their bloated, fragile bodies upstairs, my hope got weaker.

Much to my surprise, it was Tyrinie's brilliant idea to keep all of the fusions, including the fifteen in the worst condition, in Lelani's estate until we found a better way to help them. There was plenty of room, plenty of beds, and they would be safe and cared for while we looked for their families. The area was also secluded enough that, if they chose to stay, they could live there in peace and comfort.

After calling in a favor from Tetsuzo, she and Arai agreed to spare some of their team members to stay at Lelani's estate to watch over the fusions. With Tetsuzo having some of the most brilliant minds aboard her vessel, I knew they would be in good, safe hands.

If anyone could find a cure, it would be them.

Within a few hours, a large group of Tetsuzo and Arai's rebels had already arrived and got to work. A group of them cooked, others began assigning rooms, while some of the older rebels got to work on the unconscious fusions.

Their reputation served them well, they truly ran like a well-oiled machine.

"We'll handle everything from here Captain Scarlet, per Captain Tetsuzo's orders." A young woman in her twenties, who I assumed was Tetsuzo's first mate, spoke in a commanding tone. "We will keep the fusions safe while trying our best to reverse their conditions. Nothing is promised, but we will try."

"We appreciate all of the help, and we will be back as soon as we can to check in. Please give my regards to Captain Tetsuzo."

The women gave me a salute before heading back into the house.

I felt relieved to be out of that place, and I could tell my team felt the same. Despite what Lelani said earlier, and despite the fact I was "made" for destruction, the team and I just saved a lot of lives. It felt good.

But it wasn't over yet, we were about to hit our hardest target yet. It was time to take the fight right to Salem and end this once and for all.

The shifting on my back brought me out of my thoughts.

"So, that means you're staying here now." I tried to, as gently as possible, pry the girl off of my back. Oddly enough, she just clung tighter. I pulled again, but this time she shook her head, tightening her grip around me. I could hear the others chuckling.

"Come on now, you'll be much safer here. They'll take good care of you, and maybe even find you a cure." She shook her head again, huffing angrily and tightening her grip further.

I groaned, giving another halfhearted pull. When I stopped, she relaxed and plopped her head on my shoulder

I glanced over at the others. "Any ideas?"

They all shrugged, except for Faylin who was looking just as exhausted as I was. "Well, perhaps your little friend, Emme, could use a big sister."

Emme would be thrilled. I supposed it could be a temporary solution until we find out if the girl had any family looking for her.

"Okay, you win. I guess you're tagging along for now." I smiled as she snorted happily and kicked her legs. I guess she did understand some things after all. "Team, let's head back to the ship. It's time to finish this up."

We started down the broken path from Lelani's estate, the sun now rising over the horizon. I was exhausted, but I knew sleep would be the last thing on my mind.

"Do we know where Salem is, Captain?" Faylin asked. "There is a chance he is in this same sector."

There was a chance he would be in the south. After all, that was where the majority of his supporters were. But he wasn't here. I couldn't explain it, but I just knew he wasn't

No, I knew in my gut *exactly* where he was.

He was where it all began.

He was waiting for me in the ruins of Xenon Tech…and I wouldn't keep him waiting.

END OF CHAPTER 17

18

ENDLESS

―――――――――――――◇――――――――――――――

It was around 9am by the time we got onboard, needless to say we were all exhausted. Lanker, thankfully not needing sleep, got the Seven Seas airborne and on course for the ruins of Xenon Tech. At the rate we were going, it wouldn't be more than a few hours.

After everyone retired to their respective rooms, I dragged my feet to my quarters, still hauling the heavy girl on my back. I figured she would have fallen asleep, but to my surprise, she was up and active, looking at everything around her with fascination. Every once in a while, she would kick her legs if she saw something particularly interesting. I kicked the door behind me closed, trying again to gently pry the girl off my back.

"Okay, time for you to get off. You can stay here, but my back needs a break."

Thankfully, this time she let go, only standing on bent legs for a moment before going back to her hands and knees. She rolled into a sitting position and looked at me, cocking her head to the side.

"I need to figure your name out…" I murmured, stifling a yawn. "Hopefully Marcus found something in the archives."

I pointed over to my bed. "You can stay there; I'll sleep over here." Thankfully the chair in my room was huge and would be more than sufficient. Besides, with how sleepy I was, I could literally sleep on the floor.

Thankfully she seemed to understand this, and scooted herself over to the bed before hopping on with little hesitation. With a little wiggling, she got herself under the covers and stared at me with big eyes. I couldn't understand what she was trying to communicate, but something told me she'd be stuck with us for a while.

It had been more than an hour, the girl was asleep, and yet I was still wide awake. The gravity of what I was about to do weighed heavily in my mind. This was it; this was the end of the line. Once I got to the ruins, I would face off with Salem, and all of this would end.

I would, somehow, assert myself into Salem's place and run Neutopia peacefully. I had no idea how to run a planet…but I would have to figure that out on the fly.

I didn't even know how I was planning on taking out Salem, but there was something even more pressing on my mind. Salem had a power I didn't have; he had that mind control shit that I couldn't get out of my head. It had such a potent effect on me. If Salem simply *commanded* me to open up the mainframe…, would I?

"Well, that is a good concern, kid."

R floated above the bed, not far from the girl's head. "Cute girl, are we keeping her?"

"Leave her alone, R." I whispered, folding my forearm over my eyes. "The poor girl has been through a lot.

I don't even know how long she was down there. I don't know anything about her, not even where she originally came from. She didn't want to leave though, so it looks like she's tagging along with me for now."

"Well, I like her." R shrugged. "But, on to pressing matters. You're right, E-129 still has skills you don't have, but there is one way I'd be able to help it. You might not like the idea though."

"Oh yea, what's the idea?" I asked, still stretched out in the chair.

"Well, E-129 can get into your mind, but he can't affect me." R stood, heading over to my chair. "So, I know we've never done it before, but E-129 won't be able to affect your mind if you will allow me to take full control of your body. You'd have to drop all of your barriers and give me full control."

That definitely caught my attention. Give R…complete control?

"Would I be able to control anything?"

R shook his head. "You'll be fully conscious, but you won't have any control. You'd basically be watching me pilot our body. It's the only way I can fully promise E can't control us; E's words can't affect me."

It would be a perfect plan, but…what if I couldn't trust R. What if R used this chance to open the mainframe, and all I could do was watch helplessly. Or even worse, what if R never gave me control back?

"Geez kid, do you really have such little faith in me? Do you *really* think I would use this against you?" R leaned up against the chair. "I can hear your thoughts, so there is no need to lie. Listen, I know this is new for you, but it might just be our only chance. Remember, if you die, I die, and I don't want that."

"What do you want, R? What do you truly want? Do you want to help me and actually save this world? Or do you want to go back to the cyberworld, or fulfill Galaia's wishes?"

R paused for a moment, taking a long look at me. "Well, I'm not going to lie to you and say I *want* to stay here, nor do I truly want to save this forsaken place…but you do, you've always wanted to." R shrugged, "I wouldn't have ever been able to talk you out of it, so I never tried. I watched you grow, and allowed myself to be influenced by you. I'm willing to stand by my vessel, even if I don't fully agree, and even if it means never truly going back home."

For just a moment, R sounded so disheartened. He was right though; this decision would truly mean any plans he had of returning home would be permanently closed. I felt bad for him, I truly did.

"There's no need to feel bad for me kid, you have bigger things to worry about. Now, did you want to test out giving me full reign? Might as well see what it feels like now, right?"

R stood up straight in front of me, cracking his fingers. "It might feel a little weird at first."

I reluctantly nodded, standing up as well. I wasn't sure what to do, and I knew the feeling wouldn't come naturally.

I took a deep breath, releasing my barriers one by one. R was out of my field of view now; I felt his power flooding through my veins as he always did. Haze started to gather in my palms and under my bare feet.

"I'll need more than that, kid. You're only about a quarter of the way there." R cheered me on from the back of my mind.

I took a deep breath in, pushing out more and more power, allowing more of him to flow through me, dropping as many barriers as I could. I held back the choking sensation as haze began to seep out of my mouth, pouring down my shirt, just like at Cyryl's lair. I felt anxiety kick in, and I subconsciously began to slow myself down.

"That's just your fight or flight kicking in, you'll need to keep pushing. You're almost there."

I nodded, focusing hard with one final push as I let the heat completely take over me, and for a moment, I felt nothing.

I felt my body go limp as if I was losing consciousness, but my vision never faded out. I just simply couldn't move, or speak.

It was like I was paralyzed.

Suddenly, my limbs began to move. I stood to my feet, and began to move forward with no control over myself. It was terrifying, there was no other word for it.

"Well, how does it feel?" R responded in *my* own voice. "You can still see right? I can still hear your thoughts, so, I know you're still alive in there." He laughed, working the kinks out of all of limbs and walking over to the mirror.

Just like previously, my eyes glowed almost the same as R's with code ghosting over my thin-slitted pupils. I had foreign markings down the side of my face and neck, down to my arms. It was unnerving to look in the mirror and see a face that isn't yours.

"Do you know the power you have like this, kid? In this form, we could do everything E-129 can do, maybe even more."

R raised his arm, swinging it towards the wall and instantly bathing the room in red code. Instantly, all of the items in the room began to tremble and shift, fizzling in and out of view in bursts of code. Thankfully the girl was still sleeping, blissfully unaware of the items floating over her head.

My feet lifted off the ground with ease as more haze poured out of me.

"If we were on the ground, I could show you some incredible things. You'll get a show of it soon enough." R laughed as he lowered me back to the ground, sensing my panic. "I wouldn't want to wake your little friend up after all."

R took a deep breath, and I slowly felt myself back in my limbs.

"Okay, you can have the driver seat again. I just wanted to give you a little taste of what it'll feel like down in the ruins. Not too bad, right?"

When the feeling came back to my limbs, I collapsed, utterly exhausted. Every part of my body felt heavy and foreign and I had a pulsating headache.

Thankfully the floor was comfortable enough, I'd just have to nap right here until we arrived at Xenon Tech.

~

I awoke to someone sniffing my face. The sky was still a murky gray and light snow fell on my window. The gentle rocking of the ship alerted me that we were still airborne.

I turned my head, causing the girl to reel back for a moment before nudging my arm.

"I'm fine, I just decided to sleep down here for a bit." I yawned, stretching my arms far above my head. Thankfully I felt much better, my limbs felt like my own again. Letting R fully take over was terrifying, but there was no doubt we would stand a chance against E if we used that. I would just have to trust that R had my best interest in mind.

I did trust him…but he was still a nanoid at the end of the day.

I stood, shaking out my leg that had fallen asleep. "You just hang here for now, okay?"

The girl gave a light snort before shuffling back to the bed and jumping up on it, burying herself under the covers.

If things went south today, which I had no plan of them doing, she would definitely be much safer on the ship.

"So, her name is written down as Pip. Full name is Philippa Eleanor Ainsworth, and it looks like she's 16." Marcus flipped through all of the files he took from the Pig Farm's office. "Looks like there isn't much information on her though."

"Wait! Pip Ainsworth? *The* Philippa Eleanor Ainsworth?" Tyrinie jumped up from his seat across the deck, sprinting over to us. "Are you kidding me?"

"No…I am missing something here?" Marcus laughed, handing over her file.

"Y-yes, you're missing a lot! She's the only child of the Ainsworth family, and a huge name in the Southern Region. Her parents, Thane and Eleanora Ainsworth, are the heads of Ainsworth Enterprise, one of the top CHEM production companies in Neutopia.

My parents knew them very well. The Ainsworth family went missing about a decade ago or something, Philippa was the sole heir to the company."

Marcus looked starstruck as he took the files back from Tyrinie's hands, flipping again through all of the files "Well that makes no sense…I thought the captives were people off the books from Sector 6. Why in Neutopia would another heiress be stuck in there?"

"Beats me, last I remember, their family never got into any confrontations. They were quiet, kind, generous people…unlike most people down there. But they must've done something to rub Lelani or Salem the wrong way." Tyrinie paused for a moment, shaking the snow from his ears. "It's a pity, from what I remember Philippa was a really kind girl, we only really met a few times."

"I have faith Tetsuzo's people will be able to figure out some way to help Pip along with the other captives. I doubt if they'll be able to repair all of the damage done to her, but I'll be happy if she can even get a little bit of her life back." I spoke, waving the rest of the team over. "But first things first, we are going to need to have a game plan for when we land. That takes top priority."

The others nodded. Faylin joined us, soon Casteri and Lanker did the same, all looking at me expectantly just like when I gave my first speech. The snow continued to fall, coating the deck in a light sheet of white. Over the horizon, I could see the remains of Xenon Tech in the distance. Somehow it looked even more desolate than the first time. If I strained my eyes, I could see some sort of motion below.

"This is it team, this is the end of the road. Once we pull this off, we'll be free. No more running and hiding, no more dodging Salem's men, it'll be over. I want this to go smoothly, and without any hiccups. Salem is waiting down by the mainframe; I'm planning on going down there alone-"

"Wait, alone?" Lanker suddenly jumped up, "You're going to face Salem alone? That sounds like suicide, Cap…one of us should go with you at least."

I shook my head. "This is going to be tough, and the only way I will even be able to pull it off is by giving R way more power than I'm used to. If anyone else is down there with me and Salem gets into your head, it could be fatal for both of us."

"But don't I have R's power too, are you sure I can't follow you." Lanker persisted in an out of character fashion. I wondered what was worrying Lanker so much. I mean sure, we were about to go into the most dangerous fight of our lives, but…surely, he had faith in me that I would live through this, right?

I patted Lanker's shoulder, giving him the most reassuring smile, I could. "Hey, I'll be fine, okay? Don't worry about me. If anything, I'll need you all to guard the outside of the facility, there is no way Salem came here alone, and I don't want us walking into another ambush."

Lanker nodded reluctantly, still looking uneasy.

"Let's go ahead and take her down to the ground nice and easy when we are within range." I continued, "But don't have the ship too close to the building, just in case this is a trap."

"You got it Lil man, Casteri and I are gonna head below deck and make sure our weapons are all charged up and ready to go. If we are walking into a fight, we're gonna be prepared." Marcus smiled his signature smile, and gave a thumbs up.

"Lanker and I will watch the helm then." Tyrinie added in nonchalantly, despite the anxious twitching of his tail.

"Alright team, let's make the most of these few minutes, and get ready to kick some ass."

The team yelled in unison, already pumped up for the fight ahead. Their energy was contagious, and I couldn't help but be excited as well. This was almost over. We did it, amidst all odds, we're going to pull this crazy mission off.

Mrs. P,

We should be to Salem in a few more minutes, then this will all be over. I'll be coming home again! I can't wait to hug both you and Emme. Speaking of which, Senna and Dante should have arrived at your house by now, so I'm sure that Emme is feeling much better under Senna's care. After Salem is dead, I'll be in charge of caring for this world, so I might not be around as often as before, but I'll definitely be back in the West. I miss you both and can't wait to see you again.

-Scarlet

I sent off the message in the cypher, leaning back in my chair. My office was silent, save for the small sounds Pip was making over on the couch. She was sitting up properly, albeit a bit hunched, and was staring over at the window, watching the snow fall with curiosity.

"How long has it been since you've seen snow, Pip?"

Her ears twitched at the name, almost as if there was still a tad bit of remembrance there. However, she just continued staring, letting out a quiet snort.

"Are you ready for this R?" I spoke aloud, fiddling with the compass King gave me at the beginning of my journey.

"*I'm ready whenever you are, kid.*" R chuckled, "*Someone is about to come through the door.*"

I popped my head up as Faylin came rushing in.

"Scarlet, we've landed, but there is something you need to see." I could hear the uneasiness in his voice, and it immediately had me on guard. Without another word, I jumped up and sped over to the door, startling Pip.

"Stay here Pip, okay. It's safe." After closing the door, I locked it from the outside. It seemed cruel, but if there was some sort of danger, she'd be safer staying put.

When we hit the deck, everyone was hanging over the railing, staring down towards the entrance to the ruins.

There, on the ground, were creatures I had never seen before, but the sight of them made my skin crawl. They were abnormally lanky, so much so their ribs jutted from their inky black bodies. Pulses of blue veins flashed across their limbs like lightning, highlighting geometric patterns across their skin. Their eyes were pure black, and they didn't seem to have mouths or noses. Most of them, about sixty or so, walked in odd hunched forms, seemingly fizzling in and out of sight. Being visible one moment, and then reappearing three steps backwards only a moment later. The rest of them crawled on the ground, stretching out grotesquely long arms and dragging themselves out of the ruins.

These creatures…there's no way.

"Are those…nanoids?" Marcus asked, getting his gun ready without hesitation. "There are so many."

"They must be." Faylin added. "But how are they coming out of the mainframe? Nobody else can open it except for Mr. Scarlet."

I was about to speak when a gruff voice behind me cut me off.

"The gateway wasn't opened, trust me, if it was there would be many more nanoids than just this, millions more." Behind me stood R, fully visible and completely solid. "No, this is Galaia trying to slow you down, the nanoids are leaking out of the mainframe. Remember, I mentioned Galaia is able to pass small quantities of these guys though. She must've been holding these nanoids and waiting for the perfect moment to release them all at once.

They're not yet acclimated to this world, so, you'll have a chance to kill them if you act fast. But don't let them touch you, they can absorb into your body within a matter of seconds."

The team seemed too shocked to even respond, but nodded.

"You must be R, right?" Casteri asked. "How fascinating, how long are you able to keep that form?"

"Not very long, so we can have official introductions later." R looked back at me, holding out his hand. "You and I need to get down to that mainframe right away and end this quickly."

I nodded. "Team, you know the drill. Stay safe, and call me for backup if things get too dangerous. Both Arai and Tetsuzo are on their way to provide cover fire, we are taking no chances after what happened with Nyx."

They took their battle positions, and Faylin gave me a salute. "Go ahead Captain, I'll make sure we keep this area secure."

"I know you will, be careful, Fay." I looked back at R, who looked more than ready to get into the ruins. "Let's go, R."

Without another word, R and I were airborne, heading at breakneck speeds back to the place where it all began.

END OF CHAPTER 18

CASTERI

19

WHERE IT ALL BEGAN

As R and I got a view over the soon-to-be battlefield, I could see the sheer number of nanoids that were flooding from the building. There had to have been at least a hundred. Fear for my team began to creep in.

"They'll be fine, kid. Try to have a little faith in them." R shook his head. "Haven't they proved themselves by now?"

"I don't doubt their ability, I just don't want to lose anyone again. It was enough of a close call with Lanker…I don't think I could handle that again."

"Well, you won't have to, and honestly you should be focused on the fight ahead. Despite how it looks, your friends have the easier battle here. All they have to do is headshot a bunch of nearly braindead nanoids, you on the other hand, have a highly corrupted nanoid who is not very fond of you, on your hands."

R and I landed a few stories up through a shattered window. With the ground level being filled to the brim, this seemed like the safest option.

Instantly, I was overcome with a *heavy* feeling. Heavy was the best way to describe it. So much happened here, the walls were practically screaming their stories to me. Much like the same effect with Nilya's photo. I knew there was no time, and either way, I doubted if I wanted to see what had actually happened that day.

It must've been horrifying. "Are you ready, kid?" R stood behind me, his presence looming over me like a dark, immovable cloud.

"Yeah, I'm ready." I took a deep breath like I practiced and began releasing my barriers, instantly feeling R's heat flow through me, burning me from the inside out. I kept pushing through, past my conscious telling me to stop. I allowed the haze to flow freely from my hands, feet, and mouth. I steadied my breathing, trying to not choke as my vision began to go red. Everything hurt, it hurt so badly but I knew I had to keep going.

I felt R step closer to me. He bent down and wrapped his arms around me, saying nothing. But somehow, I understood perfectly.

Within a second, my limbs went numb, and R's presence went from behind me to inside of me.

I felt my body stand up straight and head towards the door, feet not even touching the ground.

"You did well, kid. You just hang back and relax for a bit. I'll handle things for as long as I can. Maybe I'll be able to convince E to stop this and leave E-129's body."

I didn't need to be in R's mind to know he didn't even believe that statement. But through his mind, I could also tell R didn't truly want to hurt E-129 if it could be helped.

"That's right, and I know you were thinking the same thing," R spoke up as we weaved through the rusted corridor. Out of the corner of my eye, I could see my team fighting valiantly outside, they were doing well. I couldn't have been more relieved.

"I know you were thinking of ways to *extract* E from E-129. The thought isn't all that crazy, and in a way, it's actually possible. We'll have to use the mainframe."

The mainframe? Truth be told, knowing I was the only one with the ability to open the mainframe made me paranoid about getting too close to it. But more than that…how would the mainframe help to extract E from E-129.   Further ahead of us was a steep, open staircase.

The type of staircase that allowed you to nearly see every level of the facility if you looked over the railing. However, with the lack of power, the staircase just looked unsettling.

"Well, it's a bit confusing, but the Gateway is only supposed to work one way - from the cyberworld to the human world…or whatever realm you are trying to reach. That's why you were only able to go by having your consciousness, very painfully, pulled there. Think of it as going up a slide. However, that might work in our favor. You see, if nanoids can come out one way fully intact, then going back in the opposite way, physically from the human world to the cyberworld, should disrupt the nanoids form enough to separate it from a host."

Was that true? To pull E from E-129, I would just need to cross through the gateway.

But what would happen to me and R? Obviously to drag E through the mainframe, we'd have to go in ourselves. So, what would happen?

R chuckled dryly as we reached the ground level. To my surprise, all of the nanoids had made it outside, practically surrounding the ship. The team, led by Faylin, was shooting them down like they were nothing. Every few moments, I would see a burst of green energy, and a nanoid would fling back into the building, dissipating into code on impact.

R turned me down the corridor and down the stairs that led to the first lab.

"Well kid, it won't be painless, but as you can guess, we'd be torn from each other as well."

Torn…from each other?

R nodded. "Going through the mainframe would separate E and E-129. In the same sense,

you and I will be split apart due to me becoming unstable. For a few moments, you'll be on your own. But as soon as I can stabilize myself, I can go back inside you. At that point, you'll have full control.

I won't be able to take over you like this the entire time. Does that make sense?"

The thought of being fully without R was terrifying. After I had gotten injured in Cyryl's lair, R was just 'asleep' inside of me, and that was horrible. I felt so weak, I couldn't even see clearly or walk straight. But having R actually removed from my body…

What would happen to me?

I took a deep breath. I had no time to worry about such things, I couldn't lose my nerve. Not now.

"Let's go see our friend, shall we?" R sped up, as we hit the lab floor and headed over to the entrance to the secret lab beneath the ruins. From the staircase, I could feel an ominous air that, if I was in control of my body, would have made me stop in my tracks. But onward we went…off to meet the parasite.

~~

We stopped in our tracks at the bottom of the staircase, on guard and ready for all attacks. However, the room was silent. Silent, but not empty.

Across the room, standing dangerously close to the mainframe, stood the man that made my veins turn to ice. Calm and collected in his ever-present black suit, hair slicked back, and steely eyes that reflected the ominous purple hue of the mainframe's light. Despite being so close, he seemed completely unaffected by the euphoric aura that surrounded the machine. For the first few moments, he said nothing. He just watched with an expectant look in his eyes.

"So, you finally arrived, child." His tri-toned voice vibrated in the back of my head, sending chills down my spine. He paused for a moment, taking a step closer with a slightly intrigued look on his face. "Well, it isn't the child after all, but *you*, brother. How interesting."

"I wish I could say it was good to see you, but you know how this is going to end, don't you?" R stated in an odd tone, not exactly confident, but at the same time completely unwavering.

Salem looked partially amused, stony expression still not breaking. "I must say, out of all the possible scenarios, the chances of you siding with your vessel were very slim. Yet here you are. I don't know if I should be disappointed or amused."

"It doesn't have to go this way though. We don't have to follow through. You and I were both forced here by *her* hands." As R spoke, the lights began to flicker ominously. "Why don't we stop playing her game, and make our own decisions here."

By the slight twitch of his lip, I could tell Salem's expression was fighting to remain neutral and unbothered. "Have you lost what little bit of a mind you have left?" He hissed out. "What reason could I possibly have for wanting anything other than what our mother desires of us? Have you forgotten where you came from?"

R shook his head. "Maybe there's more than just our world? Maybe this world deserves a chance, E."

"Your vessel truly has changed you, and I fear that it wasn't for the better. These creatures and their dying planet will more than likely not survive the next century. What would be the point of allowing them to continue existing?"

"What if they do though? You already said the chances of me siding with Scarlet were rare, so what if your predictions on the fate of this world are wrong too? You don't know everything, E. Scarlet has surprised you time and time again, perhaps you aren't as all-knowing as you think you are." R began to step closer, past the haze that hung heavily around the mainframe. Just like with Salem, it seemed to have no effect. "Back when this all began, you fought against it as well. So why are you so against the idea now? Don't you want to be free of this?" "You know nothing of freedom, brother." Salem loomed over us, his unblinking eyes unnerving every fiber of my being.

"Is being confined in a vessel, and forever banished from our home your true idea of freedom? If so, then you are more lost than I could have imagined. Do you not remember the lifetimes we spent together under our mother's watchful eye? Would you really throw all of that away for a child and his foolish attempt to save a planet that isn't even worth its spot in the universe?"

"You wouldn't understand even if I explained it to you until the end of time. This isn't about war and glory, this isn't about Galaia, and this isn't about us. This is about giving this world a fighting chance and a choice, something we never had. I'm done being Galaia's puppet, I'm making my own decision." R stepped forward once again until we were only a foot away from Salem, only inches away from the mainframe itself. "When you've spent the last 16 years inside of the mind of someone who just wanted to survive so badly…it changes your view on things. But you would know nothing about that."

Being that close to the machine made my heart thump wildly, I was only a step away from physically being pulled from this realm for the first time. I could only hope that getting back would be just as easy.

"But I can honestly say…" R reached out with lighting speed, grabbing Salem's arm with a vice grip. "I am starting to like it here."

Without a moment's hesitation, both of us were flung into the mainframe.

~~

For a moment…maybe two or three…I couldn't breathe. All I felt was the sensation of freefalling through an impossibly bright purple light. The color surrounded me, making me void of all physical sensations. At moments, I couldn't tell if I was still falling, or simply suspended in space.

The feeling of claustrophobia was beyond anything I could put into words. I opened my mouth, but no words came out, not even a whisper.

"R" I thought as loudly as I could. "Can you hear me?"

Nothing came, there was nothing but silence.

Then suddenly, a *whooshing* sound began to surround me, and the blinding purple light faded into a blood red. Lightning bolts zipped across the cloudy sky in intricate patterns, and the cyberworld fizzled into view.

As I continued falling, the picture got clearer and clearer, until I was suddenly flung forward and crash-landed into the red grass that I knew all too well.

But this time, it was different. The grass didn't just *feel* real, it was real. The grass was cold and damp against my fingertips, and I wasn't in the bodysuit I normally was in, I was just in my normal clothing.

I stood on shaky legs, trying and failing to quell the nausea in my belly from the trip.

"R?" I coughed out before covering my mouth. I was in enemy territory, and completely defenseless. I had to think fast and stay quiet.

The city was in the distance, perhaps a few miles out.

"Anything is better than being in the open." I just prayed we were alone. Every other time I came here, it seemed somewhat void of other nanoids, hopefully that was still the case.

As I started down the hill, my foot kicked something hard, causing me to trip and tumble down a few feet.

"Dammit…" Everything on my body hurt and I felt so tired. I could only hope R would restabilize and find me soon. I looked over at what caused me to fall, and nearly shouted in panic.

It was Salem.

Or rather…it was E-129. His body was completely still and his face was blank. I knelt down and shook his arm cautiously, but nothing happened. I pried open his eyes, and to my surprise, the color was different. As opposed to the steely gray, they were a deep ocean blue.

That was it then, E really was torn from E-129's body. It worked just like R said it would.

I left him there. I would come back for him when we were done. As long as R and I could take down E before he tried to take over his body again, there was a chance we could save E-129. I turned on my heels and began running as quickly as possibly down towards the city. I had to find R, and fast!

By the time I reached the city, it felt as though an eternity had passed. I had to stop running after only a few minutes, and was still trying my best to not pant too heavily. I felt dizzy, and the muscles in my legs felt so weak.

Not to mention the fact my vision was just blurry enough to be uncomfortable. There is no doubt I would have needed glasses or something without R.

What a pain.

I reached the window of one of the unmarked buildings, leaning up against it in exhaustion, before looking over and jumping back in shock. There, in my reflection, was a person I had never seen before. Obviously, it must've been me, but...I looked so different.

My hair was the biggest change. It went from its usual red to a deep brown, nearly black, hue. The shade was exactly the same as my mother, just like my eyes, which now were a hazel brown color. It was all the more apparent that I really took after my mother. Never had I ever yearned for my red eyes and hair so badly.

I turned my back on the reflection and slumped against the building. Where would I go? Where was R? For all I knew, he could be on the opposite side of this forsaken realm.

More than ever, I wished for Faylin to just pop out of nowhere and offer me guidance.

But he was quite literally in a different dimension, and I was on my own. The realization of being in a different plane of reality made me nearly vomit.

The best thing I could do was to just keep walking.

"Why are you here?" A familiar voice pierced through the silence. I froze.

"Hello?" I whispered back, checking my surroundings.

"Why are you here, child?" The voice answered back. "You don't belong here."

I froze in the middle of the road, staring straight ahead at the source of the voice. It was the man in white. He stood in full view, but this time he was clothed in what looked like a long white coat.

His head was still pointed downward, and he made no motion to come closer. I walked forward, thanks to my blurry vision, I could hardly make out any distinguishing features.

"You don't belong here." He spoke again, unmoving.

"I know I don't, but this was the only way I could save E-129, and destroy E. I've made my decision about my future, old man." I stopped, only a few feet away from him. "I'm handling things my own way now, I'm going to keep this place hidden, and destroy any nanoids that Galaia tries to send into our world. I'm going to be Neutopia's protector."

"Your heart outweighs your mind. To think you would willingly come to this place to save my humanoid is…baffling."

"Your humanoid? What do you-"

The man in white looked up, staring at me with blinded eyes and a hauntingly blank expression.

But I recognized him. I knew exactly who he was from the pictures in the basement.

"You're…Dr. Xenon, aren't you?"

"I made a terrible mistake creating E-129. The deal I made with *her*…I trusted her, and she brought me here, trapping me in this place for all eternity. And you came here willingly…thinking there was a way out, and all just to save a humanoid's life?"

I went cold, my heart beginning to speed up. "There's…no way out? No, there has to be, I came in through the gateway, surely, I can get out the same way, right?"

"Return back to the field, child. The place where you first landed. Finish this fight, and pray you can find your way back home."

Without another word, the man fizzled out of sight, leaving me alone in the city.

Surely there was a way out…there must be. I fit my thumb into my mouth and bit down hard, until I drew blood. The action did little to calm my nerves. I couldn't focus on that possibility, I had to keep pushing forward.

All I had to focus on was killing E. Once I did that, I would find a way out of here!

I stopped in my tracks as a loud fizzling scream pierced through the silence, making me cover my ears and duck down. The sound was horrendous and unlike anything I had ever heard. The sheer volume made the ground tremble, and the sky to flicker.

With ears still covered, I ran faster towards the fields. Whatever was making that sound was coming from there.

It was time to finish this, and get back home.

END OF CHAPTER 19

20

FURTHER, FURTHER STILL

I ran as fast as my legs could take me to the clearing of the red-tinged field. I saw the torn patch of earth where I had crash landed, and not far from there sat R, skin still glitching and fighting to stabilize.

The horrible piercing sounds continued to reverberate through the air, making my ears feel as though they were going to burst.

"R!" I released my ears, lunging forward to grab onto the only familiar face in this wasteland. "I'm so glad to see you!"

As I yelled, the sound stopped and a dead silence fell over us. My ears were grateful for the break, but I couldn't help the anxiety that continued to creep in.

"Are you okay, R? Are you stabilized now?" I didn't want to rush him, but I hated feeling defenseless. The sooner this fight was over, the sooner I'd be able to get out of this place and put all of this behind me.

R sluggishly looked over, a tired grin coming over his face. "Well now, you look worse than I do. I dig the hair though. You look like your mom, it's kinda hot." He slurred out, his eyes partially unfocused.

"Ugh, if you have energy to goof around, you have energy to fight. Let's go." I stammered, pulling R up to his feet. He wavered slightly, leaning heavily on my shoulder, but eventually got his footing. If it wasn't for the fact we were about to fight for our lives, I would have marveled at the fact this was the first time R truly felt real to me, and not just like a part of my mind or an extension of my body.

This was his element, his home. He was real here.

He even looked different. While he still resembled me slightly with his red eyes and hair, he was much taller than usual, at least by a foot or two. He was larger, and had the same markings I would develop down his face, chest, and arms. He had the same bodysuit I would usually wear when I was brought here, but instead of looking like an outsider, he looked like he belonged.

It was a lot to wrap my head around, but I had no time to sit and contemplate.

Further down the fields, as far as I could see clearly, I saw who I assumed was E stalking closer.

My breath caught painfully in my throat. The sight of him was something I knew would stick with me for the rest of my life. His body was the same size and build as R's, but instead of R's brown skin, E's was pure black and dripped like tar off of his body. Pulses of purple veins flashed in increments, and a churning purple light could be clearly seen through his chest.

His mouth was now a dripping, gaping hole, and his eyes were beads of white. At that moment, all I could remember was when we did that autopsy on Myrah, and what the inside of her corrupted body looked like.

Closer and closer he stalked, leaving heavy drips of the tar-like substance with every step. Every few moments, his form would fizzle and glitch out of sight, only to pop back up a moment later.

"The corruption…is so deep inside of him. No wonder I couldn't talk any sense into him. That's not 'E' anymore." R sounded shaken, and I could understand why.

"That's corruption?" I could recall back after the fight at Cyryl's lair when R said we almost became corrupted. I remembered the dark pulses that ran through his arms, and how he said it almost killed me. Is this what I almost became?

"I thought you said nanoids were the manifestation of corruption…" I spoke quietly, eyes still stuck on the monstrous image on the horizon.

"We are. It might take lifetimes, but eventually, all nanoids have the ability to become *that*. That is what happens to a nanoid when they lose all sense of control, when they allow their true nature to take over. The corruption spreads like a damn disease, affecting every part of their being."

Within a blink, E began to charge at breakneck speed, his body flickering in and out of view. R grabbed a hold of me, launching us both high into the air, keeping out of his reach.

"Usually, Galaia steps in when her children become too far gone from corruption, but something tells me she won't be stepping in this time."

Before I could respond, R's arms around me were gone, and I was floating freely. An all too familiar heat flooded through my body, and I took a deep breath, feeling completely rejuvenated. My hair turned red once more, and my eyes sharpened enough that I could see E's every moment despite the fizzing and glitching.

The markings ran down my cheeks and arms, and haze poured out of my hands. I tried to summon my tendrils, but they didn't respond.

E came closer, trampling right over E-129's body without a second glance before becoming airborne. I dove to the side, dodging him by only an inch, before landing back in the grass.

"R, have you ever fought someone with this level of corruption?" I was hesitant to run forward and strike. For all I knew, the corruption could spread by touch alone. Of all times, I wish I had my father's sword with me.

"Never. Like I mentioned, Galaia would handle them when they got to this level. All other nanoids knew to stay away when the corruption became irreversible."

I dodged another attack, running full force towards the horizon trying to get as much distance as possible. Even while going full speed,

E was a second faster. He swiped his claws at my back, close enough to tear my suit but not touching my skin. It was far too close for comfort, and I could feel the cold sweat dripping down my forehead.

"Well, do you have an idea? Can we even touch him?" I rocked on my heels, ready to dash in either direction as E's mouth began to stretch open far larger than a normal jaw.

"What could you possibly know of freedom, you traitor!" His voice screeched out in a tri-toned voice, causing my footing to stumble. *"How dare you stand in the way of The Eternal One. You will pay with your life!"*

"Scarlet, there is no corruption in you and your resolve is strong. The corruption shouldn't be able to spread to you if you're careful." R responded with hesitation. "His heart should be where he is most vulnerable."

I honed into the purple light that was barely visible through thick layers of black muck. If getting out of here meant I had to rip light out from inside of him, then that's what I would do.

He began to charge again at full force, and this time I charged back.

With a shout, I harnessed as much haze as I could, aiming my fist directly at the faint, flickering light in his chest cavity. As soon as I made contact, the blackness wrapped itself around my fist in a vice grip.

"Wha-?" I tried to yank my arm out, but it wouldn't budge. A searing pain began to rip through my veins, causing burns to rip through the skin of my arm from the inside out. "R, what's happening!"

It took everything in me to not scream out in pain. I focused a blast of haze through my hand, but it didn't do a thing.

After another, and finally another blast, the muck loosened, allowing me to rip my hand free.

My hand, or at least what was left of it, was burned down through the flesh, exposing the bones of my fingers. I gripped my forearm and looked away, willing the nausea away. Slowly, I could feel R working on the damage.

"What the hell, R?! I thought you said the corruption couldn't hurt me?" I dodged another attack from E, reluctant to touch him. This was bad. If I couldn't touch him without literally burning alive, how would I kill him?

"I said the corruption couldn't corrupt you, I never said it wouldn't hurt you." R stated in a matter-of-fact tone. "I told you to be careful, didn't I?"

"Well now is not the time to fight semantics, R! I need you to tell me straight how to kill this thing!" I focused the haze into my good hand and punched it into the ground, sending a shockwave of energy straight into E, knocking him back.

"I told you already, I don't know how to fight a corrupted being. There is some knowledge even beyond me. My best advice is that you'll probably want to use a weapon."

I stood back up and dashed over to E, who hadn't gotten back up yet. I might not have been able to touch him,

but other things could touch him. I sent more shockwaves into the ground, pushing him back further and further until he went tumbling down the hill and towards the cityscape. I knew it wasn't hurting him much, but it was all I could do.

"Well, that's great advice, R, but I don't have a weapon. Nothing traveled through the mainframe with me."

"Are you forgetting where you are, you dumbass? This place is where we are at our strongest. If you don't have a weapon, make one."

Make one?

I looked down at my hands. Thankfully, despite the pain, the damaged one was about halfway healed. The bone was no longer visible, and the pain wasn't nauseating. I released more of my barriers, allowing R's powers to nearly push me to the edge. R didn't have the strength to fully take me over again, but he didn't say I couldn't use as much of our power as possible.

The markings down my face began to glow red and wisps of red haze formed around my palms as something solidified.

It was a sword, and oddly enough, it looked identical to my father's sword. It was larger, covered in code, and glowed a bright red. Despite it being made out of thin air, it felt heavy in my hands, and took effort to swing.

"Alright, now let's go." In a burst of energy, I zipped down the hill as E was beginning to stand. Raising my sword high, I swung as soon as I was in range. It barely grazed him, giving him ample time to backpedal further into the city.

"You're fighting a senseless battle, R" He screeched out, causing the buildings around us to fizzle. *"Trying to defend a dying world...stopping their only chance at survival."*

I charged again, swinging but only hitting the wall where he once stood. He was fast, not as fast as Lelani thankfully, but faster than my reflexes allowed.

I looked around, spotting him on the wall, the black tar holding him in place. *"Do you think our mother will ever allow this rebellion?"*

"You're acting as if I should care Galaia is pissed off. Why should I care? She should have left my planet alone!" I steadied my blade in front of me, encasing it in a red haze. "Now quit bouncing around and face me like a real man!"

His form began to vibrate, and within a second, he was within striking distance. His mouth began to stretch, threatening to devour me whole.

Despite my entire body screaming at me to move, I couldn't get out of the way fast enough. All I could do was pivot as my entire left arm was engulfed into E's mouth.

The pain was almost instantaneous, the searing burn was tearing my flesh from the bone. It was so intense I couldn't even scream; I just went numb.

"I have you…right where I want you, you bastard!" I screamed out, plunging my sword deep into the murky chest cavity.

A scream ripped through as his body convulsed, releasing my battered arm and scurrying backwards once more.

I could feel the heat radiating off my arm as I tried my best not to look at it.

"Damn it…I missed his heart, didn't I?" I swore that would work, I had it lined up perfectly. "He's injured, so this is my chance!" I charged back, feet barely touching the ground as I went straight towards him. This time, I watched closely as he moved with his insane speed, nearly biting at me again. I barely dodged him, sidestepping myself against the building beside us, before slipping behind him. But before I could catch my footing, E was right in my face again, pinning me against the building's wall.

"Urg!" I bit back a scream as the corruption began to burn into my shoulders and neck. This must have been what acid felt like, but instead of running off like water, it stuck and clung like honey.

"Child, this was all your fault! You twisted my brother's mind. You caused this rebellion, just like your father."

He screeched in his tri-toned voice, pressing his full body weight into me with such force I could feel the wall behind me cracking. My clothing was blocking the majority of the corruption from burning more of me, but it couldn't hold it off forever.

"I am nothing like my father. Unlike him, I'm saving my world." I bit back, trying to free my limbs.

"My father may have been a hero in his day, but time has corrupted him. I refused to stand by as a genocide happens!"

"Do you really think you are that important, child? You would have been better off destroying the mainframe instead of coming here. If only you had chosen one of the options laid in front of you." He leaned his dripping head in closer, placing his acidic mouth against my ear. *"Do you really think you were our last resort? Oh no, child...you will easily be replaced. If not by a new creation, then by your friend. The one you, so predictably, injected us into."*

I stopped my thrashing and fighting back, allowing his words to penetrate as he crushed my body further into the wall.

Replaced?

No...that's impossible. I was the one that was going to end all of this. Despite what I did with Lanker, I was still Galaia's prophet. I was the one they needed to open the mainframe.

This ended with me!

He couldn't have meant...

"You were always just a prototype. An experiment."

No, there was no way. There was no way they knew Lanker was going to be killed, and I was going to bring him back to life using a nanoid? I thought R always said I wasn't bound by the strings of fate, but then...

Did I play right into their hand?

R.

Did R know this would happen? Did he plant that idea in my head so I would implant both some of him and some of E into a new vessel?

No...of course not. R has been on my side this entire time. R was willing to permanently give up his home in the cyberworld just to save my world. R cares about me and my team.

Right?

"And like any prototype, you are now obsolete. How does that feel? Thinking your entire life the world's survival depended on you, pushing yourself on with the belief that you were this world's savior...only to discover you were just a trial run for the nanoids." He grinned a murky grin, tar dripping from his unhinged jaw. *"Don't you dare die yet, I am nowhere near finished with you."*

He was a grotesque immovable object, and my brain was focused on everything else but on this fight. My arms and legs were completely pinned, and I could feel the corruption beginning to eat at my flesh. Breathing was becoming nearly impossible.

Suddenly all of the words from my past began flooding back to me. I was the first of my kind. There was nobody else like me out there. I was a prototype, which was why my powers would fluctuate so often. I was an experiment.

I knew the entire time but...but now that world held another meaning.

I was *just* an experiment.

E and Galaia knew I wouldn't choose either side. Here I thought I was building my own path, but I was just playing into their hands the entire time.

A fire rose in the pit of my stomach, bubbling up to my throat in an uncontrollable rage. My breathing came out in quick pants as the corruption from E added to the pain that was searing my entire body. My head was spinning, thinking about everything and nothing at the exact same time.

I was a puppet; I was their puppet for years. Mother, Father, Galaia...

I. Was. Done.

I was done being everyone's fucking puppet!

I was an unstoppable force.

And I wasn't about to let some corrupted mass of tar take me down. Not now.

Not after all I had already been through. I was more than they could have ever bargained for. If they thought they could control and predict me any longer, they were about to be disappointed.

And I sure as oblivion wasn't about to let them drag Lanker into their twisted prophecy. If Lanker truly was their Plan B, then I would protect him with everything I had.

"Fuck you...you disgusting sack of shit!" I gritted out, harnessing as much haze as possible throughout my entire body until it was flooding from my pores. As soon as he caught sight of it, I threw myself into him hard as I could, and with a flash of haze, blasted him backwards with every ounce of strength I had.

If anything, the look on his face when he went ripping through the street and crashing into the next building made the sickening decay in my arms, stomach, and legs worth it. The pain was making me feel nauseous and dizzy, but more than that, I felt rage.

More rage than I had ever felt in my life, like every part of my body was on fire.

I could feel more and more of R's presence wrapping around me as those same symbols began to carve themselves across my face and arms.

Fire flowed through my veins as something similar to my tendrils began to come out of my fingertips. They were thin, like whips, and had the same inky blackness E himself had.

I stalked closer, shooting the whips forward and wrapping them around E tightly before hoisting him up into the air and slamming him back down on the remains of the crumbled street.

Haze leaked out of my mouth as I tossed him like a ragdoll, crushing him further and further into the ground. However, he just continued to laugh, making the rage in me burn even brighter.

I didn't stop my assault though. I didn't *want* to stop, even when I heard what sounded like bones shatter, even when I saw the inky tar splashing on the streets like black streaks of blood.

"Kid, take it easy! You're pushing yourself too far!" I ignored R's protests, increasing the intensity of my swings.

Surely, he still had plenty of life left in him.

"Did you really think you were going to break me by spewing those lies?" I laughed, flinging him within all my strength into the body-shaped dent in the ground. "You aren't going to save yourself that way."

A sickening crunch resounded as E hit the ground once more.

I walked over, crouching by his side. "I am curious though…since I'm so predictable, what do you think I'm going to do next?"

E pulled himself up to his knees, laughing and spitting up tar as the light from his eyes began to flicker.

"I suppose you're going to try and kill me, won't you? That is what you believe you were created to do."

I smiled brightly, stabbing the whip-like tendrils through his shoulder blade before ripping the limb off completely and throwing it far behind me.

"Nope, that's wrong." I chuckled over his screams. "Since my existence has been nothing but a game to you, I think I need to make you feel what you've made me feel for all these years.

~~

There were some things I didn't think I was capable of, and others I hoped I wasn't capable of.

I wasn't sure what category this fell into.

R had gone silent long ago. To be honest, I wasn't even sure how long "long" was, it felt as if I had been here for an eternity.

The demolished street that I sat in the middle of was coated in tar. Limbs and chunks of inky flesh littered all around me, while E's head and pulsing heart sat right in front of me. He was still conscious, oddly enough, but a part of me expected that.

The worst part was…I didn't feel any better. None of this helped the gnawing pain in my gut, the pain of realizing that no matter what I did, I still didn't succeed in escaping this damned prophecy. The pain in realizing that my entire existence was meant to pave the way for someone else. The pain of knowing that I existed as nothing but an experiment. When the anger and rage subsided, the pain seeped back in from the recesses of my mind.

"Why didn't you fight harder against your destiny?" I asked absentmindedly. "Last time I saw you here, when we were at the statue, you told me that you fought against your destiny but you gave in."

I glanced down at E's head. He didn't respond, all he did was stare.

He couldn't respond, the corruption had him too far gone.

"I can't let this be my destiny, I won't end up like you." I stood, placing my foot on his heart. "I won't let you bastards win, no matter what your expectation of me was."

With more pressure than was needed, I stomped down, splattering black and purple fluid all over my boots. And just like that, all of the bits of tar on the street began to fizzle away, fading into nothingness.

"Whether you like it or not, I will be the one to take you down." My fists tightened as I looked up into the red sky. "Do you hear me Galaia, you're next! I'm coming back for you, bitch!"

I could feel *her* presence in the air. I couldn't see her, but I knew she was watching me. I could feel her void-like eyes on me.

I panted in the silence, allowing myself to breathe.

It was over, for now at least. Salem was dead.

I won.

I did it.

I killed him.

I headed back for the hills where E-129's body lay strewn. Grabbing a hold of him, I hoisted him onto my back with a grunt. He was much heavier than I thought he would be.

"R…I think I'm ready to go home now."

Wordlessly, R caused a portal to swirl open in front of me. My heart jumped in thankfulness that this didn't end up being a one-way trip. Without hesitation, I stepped in, allowing the purple weightlessness to engulf me.

END OF CHAPTER 20

SENNA

21

HAND IN HAND

Before long, my body was thrown mercilessly to a cold gray floor in a loud crash. Unfortunately, my head broke my fall, causing my vision to go out only for a moment. But nevertheless, I couldn't help the overwhelming bliss of knowing I was back in my own dimension. I was back. I was home. The thought I might have gotten myself stuck in the cyberworld was more than I could bear.

Perhaps since I got out, there was a way that I could get Dr. Xenon out as well.

My thoughts were cut short when footsteps began coming down the steps, they faltered for a moment, before speeding up.

"Scarlet!"

Instantly, I was grabbed, pulled into a tight hug with white hair obscuring my vision. I sighed, allowing myself to completely melt into his embrace. After everything that just happened, this was what I needed.

"We were all so worried, thank goodness you are alright. You suddenly vanished down here, and nobody could find you. We could only assume you went into the mainframe. We feared for the worst." Faylin rambled on, the nervousness in his voice was more than apparent. After a few moments, he finally pulled back, checking me quickly for any obvious signs of injuries since I wasn't moving. "Are you alright? Can you speak?"

Faylin looked arguably worse than I did, not physically though. Instead, he looked tired and worn out, like he had been stressing himself out for an indefinite amount of time.

I coughed, nodding slowly as I got my bearings "I'm okay, I'm good. Just a little tired."

I laughed, noting that dull pain in my body from my fight not too long ago. "It's over, it's finally over Fay. We won." My laughing got louder as Faylin pulled me to my feet. I couldn't help swaying a bit, still feeling weak.

The worry began to slowly melt off of Faylin's face as my words sunk in. I smiled, shaking my head as I glanced over at the mainframe.

"E is dead Faylin, Salem is gone."

Faylin looked at the prone body that was against the wall, unmoving.

"So then, is that..." Faylin questioned.

"Yeah, that's E-192. With the nanoid ripped from his body, he should just be a normal companion humanoid. I don't know how much memory he will have, or even how functional he will be.

But E-129 will have a chance at life now...whatever that might look like for a humanoid."

"Your kindness will never cease to amaze me, Scarlet." Faylin smiled, eying all of the tears and burns through my clothing. "Will you be able to walk?"

"Yea yea, don't worry about me. I just might need a moment to breathe." I laughed. "Would you mind carrying E-129 for me though?"

"That is not a problem." Faylin scooped E-129's large form into his arms, walking closely behind me as we navigated ourselves up the stairs and towards the outside.

~~

Bright lights assaulted my eyes as we stepped out into the snowy morning. The wind blew heavily, sending chills down my spine. Trudging through, I noticed the snow was up past my ankles, far higher than I remembered.

Along the ground were chunks of blown debris and patches of ground where the snow had been melted away in the heat of battle.

"Everyone fought valiantly, you would have been proud," Faylin said with a smile as the Seven Seas, and all of her glory came into view. "It was difficult for a while, but we all knew what we were defending, and fought all the more. Arai and Tetsuzo were of much assistance as well. They fought well, even without receiving a full explanation of what they were fighting."

I laughed. "I guess I owe them an explanation later then."

I would keep the cyberworld, Galaia, and the nanoids a secret for as long as I could. The fewer people I had poking around the mainframe, the better. All we needed was another Dr. Xenon to come along and try to harness the power of the nanoids…but realistically, I knew this secret wouldn't stay hidden forever.

I would have to, for as long as I can, keep it top secret until I'm able to kill Galaia. When Galaia is gone, no other nanoids should be able to exit the mainframe. Sure, R was able to make a portal back to this dimension, but I'm sure that was only because he spent so much of his life here with me. He already has a connection to my world.

"Fay…the fight with Salem is over, but Galaia is still out there," I said, staring ahead as we got closer to the ship, my team coming into view.

"I know, I figured that would still be the case." He smiled, patting my shoulder as my team began to cheer and wave. "But for now, let's enjoy this victory, Captain. You deserve it."

"Here here!" Marcus yelled, patting me far too roughly on my still healing shoulder. "Dimension traveler, Nanoid slayer, World liberation, Dictator killer…have I missed anything?"

We all sat in the War Room, drinks being passed around as everyone grilled me for answers about where I had been for the last few days. Apparently, time moves differently in the cyberworld, something I didn't know but should have guessed. Thankfully, on this side of reality, I had only been gone for about a week. However, that was more than enough time for my teammates to be certain of my demise.

"Don't forget, new leader of Neutopia." Lanker cheered. "Supreme Overlord Scarlet has a pretty nice ring to it. When are you going to make the big announcement, and what will your first decree be?"

"Ha, right." I laughed, taking another swig as Pip slid over quietly and sat by me. "Just like when we were in the Northern powerhouse and made our first announcement to the world. It seems like ages ago now, doesn't it?" I smiled, looking over at my team, my gaze staying on Lanker for just a moment too long.

"It does." Lanker laughed, taking a swig of his drink. "In fact, for old time's sake, you should make your first announcement as leader from that same powerhouse,

or at least from the powerhouse in the West if you don't want to travel all the way back to the North. No better way for you to make a statement."

"I still don't know how everyone will react to me suddenly asserting myself. The last thing we need is a huge rebellion on our hands." I laughed.

"Well, you already have more supporters than you know. You have all of the fusions down in the South, you have both Arai and Tetsuzo's teams, not to mention us and the majority of your hometown." Faylin spoke up. "Not to mention, I sent word of Salem's demise and the safe state of the mainframe over to Aztec…he's impressed, and would like to discuss a long-term arrangement."

A chorus of "ooo's" and "aahs" flooded the room.

I didn't know if I should be more upset or understanding it took Salem's death for Aztec to start taking me seriously. Either way, I accepted the compliment.

"There will be a lot of that happening…believe me." Tyrinie smirked. "Now people know what you're capable of, and now Salem is out of the way, you'll be gaining lots of 'allies. Everyone rushing and trying to get into your good graces so their past doubts in you won't be brought up. I would even say it's a matter of time before Captain King comes to you with that same attitude."

"Ah, now that I doubt. Captain King is much too proud for that." I laughed, setting my drink down. "But you guys are right. It's time for us to make our announcements, and to start solidifying some alliances before word gets out that Salem is dead. And for my first decree, I'll be commanding everyone to remove those collars from their necks. I had been waiting to do that for a long time."

Since we removed ours at the beginning of our journey, it was almost hard to remember what it was like wearing them.

"Aww back into action again, Captain? You just finished the fight of a lifetime, take the night off, why don't you."

Marcus patted my shoulder, offering me a smile. "You haven't even told us how the fight with Salem went, you were gone for days."

I smiled, but slowly the smile became more and more forced. Did I want to tell them about what happened in the cyberworld? Did I want to tell them how I lost it and completely decimated E? The more I thought about the rage I felt at that moment, the more I could feel the black sparks begin to crawl uncomfortably up my hands, leaving a burning sensation on my palms.

"Ah, well. I suppose I do owe you guys a full story." I forced a laugh. "But I'll give it to you tomorrow, I really think I need some sleep first. Our duty is far from over, just because Salem is dead, it doesn't mean we won't have hordes of Salem supporters and his personal military to sift through first."

I laughed at their groaning as I left the room, trying to cover the growing weakness I felt in my body. Obviously, I had pushed myself pretty hard, harder than I ever did before, but…the immediate fight was over.

It was over.

I just had to keep reminding myself of that.

I pushed my door open, glancing over my shoulder in surprise when I realized Pip wasn't following me. I was glad she was comfortable with the others, perhaps that meant she was starting to get better as well.

Once my door was shut, I stripped off my burnt and bloodied clothing, tossing them in a far corner before plopping on my bed, allowing all of the thoughts from the past few hours to come flooding in.

This was nothing like how I thought my journey would go…

Months ago, when I was blissfully unaware of the weight I would have in this world, I thought I would kill Salem in an epic battle. Just me and him, sword to sword, in his castle that overlooked the city. I would come out victorious and father, who would have been waiting for me outside, would come in and congratulate me.

He would hug me, pick me up and swing me around in his arms. He would pat me on the head and tell me just how proud he was of me. From there, he would take the throne as Neutopia's leader, and take the human race to a whole new level of prosperity. And I, his son, would enthusiastically watch him from the sidelines, enjoying my newly found freedom and living out my days exploring the corners of this world.

But that isn't what happened.

It was almost comical how naive I was.

No, instead, I was a pawn in a game of madness and blood that was started by an ancient being, who found the right naive human to play into her will.

I was an unwilling prophet whose sole purpose was to bring my "true" mother into this world to bring about the mass genocide of humankind. In essence, my entire existence was a result of what happens when humans try to play God and attempt to possess things far beyond their control.

In the end, I won the battle, but the war rages on.

"Are you still pouting, kid?"

My ears perked up as the familiar voice broke my room's silence. I rolled over on my back, folding my arms across my stomach as I stared at the sunset-bathed ceiling. It had started snowing again, and the temperature was dropping by the minute.

"Contemplating...not pouting." I groaned; I was too tired for R's lectures. "Hey, R...can I ask you a question?"

R didn't respond, but I knew he was still there, so I continued.

"What was the '*but*' you mentioned when you mentioned I would win. I know we talked about this already, but now the fight with E is done, can you tell me more?" I sat up, watching R who was currently standing at the foot of my bed. "I mean, at this point I basically know everything, so there isn't anything you could say to me that could damage the timeline or whatever, right?"

R watched me closely before shrugging. "You won, why does it matter now?" He walked over and sat down, still staying close to the foot of the bed. "You can't afford to be dwelling in the past anymore, you have a world to run, and some of your hardest decisions are still ahead of you. As you'll soon realize, taking care of a world is a little bit harder than managing a group of runaways." R chuckled.

"I know, I guess I just want some closure, or...maybe I want to know if I did the right thing. I mean..." I paused, taking a deep breath. "I know I did the right thing, obviously, I just...maybe if I knew all the ins and outs I missed-"

"Then you wouldn't feel the need to question yourself on whether or not you messed up anywhere down the line, right?" R shook his head.

I nodded as R stood and came closer to me, kneeling down until we were face to face.

"Listen, you won." R grabbed my face, forcing me to look at him when I began to roll my eyes. "You won a battle that, for all intents and purposes, was unwinnable. The one thing I can tell you is that you chose the *best* outcome with what you were given. Yes, there was a *'but'*, but that is just a part of war. Nothing about this was clean and pretty. However, if you have to know for your own peace of mind what that *'but'* was, I'll tell you, but you're not going to like it." R paused again, almost debating with himself.

"You won, but you'll have to kill your parents, redeeming them was never an option. You won, but your friend would have to die first, Lanker was destined to die on this mission no matter what precautions you could've taken. You won, but in bringing Lanker back from the dead, you gave Galaia a new prophet. The only way around that was to not bring Lanker back. You won, but you would have to become corrupted first, and now that corruption will always be a part of you. The more uncontrollable rage you allow yourself to feel, the more it will grow, so you will have to always watch out for that. You won, but I'll never be able to go back home again, either of us going back to the cyberworld would be a death wish.

You won, but absolute, 100% freedom will most likely never be in your future." R paused, taking a deep breath. "There were a lot of catches to your victory, but that is just reality. It doesn't take away the fact you won against impossible odds, and altered the course of history for mankind, kid. Don't forget that."

I let R's words seep in, ingraining every syllable in my mind. He was right, I just fought a silent war, one that many people won't ever even acknowledge. But we won…and this world is safe because of it.

I had a future to look ahead to.

"R… we will be together forever, right? I mean, I get you are me and I am you in some sense, but even centuries down the line…you'll still be here with me, right?"

R smiled gently and ruffled my hair. "I've been with you since the beginning, haven't I? I'm not leaving you now. Besides, where would I even go? Nobody else wants to be my vessel."

I laughed. "Nobody else would put up with you, you mean."

"Now that's rude, I'm sure Faylin would let me use him as a vessel." He smirked, effortlessly dodging a perfectly thrown book.

"Leave Faylin out of this, you pervert!" I laughed.

It hadn't even occurred to me…but the best part about all of this was I could finally go home. Emme and Persephone were waiting for me, and now they wouldn't have to wait much longer.

~~

"So…Salem's reign is finally over now. I had faith in you that this day would come, but I know you exceeded everyone's expectations on how quickly you ended this. You, Scarlet, never cease to amuse me." Faylin smiled lightly, taking a sip of his drink while keeping his eyes trained on me.

We were on our way back to the West when I decided to take a midnight visit to the upper deck. To my surprise, my favorite white-haired companion was there already waiting for me. Apparently, I wasn't the only one unable to sleep.

"To be completely honest with you, I don't really know how to feel." I chuckled to myself, taking a sip of the sweet wine, my stomach protesting after I already had so much to drink. "It's finally setting in that this part of my journey has come to an end, but I suppose I'm not sure what to do next.

So much of this journey was laid out for me, even the moments I had to discover on my own seemed to fall into place naturally. But now, I feel like I could use a little direction."

Faylin leaned against the railing, pulling his coat tight. It was late in the evening, and the moonlight illuminated brightly on the snow that coated the sea in white.

"Well, I suppose it is time for us to start building our empire." Faylin smiled, looking out towards the distance. "Afterall, you did want us to do this together, right?"

I nodded fiercely. "Absolutely. I am not doing this alone."

"So here is what I presume. After landing in the West, and reuniting with your friends, we should begin assigning jobs for our team on every corner of Neutopia, not to mention we should rally with some of your allies. The more influence you have, the better. Also, you'll need a base of operation. If I may give an option, I would say the powerhouse in the Western region would be a prime location. It will also provide you with means to make announcements. What do you think?"

"I think that is as good a plan as any." I patted Faylin on the shoulder. "This is why I need you around, you always know what to say."

Faylin laughed as he began to walk away. "No Scarlet, I am quite certain you would have come up with a plan on your own eventually. I simply helped you lay it out."

"Well, I need you around anyway. Thankfully you're stuck with me now." I followed Faylin inside, feeling my hands go numb from the cold.

We were only a few hours away from the West. By daybreak, I would have my arms around Persephone and Emme. I would be able to hug them and tell them that from now on, life would be better, just like I promised them.

~~

In the snowy distance, up on a hill, stood the house that embodied all of the pleasant parts of my childhood. Every fond memory, every tasty snack, every sleepover, and every bread delivery. I knew I had been working up to this moment, but I didn't expect my heart to be racing as fast as it was. My eyes stung with happiness, but I quickly rubbed the brimming tears away before racing as quickly as my feet would take me up the snowy bank, my team following behind me.

As I passed my favorite tree in the front yard, I skidded to a stop, trying to contain my excitement as I calmly knocked on the door.

Once. Twice. Three times. Any more than that would be unnerving.

I quickly brushed my hair down and straightened my coat before nervously ringing my sweaty hands together.

"Rose residence." Persephone's soft voice called out cautiously. It didn't take my enhanced hearing to hear the other set of footsteps closely behind her.

Looked like Dante was doing his job properly.

I smiled. "Hey…Mrs. P."

After all those months, I still couldn't think of something cool to say when we reunited, but that didn't matter. Within a moment, the door flew open, and Persephone, smiling through teary eyes, dove into my arms and held me tight.

At that moment, all of the anxieties left my mind, almost as if the past few days never even happened.

Persephone didn't even say anything, she just laughed and laughed, hugging me tighter until I had to breathe.

Upon hearing the commotion, little feet pitter pattered to the door and a loud voice exclaimed. "Hubby!" Before I felt another pair of arms wrap around me.

"Hey Emme!" I smiled, hugging them both back tightly, willing myself harder than ever not to cry.

After minutes passed, Persephone stood back and wiped her face. "Look at you! You look like you've grown so much, have you gotten taller on me?" She smiled, holding my face in her hands.

Despite the fact I was only gone for a few months, I can't help the fact I did feel like a completely different person.

"Hubby looks like a grown up now." Emme laughed, gap-tooth and all. I picked her up, noticing immediately how light she had gotten. Sending Senna here to look after her was a good decision after all.

"Hey now munchkin, I've always been a grown up." I pinched her nose, laughing as she squirmed and tried to get away.

"Well, this blizzard is picking up, we had better head inside." Persephone laughed. Unbeknownst to me, the team had already made themselves comfortable in the living room while we were all still outside crying and laughing. They all looked at home, which made me smile. Persephone's house just had that effect on people.

~~

"Lastly, this is Faylin, the one I've told you so much about." I smiled, concluding the introductions by pushing Faylin forward.

"It's a pleasure to meet you, Mrs. Persephone. I have heard many wonderful things about you and your daughter."

Faylin responded politely, almost sounding more like a humanoid than I've heard in a while. Perhaps he was just nervous.

"It's wonderful to finally meet you as well, thank you for keeping Scarlet safe. I know he can be a handful." Persephone gave him a hug, causing poor Faylin to stiffen.

To my surprise, Senna and Dante fit in perfectly in the West. Dante stood erect at the door, constantly keeping a sharp eye outside towards the walkway. Despite him being unmoving, I could tell he would jump into action at any unwelcome guest. Senna, on the other hand, sat comfortably on the large couch with Emme sitting on his lap.

He bounced her on his knee with a smile and chatted with her about how she was feeling. Returning the smile, Emme leaned into him and rested on his chest. It was a picturesque moment, Senna looked in his element; at home taking care of a family. Despite the slight pang in my chest, I noticed the happy glances that Persephone made over to Senna every now and again, ones that he returned without missing a beat.

I was simply happy to see her happy, and that would have to be enough. And realistically, it's not like Persephone and I would've ever worked out. I was basically an immortal human embodiment of a nanoid, and she was a normal human woman who wanted a normal human life.

While I might not be able to give her that life, I can at least keep her safe.

"So…" I sat back down on the now almost vacant couch. "It's all over Mrs. P, Salem is gone. We're free."

She folded her hands, giving me a light smile. "I can't believe you did it, sweetheart. I wish I could tell you I believed in you this entire time, but…"

"It's okay! It would have sounded crazy to anybody. And it's not like I was completely honest with you from the start."

"So that means," Persephone reached for her neck, stroking the collar with her fingertips. "These can come off now."

I nodded with a smile, standing and rushing to her side. "I'd be honored to help."

Before waiting for an answer, I slid my hands under Persephone's curly hair, and with a light flick, removed the collar for her neck. Senna followed suit, doing the same for Emme.

"How does it feel?" The skin that was under the collar was shades lighter than the rest of her face, she touched it anxiously, seemingly afraid the skin would fall off at the touch.

"It feels…free." She smiled, releasing a huge breath. "We really are free now, aren't we?"

I smiled, pushing all thoughts of Galaia out of my mind. "We are."

~~

Morning soon became nightfall as we spent the majority of the evening around Persephone's table sharing the tale of the last few life changing months. Persephone and Emme listened intently, laughing at some moments, eyes-widening at others, and Persephone covering Emme's ears at the memories regarding Ginseng. Some of the memories were unspoken and omitted, such as my mother's death and of Galaia's existence.

After Persephone excused herself and Emme off to bed, it was just me and the team seated comfortably around the backyard swing set. The moon was high and the night was clear and quiet, silent like the world was taking a breath of fresh air.

"Well team, it's time for our new assignments. You might not like what I'm going to say, but try to keep an open mind." Everyone remained silent as I continued speaking. "It's time for us to build the Seven Seas Empire, and I need all of you to help with this, and that includes, if possible, returning to your hometowns.

Having our team spread across all corners of the globe will help our influence spread, not to mention will work in limiting possibilities of rising Salem supporter groups.

Ideally, I would have Marcus return back to the North, and run the Seven Seas Empire Northern sector from the Myrah's powerhouse. Tyrinie, I would want you and Casteri to return to Lelani's estate and not only assist with keeping the fusion prisoners safe, but run the Seven Seas Empire Southern sector from there. Lanker, since Cyryl's powerhouse was destroyed, you'll be going with Marcus until we can get you stationed in the East. Faylin and I will rule from here, turning my mother's powerhouse into our main base of operation."

To my surprise, there were no moans or cries of outrage. Mostly, they just looked around at one another, nodding.

"Well, I would assume as much, that would be the most reasonable way to keep the sectors under wraps." Marcus spoke up from the swing, kicking his foot into the dirt. "I gotta admit though, I'm gonna miss you guys."

"Never thought I'd be going back to the south." Tyrinie replied, crossing his arms behind his head. "But I wouldn't mind the thought if I get to be in charge of all those prissy ass aristocrats down there."

"Aren't you one of those prissy ass aristocrats?"

"Shut it, Lanker." Tyrinie retorted, chucking a nearby snowball right into the back of Lanker's head.

"Don't think of this as a goodbye, because our true mission is far from over. This is just the next phase. We will keep in touch daily, and I will constantly be on the move visiting each of your sectors as much as possible. We are family now, so even though we won't be seeing each other every day, that bond won't change. And…it's not like we have to leave right now." I paused for a moment, taking in all of my teammates' faces, all of these guys who, a few months back, I didn't even know existed. And now, I couldn't imagine my life without them.

For the longest time, I thought the only people who existed in my world were my mother, father, Persephone, and Emme…and now, I have seven amazing men who left such an impact on me.

"I don't even think that 'thank you' would say enough." I smiled, voice cracking lightly. "Thank you, guys, for believing in me and my cause, for sticking out this suicidal mission to save the world with me. So many people never gave me the time of day, but you all accepted me for all I was, and still stood and fought by me. I will forever be in you guys' debt for that."

"Aw Cap'n…I can't speak for the whole team, but I should be thanking you." Lanker spoke up over the silence that fell over us.

"I was at a dead-end job in a dead-end town with no way to reach my dreams, and you gave me purpose. You waltzed right into my family's shop with your big dreams and gave this small-town boy something to believe in. Heck, we got to watch real life miracles happen time and time again while we were with you!"

"Yea, like Lanker said it's not like my life was much happier before you. If anything, … I guess I can really be myself around you guys." Tyrinie spoke up as well, the tips of his ears going red. "But that's only because you guys are bigger freaks than I am, but you guys accept me…so, I guess I'm thankful for you as well." The last part was mumbled into his tightly pulled coat sleeve.

"And Senna and I were about to be shipped off to prison, or worse, the Pig Farm if you guys didn't swoop in and rescue us. Throughout all my hacking days, all I wanted to do was break down these walls and make a difference, and you gave me that opportunity, Lil' man."

"I don't believe I need to give you a reason for my thanks, we simply wouldn't have enough time." Faylin chuckled, coming up next to me and placing his arm around my shoulder. "This journey has given me more meaning than I have ever had in my centuries of life, and I cannot wait to rule the Seven Seas Empire beside you, Captain."

I had no words, and whatever I thought I could say was caught in my throat. I took a deep breath, stretching out my arms wide.

"C'mon everyone, group hug! Bring it in."

There was an eruption of laughter as Tyrinie scrambled to escape the dogpile he was getting dragged into.

"Don't try to run away now Tyrinie, the hug isn't ending until you join us!" This was my family. This was what I was fighting for.

This wasn't about my freedom, this wasn't about a prophecy, and this wasn't about clearing Discordia's name.

This wasn't something that Galaia could foresee.

This was about guys like Marcus and Senna who wanted to change the world. Guys like Casteri who would do anything for their friends. Guys like Lanker and Tyrinie who never really knew their place in this crazy world. Guys like Faylin, who never knew who they could trust, but decided to venture out and trust someone one more time. This was their story.

This was about giving them their freedom, letting them have a chance to exist.

This was about taking back what was stolen from us, and letting *anyone* who dares to try and control us know we won't go down without a fight.

So let another Salem try to rise. Let Galaia try to spread her corruption to our world again.

We'll be ready.

And we aren't afraid anymore.

END OF CHAPTER 21

EPILOGUE

The harsh lights shone on my face as a whirring sound filled the air. I stood on the large metal platform in front of the camera, identical to the one in the North, wiping my sweaty palms on my pants. My team stood on the opposite end of the camera offering me moral support.

This was it; this was my big speech to the nation to let them know the 7 Seas Empire was here. Sure, there would be backlash, but now wasn't the time to worry about that.

"Now Captain, this will be broadcast live, just like last time. Are you ready? Would you like to practice what you'll say again?" Faylin asked in a hushed tone, stepping into my mother's particular filled chamber to adjust my collar.

"Nope, I got this Fay. It's better if I speak from the heart, it'll sound more genuine that way. Besides, if I read a script, I'll just start stuttering." I laughed sheepishly.

"You'll do fine." Faylin nodded, straightening my coat for the umpteenth time. He stepped back out towards the camera, clicking the button and prompting an automated voice to flood the room

"Welcome, Sabra Hakimi. You will be live in 5, 4, 3, 2, and 1."

There was a dinging noise, and I cleared my throat.

"Attention all of Neutopia. I am Captain Scarlet, leader of the Seven Seas. The last time I made an announcement, I made a promise of change, a promise to rid this world of Salem's tyrannical rule. That day has finally come." I waved Faylin over, who carried E-129's unmoving body into frame.

"Salem is dead, this war is over. Under the watchful gaze of the Seven Seas Empire, Neutopia will enter a new era of prosperity and security.

You are all now free, and we will do everything in our power to keep it that way. Salem's way is over, and any and all groups that still operate under Salem's influence or under those appointed by Salem are being commanded to disband immediately. If you will not do this willingly, we will be forced to intervene. This is for us, this is for the future children and grandchildren, for both humankind and cyberkind. Remove the collars that showed your oppression, and join us to ensure freedom, safety, and prosperity for Neutopians."

With a nod, Faylin ended the broadcast, and I let out a huge sigh, slumping against the back wall.

"So, how did I do?" I laughed, trying to get the feeling back in my feet.

"That was perfect, I couldn't have said anything better myself." Faylin nodded in agreement as the others cheered on. "Shall we see the reaction of the people?"

We all rushed over to the powerhouse's nearby window that overlooked the large curved roadways and the glass buildings. All around, people were stopped in their tracks, staring at the multiple holograms where my message played on repeat. On every building, on every hologram, on every phone, my message played.

Everybody was listening.

One by one, I saw people begin to raise their hands to their necks. There were moments of hesitation before massive clicks could be heard, and the oppressive items began hitting the ground. By the hundreds, collars were being removed.

Roars of cheering began to erupt through the streets; people hugged one another and jumped happily, they pointed at the screens cheering and shouting our names.

There was no word to describe what feeling I felt at that moment.

This…this had to have been what freedom felt like.

This was it; we did the impossible. Our job was far from over, but the future was looking bright.

But there was no time to sit and contemplate.

There was a world to take care of.

So, let's go.

Because now begins the era of the Seven Seas Empire.

ACKNOWLEDGMENTS & THANK YOU

As the first part of Scarlet's journey comes to an end, I have so many people to thank. Of Course, first and foremost, I Thank My Lord and Savior, Jesus Christ, without whom I wouldn't still be here.

I thank my publisher, Frozine, for believing in me and always helping me to see my potential. I thank my amazing husband, friends, and family for putting up with my book rants and for believing in me when I didn't believe in myself.

Lastly, but surely not least, I have to pass a heartfelt 'Thank You" to ALL of my Readers! Thank you to all of the people who chose to take a small peek into my imagination.

Thank you all for giving my books a chance!

Scarlet's journey is far from over and I hope that you all will continue reading the future series and see where our crew of misfits go from here!

Ashley

www.ingramcontent.com/pod-product-compliance
Lightning Source LLC
Chambersburg PA
CBHW052023020726
47501CB00004B/1202